See the ~~Desert~~ and Die

Ann Saxton Reh

Prospect Street Press

PROOF 2 – NOT FOR SALE

Ann Saxton Reh/Prospect Street Press
www.annsaxtonreh.com

Publisher's Note: This is a work of fiction. While the
setting of this book is real, names, characters, incidents,
and locations are products of the author's imagination.
Any resemblance to real persons, places, incidents, or
organizations is entirely coincidental.

Cover design: Karen Phillips /www.PhillipsCovers.com
Editing: Lourdes Venard of Comma Sense Editing /
https://www.commasense.net/
See the Desert and Die/Ann Saxton Reh. -- 1st ed.
ISBN-13 978-0-9996259-2-7

**To women who strive
to change the way things are**

Acknowledgements

Quotation in Chapter 17 from Verses by Kutaila, translator Sir Charles Lyall. Quoted in *The Desert and the Sown*, by Gertrude Bell, p. 146-7

* * *

With gratitude to those from whom I've learned about the Foreign Service including journalist and FSO Beatrice Camp and Ambassador Stephen Browning [ret.]. To Col. Jerry Lyons [ret.], a friend in the desert, to Prof. Eamonn Gearon for his inspiring writing about the Middle East, and to Tom Saxton for his telecommunications expertise.

Chapter 1

International Tribune
June 13, 1972

American Journalist Missing

RIYADH, June 13. Five days after her disappearance near Riyadh, Saudi Arabia, the fate of American journalist Katherine Darius is still unknown.

Darius, 49, acclaimed for her reporting from war zones in North Africa and South Asia, vanished June 8th while on an early morning photography trip.

A freelance journalist for the Associated Press, Darius is best known for her firsthand accounts of women's participation in combat and anti-colonial resistance during the Algerian War and the Vietnam conflict.

She was last seen walking into Al-Diriyah, a historic town under restoration on the western side of the capital city.

A spokesman from the U.S. Consulate said, "We are working with the Ministry of Interior to determine the cause of her disappearance, and the investigation is ongoing. Protecting American citizens is our highest priority."

Local police report they have "searched the area by foot and helicopter. No trace has been found."

The journalist's husband, Alexander Darius, professor of Classics in Washington, D.C., said, "My wife went to Arabia to visit friends, not to investigate a story." Asked if he believes his wife is alive, Darius said, "I won't speculate."

Stepson Thomas Darius, an ethnographer working in Yemen, could not be reached for comment.

In a telephone interview, daughter Layne Darius, 22, a student at Georgetown University, said she refuses to believe her mother is dead. "They won't let me into that country to look for her, but I'll keep asking questions. I can't give up hope."

Chapter 2

Arabia — August, 1980

Thomas Darius glanced up from his book. In the dimness, people were moving toward the back of the plane.

Next to him, his sister Layne stirred. "What's happening?"

He waited while two men and a woman passed on the way back to their seats. They'd gone up the aisle in stylish European clothes. Now, the men wore white *thobs*, checkered *ghotras* covering their heads, and the woman was shrouded in a black *abaya* and veil.

"Post-Ramadan return," he said softly. "Those who leave the country before it starts have to shed their Western decadence when they come home."

"It's eerie. Half the passengers look like different people," Layne said. "And those abayas are dehumanizing. You won't ever see me in one."

Thomas shook his head. The ways of the desert were familiar to him after years of studying Bedouin tribes on the Arabian Peninsula. But his sister would

3

face challenges she couldn't yet imagine.

The concerns he'd had these past months began to prickle again. Was bringing her here the right thing to do? He had no doubt about her skill as an ethnographer. Professional training had taught her to approach new cultures with an open mind, and she did impressive work with tribal women in Northern India.

Still, she was an outspoken supporter of the Women's Movement. Coming to a land with such absolutes and restrictions, where women wore veils for protection as well as privacy, would test everything she believed.

An hour later, they had landed in Dhahran and were trudging across the runway in the blue darkness of early morning, heat radiating from the tarmac.

Thomas breathed in the smell of sand in the warm wind buffeting them. He was on the desert again! For a few years, it seemed he'd never get back to this part of the earth where his spirit expanded in its unbounded space.

He glanced at his watch. A little past four. It would be daylight before they got through customs. If nothing went wrong, they'd be on the road to Riyadh by eight.

Of course, no wise person starts a half-day drive across Al-Dahna Desert later than dawn in these summer months. But he didn't regret landing on the east coast.

The all-terrain vehicles Ricky Al-Amir ordered had

been shipped by sea from Europe and were being serviced in a local garage. The guide he'd found would meet them there, and the trip would give Layne a preview of the months ahead.

A hired car and driver were waiting for them outside the terminal, and they rode through shadowed streets to an alleyway near the edge of town, stopping in front of a small garage.

The proprietor came out smiling.

"Allah be praised, you have come! All is ready for you."

He led them into the dusty back area of his garage and showed them two canvas-topped jeeps. Thomas felt the first stab of alarm.

"I understood Mr. Al-Amir ordered Land Cruisers for us."

The man's eyebrows lifted in amazement. "Here is what was delivered, none other."

Looking at the jeeps, imagining how rough their ride would be over hard sand tracks, Thomas tried to protest.

The garage owner gave him abundant assurances and then became indignant.

"Our guide is supposed to meet us here. Have you heard from him?" Thomas said, knowing more argument was a waste of time.

"This I was also told. *Insha'allh*, he is just coming."

Thomas spent the next hour in the tiny office, trying to call Ricky. First, the call didn't go through. Then he was told Mr. Al-Amir was not at home.

He hung up the phone and looked at Layne, sitting in her baggy tunic and pants on a hard wooden chair next to him. Exhausted from fourteen hours of travel, she'd dozed off.

Again, he hoped he hadn't made a mistake in bringing her. It was useless to ignore the fact that she'd really come to this desert driven only by the hope that, even after eight years, she might find some trace of Katherine Darius.

It was her determination that worried him. So much so that he was glad he hadn't told her certain things just yet. Until he got her safely to the village where they'd be working, not knowing those secrets might be her only defense against dying as her mother likely did.

He heard the slap of a sandal on the pavement outside, and a young Bedouin came through the open door. Mustafa, the guide, smiling shyly, was dressed in a starched white thob, the ends of his ghotra folded back from his lean face, his beard and mustache carefully groomed.

They greeted each other. Then, they sat and talked in the usual manner of men who meet on the desert. After a while, Mustafa rose and began to load their gear.

"It's Mustafa's extended family that we'll be living with," Thomas said to Layne. "Ricky told me he's a good man, and I believe he is. The success of our study, as well as our lives, will depend on him."

He saw fear flit across his sister's face, but she said,

"From the little I could understand, he seems eager to help us."

They had loaded the water cans and were about to leave when the garage owner called to them. He hurried from his office with a scrap of paper in his hand.

Thomas glanced at the scrawled Arabic and the map sketched underneath. It was an invitation to visit a Bedouin camp on the way to Riyadh.

"We don't have time for this," he said.

The agent put his whole body into a shrug that communicated disbelief. "Close by the highway, a matter of minutes. This family have kinship with people you study."

Thomas acknowledged his point. Though it was already midmorning and probably over a hundred degrees, one did not refuse hospitality in this society.

The jeeps seemed to run well enough as they made their way through a row of stalls already open for business and negotiated traffic on narrow streets of shops and apartment buildings.

Like most desert towns, this one had a flat, worn-out look that would last for years until one day the wind had blown them away.

Finally, there were no more buildings and the vastness of sand and scrub bushes stretched away to a brown haze at the horizon.

Layne pulled the long cotton scarf off of her head and leaned back with a sigh. "This isn't quite as bad as I thought it would be. At least we're moving. Better than sitting on that hard chair wrapped in a shroud."

Thomas knew she must be frustrated as well as tired. It was not in her nature to sit and wait for anything. "Are you regretting your decision to come?"

"No. I'm just brain-fogged from jet lag, and incredibly uncomfortable in this dusty steam bath. But don't worry. Nothing's going to make me leave."

Hearing the unspoken *until I find what I came for*, he said, "This drive is easy compared to what's coming. But once we meet our host family and settle in, you'll be so fascinated by the Bedouin way of life you won't be worried about anything else."

He glanced at her when she didn't respond. "I know you came here to find out what happened to Katherine, to have some closure. But after all this time, there isn't anything to find."

"If she'd been your mother, you wouldn't believe that," Layne said.

Annoyance tinged with guilt rose as it usually did when she threw that accusation at him. He was five years old when Katherine Darius came to live with them. He'd never loved his stepmother, and she made no effort to take his dead mother's place.

So seldom was she at home that he wasn't shocked when she was gone. Pity for Layne's grief and his father's sorrow was about all he ever felt.

"I don't know what it will take to convince you," he said. "The odds of finding any trace of her are absurdly high. Even if prying into the past in this country weren't so dangerous. We're just too vulnerable to risk it, Layne."

"I do remember you told me that. Several times."

They drove in silence until Thomas began to watch for the turnoff indicated on the pencil sketch.

"I'll have to stop at this Bedouin camp," he said. "Another delay. But we can't ignore an invitation from people related to our hosts."

"Since I came here to study women in the society, maybe I'll actually meet some. That would be a nice change," Layne said.

Thomas glanced at her, not sure what her sarcasm meant.

At last, he saw an unpaved track running from the highway toward a distant cluster of wind-sculpted hills. Slowing, he steered off the pavement.

The jeep slammed onto the dirt track so hard that he almost lost control of the wheel. Layne, muffling a scream, clung to the handhold as they bucked over the ridges and holes, throwing up a dust cloud from their wheels. Thomas glanced back to be sure Mustafa was still following. The shape of his jeep was barely visible in the sandy wake.

For another half mile, they struggled to stay on the roadway until it smoothed out slightly, but after twenty minutes the rust-gold hills seemed as far from them as ever.

"I don't think there's anything out here," Layne said. She wiped away sweat with her scarf, leaving dusty streaks on her forehead and cheeks. "You must have taken the wrong road."

"It was the only road. The camp has to be right over there." He pointed at a dark rock formation just becoming visible beyond the hills.

Layne bent to get something out of the bag at her feet, and he heard her gasp.

"I think we're in trouble." She nodded toward the dial. "The needle on the temperature gauge is right below the red line. It's just quivering there."

Thomas looked down. "I don't believe it! I checked the radiator before we left. There must be a leak. We'll have to stop and add water."

He braked, and the needle shot belligerently to the top of the red. Then, steam began seeping through the sides of the hood. Steering to the edge of the roadway, he turned off the engine and they got out.

The other jeep skidded to a stop behind them. Mustafa climbed out and sauntered over, his thob wrinkled and smudged with dirt. Unwinding the ghotra that covered all but his eyes, he brushed sand from his mustache and beard. After a flash of disdain, his face was composed.

Thomas knew he must be having second thoughts about attaching himself to people who came so foolishly into lands that were perilous and unforgiving.

Snapping the clamps open he raised the hood.

"These decrepit war relics can't be the vehicles Ricky ordered," he said. "We should have stayed in Dhahran until I could reach him."

As the steam lessened, he went to the rear of the jeep. He tensed to lift one of the five-gallon jerry cans that held their water supply but stumbled backward, thrown off balance by the nearly weightless can. He spat out a curse and reached for the other one.

"The damned things are empty! I know they were full when we left." He laid the cans on their sides. In a bottom corner of each one was a hole that had been bunged up with some kind of filler, apparently jarred loose by the bouncing on the rocky track.

Mustafa went to his jeep, hefted a can, and said something guttural in Arabic. He shook it to show it was empty.

They stood there addled by the significance of their situation.

"This didn't happen by accident. Somebody wanted to strand us here," Layne said. She glanced at Mustafa, who had walked a few yards away, staring at the hills.

"This Al-Amir family that made the arrangements, are you sure you can trust them?" she said.

"I know Ricky Al-Amir. He didn't do this! Why would he go to the trouble and expense of setting up this expedition and then sabotage the whole thing? That garage owner in Dhahran must be responsible." Thomas took off his glasses and wiped them. "I wish I'd been able to reach Ricky before we started."

Suddenly, Mustafa yelled and waved his arms. "Truck coming!" A dust cloud was racing toward them from the direction of the highway.

"They'll help us," Layne said. "Surely some code of the desert will compel them to stop."

As the dust came closer they could see a British Land Rover bearing down on them, driven by a man in a ghotra and dark glasses.

They all waved, but he careened past, spraying them with a barrage of sand.

Stunned, they watched his dust until he dropped from sight as if the road had dipped suddenly into a valley.

"So much for desert hospitality," Layne said. "Why don't we leave this jeep and go on to Riyadh in the other one?"

Thomas raised his hand to his brow and scanned the hills, trying to estimate how far they were. "The camp must be on the other side. The people there will give us water."

"If they're no more helpful than that man was, we're probably out of luck," Layne said, getting back into her seat.

Thomas seized the jerry cans and tossed them into the other jeep. "We still have a gallon of drinking water. Come on. You've got to go with us. I can't leave you out here alone."

Layne got out and jerked the strap of her bag over her shoulder.

He knew she was mad, and he tried to curb his reaction. Accommodations and protection for a woman weren't an issue in his past fieldwork. This was going to be damned complicated.

Again, Mustafa was first to see the dust cloud in the distance—a big American SUV this time, coming fast. With all their might, they waved and shouted at it. Their hope turned to outrage as it showered them with sand and roared past. Then, in one of those miracles that send thrills up the spine, it skidded to a stop after fifty yards and turned in a wide arc. It was coming back.

Two men got out and strode toward them. They wore khaki work clothes, pants tucked into thick boots laced up to mid-calf, and checkered ghotras wrapped around their heads. Thomas guessed they were a couple of the British or European technicians who work all over the Middle East, selling their skills like high-tech mercenaries.

The driver was a tall, well-built man with olive skin and the angular cheekbones one is used to in this part of the world. His eyes were concealed behind dark glasses, but he didn't look like an Arab. He pulled off his head covering and said in an accent that was clearly American, "Do you need help?"

"Yes, I'm afraid we do. I'm Dr. Thomas Darius. We're here to do an ethnological field study. As you can see, we've run into some difficulty. The radiator must be cracked. It's happened to me before crossing the desert, but we just discovered our water supply has been tampered with."

"You're studying something out *here*?" the man said.

"Not here, precisely. Our Bedouin hosts are herders in the Rub Al-Khali. We're on the way to Riyadh to finish our preparations."

"Why did you leave the highway?"

Thomas tried not to show the chagrin he felt. "We have an invitation to visit a related family camped nearby. One doesn't ignore such things in this society."

The man shook his head. "It's suicide to go off the main road without adequate supplies."

Layne, who had been standing quietly, said, "Will you help us or not?"

Her hostility seemed to catch him off guard, but his companion surged forward.

"Of course we will help you, dear lady." He had unwrapped his head covering and left it framing his face, shining with amusement.

"You must not be offended by our curiosity," he went on. "I am Saeed Bin Yousef, and my impatient friend here is Mr. David Markam. He is a member of your American Consulate in this country. What a fortunate thing we were traveling this way today."

Markam, staring into the distance where the Range Rover had gone, did look impatient. He turned and said, "Do you need anything besides water?"

Thomas told him what might be wrong with the radiator, and they all huddled around the engine, pinching hoses and testing fittings. Using his handkerchief as a rag, Markam started to unscrew the radiator cap. A burst of steam shot out and he leaped back.

Glancing at Layne, Thomas saw her smile. She was clearly enjoying Markam's discomfort. Though minutes later, when he hoisted a full five-gallon jerry can from the back of his vehicle, she looked more impressed.

"This should get you to the city if you take it easy," Markam said. He filled the radiator and added a bottle of sealant. "I'll leave the rest of this water with you."

He put the can into their jeep and looked toward the hills, frowning. "Be sure to have your vehicles checked out before you go into Al-Ramlah—the sands. You need to carry replacements for everything. In this climate, always expect the worst."

Bristling at his patronizing tone, Thomas felt the need to defend himself.

Before he could, Bin Yousef said, "Indeed, 'the worst' may be true of the climate. However, it can never be said of the natives. As soon as you reach the city, you must come to my house. Let me give you a taste of our true hospitality."

"Thank you. We'd love to," Layne said, as if she were anxious to seize the offer before he refused it.

Instinctively, Thomas knew why she was interested in this Bin Yousef. He was undeniably a person of consequence. His clothes looked expensive, and diamond rings circled two of his fingers. Such people have friends with influence. She must see in him a possible way through the implacable wall of silence that hid her mother's disappearance. He sympathized with her, but feared for her more.

"Are you still going on to that camp?" Markam said.

"These people have a tribal relationship with the family I'll be studying. As I said, it's important not to ignore this invitation."

Markam shook his head again. "I'd advise against it. There may be more risk than you anticipate."

Thomas dug in his heels. "It can't be far. I do strongly feel an obligation to honor this invitation."

After a strained silence, Markam said, "If you're determined, we'll caravan with you." He turned to Bin Yousef. "That Land Rover might have been headed to the same camp."

Bin Yousef nodded and glanced at Layne.

Markam said, "I must urge you and your wife to follow us back to Riyadh after the visit."

Thomas waited for Layne to declare that she was not his wife, but she said nothing.

The spine-jarring drive along the rutted track took another fifteen minutes. They dipped into a wadi and then began to climb again. He felt a surge of anticipation as they crested the ridge and saw below two long black tents huddled between the fingers of the hill.

The camp might have been abandoned. No people, no camels or goats, not even dogs in sight. The sun held the air in glittering stillness as they drove cautiously toward the tents.

When they were a quarter mile away, everything came to life. Four or five skinny dogs bounded out of the shadows, yelping, and the largest tent disgorged half a dozen Bedouin men, bandoliers across their chests, rifles raised to fire.

Shocked more than surprised, Thomas put his hand on Layne's shoulder. "Get down. Stay still."

Chapter 3

Mustafa climbed out of his jeep and walked cautiously toward the tent, talking and gesturing. After a tense few minutes, the men lowered their rifles.

Layne tied her scarf around her head and reached for her bag. Thomas caught her arm. "Stay here until we see what the situation is."

All of the men gathered in a group outside the tent, and she sat watching their rituals of greeting. It was interesting to see that the Bedouin treated Bin Yousef with special courtesy. He must be a man with influence. She'd need help from someone like him if she had any possibility of uncovering the truth about what happened to her mother.

They all went into the tent, though the American named Markam did hesitate and look back as if he were worried about leaving her alone.

She got out, stomped around to relieve her cramped legs, took off her scarf, and fanned herself. The hill behind the tents might cast shade later in the day. Now, a huge, burning sky flattened all life.

Why did her mother come to this place? She spent her life taking risks and surviving. Always for a purpose, a story that justified those risks. What was in this desert worth dying for?

The flap of the tent opened, and Mustafa strode toward her, his beard twitching with good will. "Drink tea now. Bring water after one hour. Work not good if sun high."

"I'd love to have some tea," she said, starting toward the big tent. "It's about time somebody remembered I'm here."

Mustafa threw out his arms. "No lady here! This place for men." He made a kind of spinning gesture with his right hand as if he were herding goats and pointed to the smaller tent. "Lady sitting there."

He looked relieved when she started toward the other tent, and he went back inside male territory.

Layne took her time getting to the *hareem* quarters, pausing at the corner of the men's tent to look around the back. An extension, a kind of garage, had been created with tarps tied to wooden poles. A whip-type antenna stuck up through an opening in the far end. She lifted a corner of the canvas and in the dimness, saw the Land Rover that nearly ran them down.

Edging closer, she wiped the glass with her sleeve. In the cargo area, metal boxes with dials lay half-concealed under a tarp, transmitters that could send and receive messages a long way.

What were they doing here? Thomas tried to get permission to bring in field radios like these. He was told no private citizen could own such equipment.

Barely able to breathe under the canvas, she moved outside, thinking about what she'd seen. This vehicle was a portable listening post. After millennia of raising camels and goats on the desert, why would Bedouin herders suddenly need electronic communication? These people must be in some other line of work. One that had to be defended with rifles. Were they bandits? Smugglers? Why would they want Thomas to come here?

A voice spoke softly behind her, and she turned, her face burning. An old woman stood like a sentry beside the smaller tent, her hands tucked into the folds of her long green and yellow skirt, and her gaunt head draped in a black scarf.

"Oh, hello. I'm just looking for your tent," Layne said.

The woman stared, a sour expression on her leathery face.

"*As-Salaam-Alaikum,*" Layne tried again.

The woman mumbled some response and motioned for her to come into her tent.

Layne bent to get through the low opening. In the darkness, she heard a clink of metal and smelled wood smoke and body scents perfumed with musk.

As her eyes adjusted, she saw half a dozen women sitting or reclining on carpets spread around a still-warm fire mound in the center. These must be the wives and sisters of the men with the rifles. They were young, teenagers or early twenties, except for the elderly woman, who might be grandmother to some or all of them.

No one spoke while they gave her cushions to sit on and produced a small glass of hot sugary tea. Then, they stared, as if uncertain of what to do. But, oddly, they seemed to have expected her.

She looked at their luxurious hair and supple bodies in fitted blouses and skirts in primary colors. The heavy silver bangles on their wrists and ankles clanked when they moved. Though they sat limply in the afternoon heat, the youngest women looked ready to leap up and dance if the impulse struck them.

In her halting Arabic, she told them her name and explained why she had come to their country. The idea of studying their culture produced smirks and doubtful glances.

Searching for common ground, she said, "Will you tell me your names?" Three of the younger women complied, but the grandmother, sitting across the fire from her, said nothing.

"Do you have children?" Layne said. Two of them answered at once. The children were with the rest of the family in the summer encampment. She wanted to ask why they were camped out here, but the grandmother said, "Where are the lady's children?"

"I have no husband, no children," she said, and she felt them withdraw from her, suspicion replacing curiosity. A woman of thirty with neither of those essentials must be a barren spinster, a person who brought bad luck. Maybe they even feared she was one of the malevolent *'ifrtah,* a spirit who did harm wherever she went.

Disconcerted, she searched for a way to reach them. The sense of being an outsider, even shunned, at the beginning of a field study wasn't new. The tribal women she lived with in India tolerated her for weeks before they trusted her enough to talk about their private lives. Wariness was expected, but in these Bedouin women's eyes, what she saw was fear.

They gave her more tea and, after the traditional three cups, she thanked them and said she had to go.

Outside the men's tent, she stood listening to raised voices, worrying about Thomas. Somebody in there was the driver of that hidden Range Rover. And the one who used those field radios.

Finally, Mustafa stepped out. Seeing her, he did more of his herding gestures to steer her away. She scowled at him but moved a yard or so and waited while Thomas and the other men came out. Two of the Bedouin were carrying big water cans, presumably from a supply they had behind the tent.

Thomas's face was flushed, and Layne could see he was not pleased. Sensing the farewells would still be lengthy, she started back to the jeep. Before she reached it, David Markam caught up with her.

"Did your visit with the women go well, Mrs. Darius?" His dark glasses made it hard to read his expression, but he sounded amused. So he disapproved of her being here too. It was interesting that Thomas didn't tell him she was his sister, not his wife. Probably she wasn't even mentioned.

"My visit was fine. How about yours?"

"Less than satisfactory," he said in a low voice.

Bin Yousef came up beside them. "Mrs. Darius, we have agreed. You and Dr. Darius are coming to my house for dinner tomorrow night. So many people will want to meet you!"

She smiled at him. At home, dinner parties were an ordeal, but this invitation might be the lifeline she hoped for.

He went back to where Thomas was still talking to the Bedouin, and another round of farewells began.

Standing next to Markam, Layne watched the men fill the jeep's radiator. She wondered if she should tell him about the hidden Land Rover. It must be important to him since he and Bin Yousef were chasing it. She opened her mouth but caught herself. If she told him, he'd want to know why she was snooping, what she was looking for. Even if this man's job was to help American citizens, he was even more likely than Thomas to disapprove of anything that went against customs or laws here.

"Your husband didn't mention who's sponsoring your fieldwork," he said after the men with the water left. "It must be a private venture. We'd have heard about it if the Ministry were involved."

So, he was already suspicious of them. She didn't answer, and he said, "I wonder if he understands how unwise it was to drive out here. The political climate is volatile these days. Under the best circumstances, this desert is dangerous."

Layne crossed her arms and glared at him. "We're aware of that. This is my brother's third field study in the region. He knows what he's doing. Somebody gave him the wrong information about this camp."

"He's not your husband?" He looked at the group of men. "You didn't falsify your visa application, did you? If you came into the country as his wife—"

"We wouldn't do anything that stupid. I'm an ethnographer, too. I'm an official part of his study team. You don't need to worry about us. We'll have everything we need in Riyadh."

Markam frowned. "It's still going to be an arduous trip. Most women I know wouldn't let themselves in for risks like you're taking. Or the discomfort of living rough out here."

Layne got into the jeep and glanced up at him. "You must know some pretty dull women."

He looked away and actually grinned. "Well, I never thought so before now."

Just then, her brother came up, and Markam said, "I think we'd better stay with you until you reach the city, Dr. Darius."

Thomas nodded and got into the jeep, but as he drove back toward the highway he was hunched over the wheel in frustration.

Layne tied the scarf over her nose and mouth and took slow breaths to tolerate the haze of dust inside the jeep as they bounced along.

"Now I'm even less certain why we were invited to visit that camp," Thomas said finally. "Mustafa wasn't aware of the kinship connections the men claimed. They're not traditional herders. They don't even have any animals."

"And they're armed to the teeth."

"That part's probably not unusual these days."

Remembering the fear in the women's faces, she said, "Didn't they tell you anything about themselves?"

He shook his head. "They talked about everything but themselves. It's possible they were inhibited by the presence of Markam and Bin Yousef. They seemed to be very honored to have Bin Yousef as a guest."

"Not sure what those two are after, either," Layne said. Why were they following that Land Rover?"

"No idea. It's a good thing they were, though. If Mustafa hadn't done some fast talking and Bin Yousef hadn't been there, who knows what would have happened."

When they reached the highway and sped up to keep Markam in sight, wind beat against the canvas cover, threatening to rip it off. The ride was less jarring, but heated air shimmered above the highway like greasy waves over a skillet of burning oil.

Her encounter with the women kept circling through Layne's mind. They were people she wanted to know more about. Why did she feel so alien among them? Granted, with only a few weeks to read about Bedouin life and learn the rudiments of Arabic, she wasn't really prepared for this work. Still, her uneasiness with what she saw of this culture was bewildering.

As if he had heard her thoughts, Thomas said, "You look miserable. I did tell you this would be harder than anything you've done before." He patted her hand. "Once we get to Riyadh, Ricky Al-Amir will put things right."

"I hope so," she said to appease him, but her ineptness with the Bedouin women was still smarting. That was one thing Ricky couldn't fix. She dug through her bag for a lozenge to soothe her throat and gave one to her brother.

"Why didn't you tell Markam that Al-Amir is sponsoring your fieldwork?" she said.

He rolled the lozenge around in his mouth and crushed it. "There are a number of conflicting factions in this country. Mistrust and loyalties run under every surface. Until we know where people's sympathies are, it's best not to volunteer anything."

After a while, he said, "We'll be fine here as long as we do the work we have permission to do. Anything else—anything surreptitious or illegal—will probably get us thrown out of the country. We could even be arrested. Or imprisoned. I'm counting on you to take this seriously."

"I am taking it seriously."

Thomas looked doubtful. "No matter what I say, you're still convinced you can find some sinister motive behind Katherine's death, aren't you? Why can't you accept that it had to be an accident? We've never heard anything to suggest it wasn't. You have to let it go."

"It's the only chance I'll ever have to know for sure."

"The past is over and done, Layne. We've got too much at stake now, in the present. What if you do find out how she died? Will it make your life better?"

Layne couldn't answer him.

What happened to my mother? The question seized her eight years ago, as if a nail had snagged the edge of her heart. Afterward, earning her degrees, building a career, she moved on, except in that one place. To stop hoping, to pull free, would leave an un-mendable tear. Katherine Darius's daughter could not let go.

Chapter 4

They reached Riyadh without any further incident, but when they left Darius and his sister outside their hotel, David Markam still felt uneasy. All his instincts told him something was threatening these people. He just didn't know how he could intervene.

Across the city, he steered the SUV through the entrance of Saeed's estate, and the massive metal gates slid together behind them. Inside these walls, palms lining the drive muted the fierce sun.

The road circled a monumental fountain, then straightened to approach the chateau, flanked by acacia trees. He experienced again the shock he felt the first time he saw this house. Despite the cynicism he'd developed in his nine years as a diplomat, this opulence still disconcerted him.

"Come in for a drink," Saeed insisted.

They climbed the wide bank of marble stairs and passed the brace of stone leopards in the foyer to reach the terrace beyond, shaded by vines and trees. They sat at one of the wrought iron tables beside the swimming pool, grateful for the moist air.

Saeed's Yemini butler came in, carrying a tray laden with assorted bottles of beer and a crystal carafe of lime water.

David wanted a cold beer, but he settled for water. "I've got to drive back into town to talk to Darius as soon as I can. It's surprising that he's booked into a hotel. I thought he'd be staying with his sponsors. They'll probably be going there for dinner, though."

Saeed drained his glass of India ale. "I see you're worried about those people. Who do you suppose told Darius he'd be welcome at that camp? The Bedouin did not know he was coming. Seems an odd situation."

"It could have been disastrous," David said. "That guy in the Land Rover knew we were following him before he left the highway. Good thing we didn't roar into that camp by ourselves. Talk about disturbing consequences! I'll bet they had that vehicle hidden somewhere. You said the antenna was the kind used for shortwave. Could the messages you intercepted at the earth station have been sent from a setup like that, if they had transmitters?"

"Without doubt, those men are not goat herders," Saeed said. Looking thoughtful, he said, "Yes, a mobile unit like that might be ideal if one wanted to avoid being tracked to a particular location. I wonder. These fellows could be remnants of the insurrection that was so badly bungled last year."

"The rebels in Mecca? I thought they'd all been rounded up. Would you say the men we met today were political radicals?"

Saeed shrugged. "A single failed insurgence will never be the end of it."

"Seldom is. Did any of the messages you picked up sound like the work of such a group?"

"All nonsense, those messages. But they've become more frequent. Restless energies gather at this time of year, sometimes greater after Ramadan than before."

Just then, the servant came to tell him he had a phone call.

David let his eyes rest on the shadows of trees around the pool while he waited. Saeed was obviously worried. He was committed to preparing his country for the future, but not with oil. It was technology and water that interested him—desalination, hydroponic farming.

Now, as the sponsor of the American company putting up satellite earth stations for the new communication system, he had become the highly visible adversary of people who didn't want such progress.

Saeed came back to the terrace, looking more serious. "Talk of the Devil. Another message. Picked up by Jenkins at the Riyadh station. It's like the others, gibberish. Except this one has something new. There's a name at the end."

"How does it relate to the rest of the message?"

"Here, I wrote it down."

He pulled a small notebook out of his shirt pocket and laid it open between them on the table.

13 – 14 – *Dhuhr* 2 – *tati* 5

No fox – No fox – Al-Amir

"Code again," David said. "Could the thirteen and fourteen be time, 1300 to 1400 hours? Dhuhr, that's the midday prayer. What's this word?"

"Tati means come. Come where? Come five? If the first two numbers indicate time, five in the afternoon would be 1700 hours."

"What do you think about 'No fox'?"

Saeed looked disgusted. "Someone's having us on, as they say in the U.K. Nonsense. It must be."

"Al-Amir? That's the name? Do you know who he is?"

"Quite a prominent person."

"You mean Asad Al-Amir? The man who was an ambassador for your country?" David said.

"That family, at any rate. It needn't be the Quiet Lion himself."

"His book *Middle East Modernization* was required reading in one of my graduate classes."

"I suppose he's still a personage in diplomatic affairs," Saeed said. "Most of the time he was in public life I was living overseas. He has not been conspicuously involved in any cause for some years now."

"Conspicuously? You mean he still has influence? Does it seem likely he'd be involved with a subversive group?" David said, not sure he believed the old man was still active in politics or anything else. "As well known as he is, how could his participation in such a group be kept secret? People in the Ministry would be aware of it."

"Perhaps not," Saeed said. "Your consulate wasn't informed that this Darius team had come into the country. Isn't that so?"

David shook his head. Lack of knowledge was never easy to admit. Whoever sponsored Darius's fieldwork must have enough power to keep the information within a small circle of his colleagues at the embassy in Jeddah. Not being included in that number was more than galling.

"This afternoon, I'm going to make some calls to find out who got Darius into the country and what kind of provisions they've made for security," he said. "I can't believe he expects to go out into Al-Ramlah as unprepared as he was today. If a political uprising is in the works, and there's violence, he could be caught up in that, too."

Saeed nodded. He reached into the flowerbed next to his chair, turned a handle, and leaned back, gazing at the undulating fountain jets that rose from the center of the swimming pool.

"How curious you Americans are. And Europeans, the same. Always wanting to travel into deserts and jungles to dig up the past or study foreign ways of living."

"It's a kind of fever some people catch," David said. His own great passion was ancient ruins, and he couldn't remember a time he hadn't longed to know all he could learn about other cultures. "I respect

Darius's interest in the Bedouin tribes. What I don't understand is why he went out to that camp in the middle of the day." He shook his head. "This is evidently not his first fieldwork in the desert. He ought to know better. Especially with that woman along."

"Ah, yes. The attractive wife."

"She's not his wife. She told me they're brother and sister."

Saeed's eyes brightened. "Oh, ho! So the interesting lady is unmarried. Well, we must certainly do what we can to make her feel welcome. I imagine she might be quite lovely in a dress."

"Don't get your hopes up. That lady's going to cause trouble. You can be sure of it."

Raising his eyebrows, Saeed said, "Your people breed difficult women, do you not?"

"It seems so. I've heard about—Darius!" The name had been flitting at the corner of his memory all afternoon. "That's why it sounded familiar. The American journalist, several years ago. Talk about difficult women. She disappeared somewhere around here. Her name was Darius—Katherine Darius."

"Hmm. I don't recall. Probably I was still in the U.K. then. Was she never found?"

"Not a trace. It's one of those mysteries that get more like legends as time goes by."

"You're supposing these people are relatives of hers?" Saeed said.

"Hard to believe it's just a coincidence. The name isn't particularly common. It happened right after I came into Foreign Service."

"Interesting. Darius. It is a Persian name."

"Sounds like it should be. Darius the Great of the Achaemenid Empire," David said.

"If Dr. Darius is related to that journalist, it's unlikely the Ministry gave him permission to enter the country," Saeed said. "Possibility of overturning old stones. No one wants an event of that sort to be brought up again. Arrangements must have been made through private channels."

David waited for him to continue. Saeed might not be one of the royals, but his family had significant influence. He knew about most things that went on, official and otherwise.

Saeed poured himself more beer, swallowed it, and set the glass on the table with a thump. "By tomorrow, I shall know. At least the identity of the rogues we encountered today. Perhaps more about these inane messages we're intercepting."

"Let's hope so," David said, getting up. "I have a feeling something important is going on. And those Darius people could be right in the middle of it."

On the way to his apartment, he thought about what he wanted to find out from his boss, Gerald Fitzwilliam. As political minister counselor in Jeddah, Gerald was senior enough in the embassy's hierarchy to know how Darius got into the country. He also had access to archived files on Katherine Darius.

He showered and dressed, musing about the woman he'd met today. *The woman.* He didn't even know her first name. Saeed was right; she probably was beautiful. It was hard to tell what she looked like under dark glasses and those baggy clothes.

Beautiful or not, she had done something to him. She mattered, more than good sense told him she should. Most disturbing of all was a strange feeling of inevitability he couldn't shake.

During his Peace Corps time in India he'd come to believe in the connectedness of events and things. Was this meeting as inevitable, inescapable, as it seemed? The thought intrigued him and simultaneously set off a warning.

He'd been in Foreign Service long enough to see people ruin their careers, compromise their work and themselves when emotions got out of control. Caution was routine. Why did he feel as if he'd walked into a cave beneath this desert, knowing it was a sinkhole that might close in over his head?

Chapter 5

The rooms Thomas booked in Riyadh were in the sort of hotel Layne had seen only from the outside. The deliciously cool lobby of the Hotel International echoed with a patter of sound rather than a bustle as men in suits and thobs moved around its green-and-white marble expanse.

Thomas ordered sandwiches and bottled juice and water to be sent up to their rooms. He gave Layne books to read and told her to practice her Arabic.

"I'll be back as soon as I can. Take advantage of this time. Relax. You'll feel better," he said as he left to meet Ricky Al-Amir.

Relaxation was unlikely, she knew, but indulging in a little comfort wouldn't hurt. Filling the bath, she stripped off the sweaty, sand-filled clothes and sank into rose-scented bubbles.

The luxury felt wonderful for a while. Then, as the water cooled, a stirring of urgency crowded out pleasure. The few days before they left the city were all she had to find some trace, some reason, for why her mother was here and never came home.

The men they met this morning were a lucky break. Bin Yousef surely had contacts. It was also tempting to think David Markam might be an ally, but until she knew them better confiding in either of them was a risk.

Finishing a tuna sandwich, she looked with disgust at Thomas's stack of books. What she needed now was to go for a walk or take a taxi downtown. In the letters she found after her father died, her mother wrote about wandering through the souk, the old market in the heart of this city, of the weavings she saw in the women's souk just past the halal slaughterhouse. *This is where real life happens in Riyadh.*

Then, that's where she'd start to see this city as Katherine Darius saw it.

She rummaged through her travel box. "Modesty is the norm here," Thomas had said so many times that the words ran through her mind like a mantra.

A long skirt and tunic she bought in an Indian bazaar would have to do because she was not going to submit to wearing an abaya for any reason. Not ever.

Wrapping one of her scarves around her head like a *hijab*, she stood in front of the mirror. Not a single sliver of skin visible except her face and hands. That was enough modesty for anybody.

The phone rang, and she picked it up. Mustafa's voice came shouting through the receiver. "Doctor go Al-Amir house. I drive you shop. Wait you downstair," he said.

"I don't want to buy anything. I'd like to see the main souk." But she was speaking into a dead line.

She knew very well what Thomas was up to. While he was out dealing with business, Mustafa had been instructed to take her to buy an abaya, whether she wanted one or not. Well, if this was the way her brother intended to treat her the next six months, they were going to have a serious talk as soon as she could get hold of him.

In the lobby, Mustafa was nowhere in sight. As she passed the front desk, the clerk stopped her and said her brother had left a message. He gave her a note that said, *Called. You didn't answer. Plans changed. I'll call you later.*

Still annoyed, she stepped outside. Within a minute, she was as flushed and prickly as if she hadn't bathed.

The jeep was parked in front of the hotel, and Mustafa stood beside it, waiting for her. He'd changed into a fresh thob and a white ghotra in place of the checkered one.

Layne climbed wearily into the passenger seat, feeling like she'd spent half her life there. Mustafa seemed uncomfortable having to sit so close to her, but with no choice, he started the engine and glanced at her as if appraising her tastes. "We shop cloth," he announced.

"Are you kidding? Why do I need to buy clothes? I've got enough. No, I don't need any more clothes."

"All ladies must have," he insisted.

She understood then what he was talking about and decided not to argue. At least they were going into the city, so she'd have a chance to see the souk.

It took some time to get out of the congested area around the hotel, but soon they were driving through a residential neighborhood of twelve-foot cinder block walls on either side of narrow streets. Occasionally, a spray of red bougainvillea escaped over wall tops. Otherwise, everything, even the haze in the air, was the color and taste of sand.

As they reached a more commercial area of the city center, the scenery began to change. Mustafa rocketed around a traffic circle, and they might have been whizzing through time. One block looked like a flashback to the fifties—single-story stucco motel or gas station type structures. The next was lined with modern steel and glass high-rises in a forest of building cranes. Dominating the skyline, a green-and-white water tower in the shape of a martini glass emphasized the impression that the city was in a kind of ambivalent adolescence, growing but not certain of its direction.

Merging from a connecting road, another driver veered within two inches of their side. Mustafa blew the horn and made a kind of chopping gesture at him. The other man yelled something that wasn't in Layne's Arabic vocabulary and Mustafa charged after him, horn blaring and jeep rattling as if it were falling apart.

Layne held on with both hands to keep from

sliding out of her seat and did some cursing of her own. They finally stopped for a red light, and Mustafa glanced at her sheepishly. But no doubt he'd do the same thing the next time.

Eventually, they emerged onto a broad avenue of Palladian-style buildings, foreign banks, and upmarket shops. Mustafa parked the jeep in an alley, and Layne climbed out with shaking knees.

It was good to walk after all those hours on a hard seat. Wandering down the street for a while, they peered into shop windows at fabrics and appliances, masses of gold chains and gaudy jewelry, and Layne's frustration grew with every block.

Certainly, her mother never spent five minutes on these sanitized, modern streets.

"I'd like to go to the old market, Mustafa," she said. "To Souk Al-Zal. Is it far from here?"

"Doctor say you no go souk."

She stared at him. "Why did he tell you that? He wants me to buy an abaya, doesn't he? The stalls in the souk will have them at much better prices than these expensive stores. Besides, I want to see that place."

He shrugged. "Doctor say you no go." That was sufficient explanation for him. Thomas was her guardian and she was expected to follow his orders without question.

Her brother's warning before he left her at the hotel room should have prepared her for this. "Religious police, *mutaween*, will probably be in the souks, walking around with big sticks to 'correct' any woman who flouts the dress codes. It's just a fact of life you'll have to accept."

Well, it wasn't a fact of her life yet. She still wanted to go there.

At that moment, just ahead of them, three women in abayas came out of a jewelry shop, their faces veiled, except for eye slits, and their heads covered by thick gauze scarves.

Layne stared at them, feeling almost as if she couldn't breathe. She'd hardly looked at the women in abayas at the airport this morning. Now, close enough to hear the black capes rustling like old taffeta, she pitied these formless figures, these women forced to be invisible. The thought of wearing one herself made her feel cold inside.

As they passed, one of them stepped from the curb and stumbled. There was a ripple of young laughter from her friends when she hiked up her cape, displaying a pair of purple Nikes and lavender socks.

Layne looked after them, shocked. Her years of study and experience told her assumptions formed at a distance were unreliable. Yet, she'd come here expecting these women to look and act distressed, as if they longed for change. These girls were laughing. It was humbling to realize how ill-prepared she was to study this culture.

Catching up with Mustafa, she saw his shoulders sagging and felt sorry for him. No matter how tired and bored he was, he wasn't going to let her go beyond this street.

They reached a window display of fancy dresses and abayas, and she made a decision. "This looks like a good shop, Mustafa. I'll go in here. Is there anything else you need to do today?"

"Must go garage. Take one hour," he said.

"Why don't you go there now? You can't go inside this shop. It's just for ladies. Since my brother wants me to buy an abaya, I'll stay here while you go to the garage."

"Doctor say must stay close you all time."

It had been a hard day, and she wasn't in the mood to be bullied. "Look, Mustafa, I've spent enough time in garages today. They probably won't have any place for women. I want to stay here in this store. I'll be perfectly safe. See? Only ladies inside."

Before he had time to think of a way to stop her, she walked into the shop and began looking through a rack of dresses. For a while, she could see him hovering anxiously outside the window. At last, he went away.

Another five minutes and she was out the door. She went into the English bookstore she'd seen down the street and, mentally thanking Thomas for insisting they exchange dollars for riyals at the airport, she bought a small map of the city. Street names were in English on her map, in Arabic on street signs, but she found her location and figured out how to get to the main souk. It didn't seem far if she took a shortcut through side streets.

She walked another two blocks and turned into a narrow cobbled lane, lined with tiny shops that looked closed. It was cooler here if she stayed on the shadowed side of the road, and soon she was far enough from the main street that traffic sounds were muted.

Turning another corner, she stopped to look at her map and heard sandals on the pavement behind her. Three young Arab men were coming toward her, two of them in dark glasses and wearing headphones over their ghotras. They began making high-pitched trilling sounds and sucking and clicking noises.

Layne knew street harassment from the bazaars in India, but there, other people were always around.

"*Imshi*! Go! Leave me alone," she yelled, pulling her scarf forward to hide more of her face.

They caught up with her. One of them slapped her buttocks, and another grabbed the end of her scarf. She jerked it out of his hand and ran, her elbow scraping the edge of a wall as she careened around a corner.

Just as they were about to catch her, she turned another corner and saw up ahead a woman in an abaya going into a small shop. In a few more strides, she reached it, leapt up the two steps into the shop, slammed the door, and held the knob.

The shopkeeper and four women standing at the wooden counter stared at her.

"Excuse me," she said, squeezing behind the women and into the tiny space at the back. Among the bolts of cloth stacked on shelves, she tried to stop panting.

"You are needing help?" one woman asked in what sounded like a German accent.

"I'm a bit lost," Layne said.

All heads turned toward the hoodlums outside, who were drifting down the street. One of the women said, "You must be careful. Better not to be alone here."

She waited until other people were walking along the little street and she felt safe enough to leave. Outside, she turned left into an alley and crossed to another street, certain it led in the direction of the main souk.

After two or three blocks, the street began to narrow, and instead of shops, there were only high, whitewashed walls on both sides. She went on slowly. It even seemed hotter here. Her heavy skirt clung to her legs like hobbles.

About to turn around, she noticed that a section of the mud-brick wall had crumbled, leaving an opening. No warnings against trespassing were posted, so she stepped through the opening into the courtyard of a ruined fortress, built of the ruddy sand on which it stood.

It was a square complex of rooms surrounded by thick walls with conical towers at each corner. The flat roofline had triangular crenellations and, below it, rooms spared by desert winds still had charm. Looking up at the row of columns along a covered portico, she imagined graceful forms gliding along that walkway.

As she pressed her palm against the rough mud wall, feeling the day's warmth, a sound like falling stone startled her. Before she could turn, there was a sharp crack and something flew past her head. Whirling to face the street, she dropped to a crouch, listening to the air reverberating with silence. In the glare of the courtyard, not even a shadow moved.

Her heart pumping in sickening jerks, she raised up and looked at the wall behind her. Just where she had been standing, a bullet was embedded in the flaking stone. It had dislodged a chunk of gritty surface, and a few grains of dust still hung in the air above the scar.

Whoever fired that bullet must be just outside the wall. As exposed as she was in this courtyard, a second shot wouldn't miss.

Grabbing a wad of her skirt to free her legs, she dashed across the open space and jumped through the wall break. The street was empty, but she didn't dare slow down. She turned in what she thought was the direction of the boulevard and ran down the alleyway.

Chapter 6

At the end of the alley, she slowed to a walk and released the grip on her skirt. Hands shaking, she found a tissue in her bag, wiped her face, and pulled at her tunic, sweat-glued to her skin.

When she reached the boulevard, she looked both ways to see if anyone was following her. Dozens of people were on this street. Any of them could be carrying a gun. Though a random shot seemed unlikely. How often did casual shootings happen in a country where the punishment for theft is getting your hand chopped off? The shot fired at her was probably deliberate and personal.

She considered finding a policeman. But that might be dangerous, too. A tedious ordeal would surely follow. And even if they believed her, they'd think the whole thing was her fault. All she could do now was go back to where Mustafa left her.

Mustafa was standing on one foot in front of the abaya store, his back pressed against the wall. His expression changed from worry to relief and then to a peevish frown.

"Where you go?" He came toward her, both hands palms up, like a teacher prompting a slow student. "You say stay in store. You no here."

"I know. I'm sorry, Mustafa. I went down an alley and got lost." She felt guilty realizing how worried he was.

His eyebrows contracted in disapproval as he looked her over. "You sick? You—" He searched for a word. "You look mess."

She couldn't stifle a laugh. "I guess this heat's getting to me. Let's go back to the hotel."

His lips tight with annoyance, he led her halfway down the block and stopped beside a blue SUV. "New truck!" he said.

"Oh, this is great!" Layne climbed in. The truck wasn't new, but compared to the jeep, it was a limousine. Her expectations about this trip began to brighten.

"Shall we turn on the air conditioner?" she said.

Mustafa didn't respond. He might not know how to turn it on. More likely, he didn't want to. All his life he'd lived in this hot climate with nothing more than wind to cool him. Air conditioning probably made him miserable. Thomas undoubtedly felt the same way. Which meant she'd have to get used to being uncomfortable driving through the desert. She rolled down the window. It wasn't actually cooler, but still a lot better than riding in the jeep.

As they moved through clogged traffic, Mustafa glanced at her suspiciously. She wondered what he really thought of her. Was she an improper woman? Insane? His wariness had one compensation, his driving was less terrifying.

It took them about twenty minutes to get back to the hotel. They parked near the entrance and got out. "You'd better come inside, too," Layne said. "Thomas is probably here now with a bunch of thrilling plans he's cooked up for tonight."

Mustafa swung the keychain around his fingers like a strand of worry beads and dropped it into the deep pocket of his thob. They trudged together up the stairs. Stepping into the hotel lobby felt like being submerged in icy water until she adjusted to its relief.

They crossed the lobby, its green-veined marble blending the clusters of high-backed chairs and potted plants into oases between the stone pillars. As they skirted one of the pillars, a man rose from a chair and stepped into their path.

"Man from desert," Mustafa said in a low voice.

He was right, but the man had changed, the dusty khakis replaced by a light gray suit, white shirt, and linen tie. David Markam seemed at home in this elegant ambiance. Without the sunglasses, she could see his dark, deep-set eyes, lit with amusement. She stared at him, disconcerted.

"Dr. Darius, it's good to see you again. Can you spare a few minutes?" he said.

Her first impulse was to refuse. She was hot and tired, aware that she must look like a wild person. But she sensed something serious behind his courtesy.

Turning to Mustafa, who was still maintaining a protective—or custodial—proximity, she said, "I'll talk to this man for a few minutes. Why don't you see if my brother has come back to the hotel?"

He glared at her and at Markam but swung toward the reception desk.

She sat down, took off her scarf, and leveled what she hoped was a serene gaze at Markam, who sat across from her.

There was no denying he was attractive—skin tanned nearly as brown as Mustafa's, the high cheekbones, and those eyes!

"You look well equipped for the local fashion requirements," he said, smiling.

"Oh, yes. Covered head to toe. I have a whole wardrobe of long cotton skirts and tunics I bought in India. It's a compromise. My brother wants me to wear an abaya. In fact, we've just been out shopping for one. I couldn't find any I liked."

He grinned, and she knew he'd caught her meaning.

"You were in India?" he said.

"I thought you people in the State Department knew all about Americans overseas. My university gave me a grant to do fieldwork in Northern India two years ago. Since I was studying tribal women there, my brother knew I could make a contribution to his work here."

"Where did you do your research?"

"Himachal Pradesh. Up north, near Kasauli. But

don't you already know this? You called me 'Doctor Darius'."

"I admit to doing a little checking, but the details we have are sparse."

"Why did you check my details?"

He seemed to be trying not to smile. "Anyone who's lived in India interests me. I did Peace Corps work on the eastern side of the country. And Delhi was my first Foreign Service post."

Thinking he was about to launch into a nostalgic story, she relaxed. But he said, "I should tell you why I'm here. I came to see your brother. We didn't have a chance to talk earlier, and I wanted to hear more about your plans."

"Why?" she said, disappointed that she'd misread his intentions. "Thomas got all the visas and documentation we needed. Did you call his room to see if he's here?"

"I tried, but I was told he's not. What I want to discuss with him has nothing to do with his documents." He frowned and seemed to decide he'd have to deal with her.

"Frankly, I'm concerned about your safety. I'd like to make him aware of a situation he may encounter."

Considering the band of men with rifles and bandoliers they "encountered" earlier today, it didn't seem like a bad idea to hear what he had to say.

"Look, I'm sure Thomas does want to talk to you. Can he call you later? Oh, here comes Mustafa. He probably knows where my brother is."

Swinging the keychain and looking smug, Mustafa said, "Doctor no here. He go."

"You mean he hasn't come back?"

"Already come hotel, check out. No coming back."

Feeling like kicking her brother, she stood up. He'd sent her out shopping; then he'd moved out and left her. What was she supposed to do?

"Did he leave a message for me?"

"He say you go Al-Amir house now," Mustafa said, loud enough for most of the lobby to hear him.

She glanced at Markam, who had also risen and was listening. He turned his head, but not before she'd seen interest and maybe surprise in his face.

"Do you know who the Al-Amirs are?" she said.

"It's a familiar name in this country. The Quiet Lion, they used to call Asad Al-Amir. How does your brother know the family?"

"One of his sons—Ricky Al-Amir—is sponsoring Thomas's fieldwork. They met a few years ago at the university when Ricky was studying in the States."

Markam said, "You don't know any other members of the family?"

"No, I was hoping—" She stopped. Once again, she'd nearly blurted out her frustration and need for help in finding anyone who knew her mother. She looked up at him, baffled by her compulsion to confide in this stranger.

"I'd better go upstairs and get ready," she said.

Again, Mustafa swung the keys around his fingers. "Doctor take you cloth," he said, clearly approving of

Thomas's high-handed behavior. "We go now."

"What? He took my clothes, too? Well, he'll just have to bring them back. I'm looking forward to at least one night in this hotel. I'll get a room myself. Wait! Did he take my passport? I need it to check in."

"They probably won't let you stay here alone even if you have your passport," Markam said. "Women aren't allowed to check into a hotel or travel without written permission from a male relative." At least he had the grace to look like he felt sorry for her.

Taking business cards from his pocket, he held them out. "I'll leave these with you, Dr. Darius, in case you need to contact me. Would you give one to your brother? I'll call him this evening. Or perhaps I can—"

"I'll give him your message. Goodnight, Mr. Markam. Thank you." She dropped the cards into her bag and followed Mustafa. Glancing back, she saw Markam standing there, watching them go, his body rigid. Something was definitely worrying that man.

Outside, the heat had flattened into a hint of evening. Layne got into the SUV, and Mustafa, his face set in lines of fatigue, made an elaborate business of checking something in the back. He got in beside her.

"You must be really tired," she said. He didn't respond and she tried again. "It's been a long day, huh?"

He grunted and gave her a look that seemed to say he'd had enough of her.

As they left the hotel area and drove along a broad road, the gray-blue twilight sky was deepening. Soon, the clear tenor voice of a muezzin hovered in the air, calling the *Maghrib*, the sunset prayer, and Layne sensed the nearness of a sudden drop into night.

She closed her eyes and settled against the seat, welcoming the wind through the open window. The experiences of the day crowded in upon her, and she shivered, her nerves still raw.

After a while, the motion was soothing. She almost dozed until she thought about arriving at the Al-Amirs' house in this dusty, disheveled state. With luck, she'd be sent straight to the women's quarters, but she'd still have to deal with a whole new bunch of people. Darn Thomas. She had so looked forward to a peaceful rest in that lovely hotel bed.

The truck shuttered to a stop, and she opened her eyes. Mustafa sat sullenly waiting for a group of women, shrouded in black, to cross in front of them. It was dark now. She could see a few lights from tiny shops and vegetable stalls along the left side of the road.

They seemed to be in an older residential area with remnants of European influence in the wide streets and sidewalks. But the biggest change from downtown was the presence of trees! Large, mature oak trees, their branches massing against the last light in the sky. The air was cooler here, too, and denser.

She caught the scent of sweet night jasmine that always filled her with a strange longing.

They lurched forward again, and she said, "Are we almost there?"

Mustafa seemed unsure but he had no intention of saying so. He turned sharply into another street. No shops lit this road. Weak streetlamps cast a hazy light, revealing nothing but high stone walls and overhanging trees.

He drove slowly past a long wall, squinting as if he were looking for an address. She was about to ask him if they were lost when he swung off the pavement onto rocky ground.

Wearily, he climbed out and disappeared into the shadows of trees. Layne grabbed her bag and was close behind him. He pushed a buzzer next to a rusty metal door in the wall. The only sound was the stirring of leaves overhead.

"This can't be the Al-Amirs' house," she hissed at him.

"This right house," he insisted. He pounded on the door, making a din that echoed in the silence.

Layne stepped back, her sleeve brushing the shabby, gray wall. In the dim light, the stone was positively mangy, covered with crumbling mud. Weeds grew in chinks in what was left of the mortar.

"What are we doing here, Mustafa? Let's go back to those shops we passed and ask for directions."

He made an unpleasant sound in his throat and pounded again.

Suddenly, metal scraped across uneven stone. The door opened a few inches and Mustafa peered through the crack into the darkness.

Apparently talking to a shadow, he mumbled something. The door opened wider. Layne saw a small, wizened man, his thob stark white against his mahogany-colored skin. He held up an electric lantern and spoke a few words that sounded like no actual language she'd ever heard.

Mustafa said, "This man show way."

"What? It's not the right place. It looks deserted."

"This Al-Amir house. We go!"

Too tired to even consider options, Layne hitched her bag over her shoulder and followed the lantern's light along a brick path through a tangle of bushes.

Chapter 7

The little porter shuffled ahead along a winding path toward the dark bulk of a stone structure. Stepping carefully on the uneven bricks, Layne caught a strong scent of roses on the warm night air. They crossed a wide terrace surrounded by flowerbeds and followed another path. This one, lit by filigreed lanterns, went around the house to a lighted circular driveway and stopped at the foot of marble steps leading up to massive double doors.

The house was designed to be seen at its dramatic best from this view. And it was impressive. Its tall Georgian windows echoed those of an English country house, but the landscaping gave it a warmth and grace that was purely Mediterranean.

A manor house in a sultan's garden. The words came to her with an uneasy sense of familiarity.

Layne glanced back at Mustafa, who waited at the bottom of the stairs when she began to climb. She was halfway up when the doors burst open. A young man dressed in a silk shirt and dark trousers came bounding toward her.

"You must be the other Doctor Darius," he said, stopping just short of colliding. "We were about to send out a search party for you. Now here you are." He bowed his head and pressed his palms together. "*Ahlan Wa Sahlan*. You are so welcome."

As exhausted as she was, Layne couldn't help responding to his eagerness. "Thank you. *Ahlan Bik*. Are you Mr. Al-Amir?"

He grimaced. "Why have I not already told you that? Yes, I am the infamous Ricky Al-Amir, Thomas's friend. And you are Thomas's lovely sister. We have been waiting to see you all afternoon." After a few words in Arabic to Mustafa, he held out his hand to her. "Please come. You must be very tired. We won't leave you on your feet for another moment."

Glancing up, she saw her brother standing in the doorway with a frown on his face. He had the audacity to say, "You look like a *shamal* blew you in, Layne. Where have you been?"

"I'll talk to you about that later, especially why you went away and left me," she said, feeling like smacking him.

He put his arm around her and hugged her. "I'm glad you made it. I was worried."

"You could have told me what you were going to do. You left me stuck there without so much as a hairbrush."

"I didn't know until I called Ricky this afternoon. He insisted that we come here instead of spending the night in the hotel."

"Oh, absolutely," Ricky said. "It was unthinkable that you should stay in a hotel—even for one night. There's plenty of room here. We meant for you to be our guests. Somehow, things got a bit confused, but now, all is well."

He bent nearer. "We wish to keep you close to us," he said, as if he were teasing. But his expression was serious, and she realized he was older than she thought, probably nearly forty, like Thomas.

Once inside the huge doors, Layne stared in awe at the cavernous marble entrance hall. French Empire chairs and tables were grouped around a gigantic Persian carpet, and on the far side, a long passageway, its walls pierced by a succession of arches, stretched into the shadows.

"Your home is truly grand," she said.

Ricky threw up his hands. "This is not my house, Layne—I may call you Layne? It belongs to my father. He is Asad bin Shirazi Al-Amir." He said the name with both reverence and complacency, as if he had no doubt she would recognize it.

"I intended for you to be *my* guests, of course. My wife, Rana, was looking forward to your visit, but my father insisted that you remain here."

A glance at Thomas's face told her he hadn't known about these arrangements either.

"My father will join us before dinner," Ricky said. "He is especially anxious to meet you, Layne."

After the stresses of this day, she wasn't sure she had the strength to sit through an evening of polite conversation. And with so august a person as this Asad Al-Amir must be. All she wanted in the world was to be clean and have a quiet, uninterrupted sleep.

"If you'll tell me where I'll be staying, I'd like to change before dinner," she said.

"Of course! How tired you must be after such a long trip." He snapped his fingers. A servant in a gray thob stepped from one of the archways.

For an instant, as Ricky spoke to the man and dismissed him with a flick of his wrist, the eagerness left his face, replaced by an arrogance of long custom. Then, he turned to her, smiling.

"This man will show you to your room. A maid is waiting there to bring whatever you need to be comfortable."

Following the man in gray, Layne felt anything but comfortable. There was power in this house, secured by generations of wealth and privilege. She couldn't imagine actually being able to relax here.

Upstairs, they went along a hallway until the man opened a door into a large airy bedroom. Her traveling box, looking scruffier than usual, was at the foot of a huge four-poster bed.

She wandered around the room, trying to get used to the luxury. Everything was white and gold— drapery, bedcovers, brocaded chairs. A scent of roses came in through the French doors that were slightly ajar.

On the wall behind the sofa in the sitting area were three watercolor paintings of London streets, muted by rain.

To remind me all the world is not a desert.

The words came to her as if her mother's voice had whispered them in the room. In her last letter she wrote,

I'm staying with friends in Riyadh. They've given me a luxurious room. I can smell roses from the garden below and look at watercolor paintings to remind me all the world is not a desert.

Elation and terror gripped her. This Al-Amir family must have been those friends. She sat on the edge of the bed, her legs suddenly weak. This was the same room. Was it the place where Katherine Darius spent the last days of her life?

Those terrible weeks after her mother's disappearance came surging back—her father's frantic efforts to get information, the reporters' calls, the waiting, hoping. The months that followed, when she went numbly through the routines of her life, feeling nothing. Except in the agonizing moments when she saw her mother ahead of her on a street or in a store, and that frozen grief gave way to joy that stopped her heart. Until the woman turned, and she was a stranger.

Now the pain, the hope and despair she'd lived with these past years was about to end. She forced herself to reject the excitement threatening to overtake her.

Thomas must have known her mother stayed in this house. Why did he keep it from her? She buried her face in her hands, trying to understand.

After a while, she got up, pulled a white caftan out of her travel box, and threw it on the bed. On her way to the bathroom, she heard tapping on the door.

"Come in," she called, and a tiny South Indian woman dressed in a white cotton sari slipped in. She might have been very old, her face like thin parchment stretched over sharp bones. But her quick, nervous movements suggested she was younger. She clasped her hands in front of her waist and stood scowling. If she was the maid, she didn't seem too happy with her job.

"Hello," Layne said. She'd never had a servant. Feeling gauche, even vaguely guilty, she waited.

The woman swung her hand back and forth to indicate ironing and pointed at the caftan.

"Oh. Yes, that needs ironing. All of my clothes are pretty wrinkled," Layne said.

Seizing the caftan, the woman hurried out the door.

Layne scanned the room, looking for peepholes. How did that woman know she needed to have a dress ironed? When she came out of the bathroom a few minutes later, her caftan lay on the bed, beautifully pressed.

She dressed and began to twist her hair into the long braid down her back that she always wore. So close to the mirror, she could see the fatigue in her face. On impulse, she brushed out her hair to hang in chestnut waves.

Downstairs, Thomas's voice reached her as she crossed the entrance hall, and she followed the sound into a large library. Her brother was explaining something, his cheeks pink with enthusiasm and his glasses halfway down his nose.

He and three other men sat companionably in big leather chairs on either side of a fireplace. It was a masculine room, dark paneled and secure, smelling of leather and wood polish. An oak desk in one corner was covered in stacks of papers and open books as if the master of the house had just been interrupted in his work.

Asad Al-Amir sat on the left side of the group, a little apart from the others, at ease in his domain. He was still handsome, though he must be seventy, and there was vigor in his tall body, pared to essential muscle and bone.

A passage from an article her mother wrote years ago came back to her.

This man has the fierce look of the highborn of this region. A sultan, dressed in the flannels of a British gentleman.

Now, she knew who that man was. He turned and looked at her. His eyes, set deep in shadow, widened.

They stared at each other until Ricky said, "Layne, how nice you are looking. Come and have a cool drink." He rose nimbly and directed her to the long couch that faced the fireplace. She sat down quickly.

Ricky, still standing, said, "This is Mr. Khalil Hassan," indicating the man on Al-Amir's left.

He was also good-looking, in his early fifties, with black, grizzled hair. His face and neck had the tautness of physical activity, but the most remarkable thing about him was a look of habitual vigilance.

"And this is my father," he said, his voice deferential.

Layne made herself meet those shadowed eyes again.

Al-Amir did not smile. "How do you do, Dr. Darius?" His voice was deep and had the clipped precision of the British public schools.

"I'm feeling much better now, thanks to your hospitality," she said.

The servant appeared beside her with a tray of drinks, and she took a lime water, grateful for the time to compose herself. Being the center of attention was intimidating and Al-Amir evidently intended to keep her there.

"Your brother tells me you spent some time working in India. And now you are braving the desert. Bold choices for a young woman."

She sipped her drink. "Women can do quite a lot if given the opportunity." Glancing at her brother, she saw wariness in his expression.

"Undoubtedly that is true," Al-Amir said.

Having put her toe into the cauldron, Layne decided to plunge in the rest of the way.

"I've heard about you, Mr. Al-Amir. Thomas told me you're an advocate for modernization and allowing all people, including women, to develop their abilities and pursue their dreams."

Al-Amir averted his face, obviously pleased. He rubbed his forefinger over the folds of an exquisitely carved wooden box on the lamp table next to him.

"You remind me very much of another beautiful woman I once knew. Have you the same fearlessness your mother had?"

The words sent ice prickles through her. She had prepared for resistance, even denial, not bald revelation.

"My mother had much more energy than I ever will."

Al-Amir held her gaze and then seemed to look beyond her into the past. "Few people have," he murmured. "Katherine Darius was a woman of great strength."

Watching the play of emotion in his face, she was angry. She was in this house because this imperious man willed it. Why? Did he bring her here to satisfy his curiosity?

"I hope to find out what happened to her, Mr. Al-Amir. Do you know?" she said, straining to keep her voice level.

In the silence, Ricky appeared to be studying the pattern in the rug. Thomas stared at her as if she'd lost her mind. Hassan waited, alert as a falcon.

Al-Amir sat with his head bowed. Then, he looked

up and, amazingly, he laughed. "You are so like her!"

His voice was warm with pleasure. "You may lack her energy, but you have her fire. Indeed you have. So this is why you have come to our desert—to excavate the past."

Trying to recover her balance, Layne said, "Thomas and I are grateful for the opportunity to do research, but I don't want to leave here without knowing why she disappeared. I have a right to know."

Al-Amir's expression hardened, and Layne realized she had gone too far.

"Perhaps we will talk of the past another time," he said. "It is the present that concerns us now, is it not?"

Tilting his head back, he regarded her down the length of his nose.

Ricky and Thomas both began talking. Layne sat in a kind of daze with no idea what to say or do. Clearly, this was Al-Amir's domain, his rules. Whatever dealings she had with him would be on his terms, not hers.

Ricky said in a loud voice, "The ladies in my family are anxious to meet you, Layne. My wife asked me to say that she will be honored if you will have tea with her tomorrow." He glanced at his father.

She couldn't tell whether the patriarch approved or disapproved of this. Al-Amir's attention seemed to have drifted.

Thanking Ricky, she tried to sound enthusiastic. She expected to spend most of her time in the women's private quarters, the hareem, just as she did with the Bedouin, but at this moment she felt like a child being sent to her room.

"Wonderful!" Ricky said. "We live not far from here. Rana will be pleased. She'll send a car for you."

He was interrupted by the servant's appearance in the doorway announcing a visitor.

Ricky turned to Thomas. "This must be the American fellow who phoned earlier to speak to you. I asked him to come round this evening."

Chapter 8

David Markam followed the servant into the old-fashioned library, relieved to find one room without the house's Georgian grandeur.

The men stood to shake his hand when Thomas Darius introduced him, except for the patriarch, who gave him only a nod of acknowledgement with a bare edge of civility.

Taking the other end of the couch where Layne Darius was sitting, David saw her staring at him, as if she couldn't believe he had come.

"It's a pleasure to see you again, Dr. Darius," he said, sending her a look that meant, *Thought you'd gotten rid of me, didn't you?*

"Good evening, Mr. Markam," she said.

Then she smiled, and he had to force himself to look away.

Her face wasn't conventionally pretty, but the flowing hair softened it. The fine bones and wary green eyes had a haunting beauty he knew he'd never be able to forget.

Hassan said, "Mr. David Markam, I have heard of you from those in the Foreign Ministry who know what goes on in your diplomatic mission. You are a political officer, I believe. One of a team who have come to facilitate the relocation of your embassy from Jeddah to Riyadh, are you not?"

"Yes. Watching this modern city rise from the desert is exhilarating," David said, not surprised that Hassan knew who he was. He'd heard a few things about Hassan, too, and knew he held a place of power in the country's national security.

Hassan nodded. "It is the beginning of a new era. Once the embassies are in place, Riyadh will truly be a capital city."

David looked at Al-Amir, wondering what he had to say about the changes in his country. Before he could frame a question, Hassan said, "You have made quite a number of friends locally, have you not?"

"Meeting people is one of the advantages of my job," David said, adjusting to what sounded like a hint of provocation.

"We were lucky to be among them today," Thomas Darius said. "Your help was invaluable."

Ricky Al-Amir flushed, the family hauteur in his face. "Thanks to God, you came to no harm! I am mortified by what happened. You were put into terrible danger by the incompetence of that thief I hired in Dhahran. It is unbelievable. The man was highly recommended!

"Giving you wrecks instead of the vehicles I paid

for was bad enough. The business of tampering with the water cans was unforgiveable. The instant I heard, I was on the telephone to have him arrested. The villain has disappeared!"

"We have already begun an investigation," Hassan said. "Though we will not be astonished if they have decamped and vanished."

David had heard of incidents like this more than once. Substituting the jeeps for the vehicles ordered wasn't a spontaneous act. Somebody with a plan was behind it. He glanced at Al-Amir, and saw he was watching him.

In the awkward pause that followed, Hassan said casually, "How did you happen to be on that road today, Mr. Markam?"

"Saeed Bin Yousef, the man who was with me, is an engineer sponsoring the American company that's building your country's new satellite communications system. He also has a large farm doing hydroponic plant cultivation in the Eastern Province. We drove out to look at his facility this morning. On the way back to the city, we saw that Land Rover stopped on the side of the road.

"He recognized the whip antenna on its bumper as the kind you need if you're using side-band radios. A Land Rover just like that was recently seen in the vicinity of the satellite station near Riyadh, so Saeed wanted to know who the man was. We pulled up behind him, and he took off like a gazelle. We were hot on his trail when we saw you folks."

"I'm sorry coming to our aid made you lose him," Darius said. "But it was in a good cause."

"An excellent cause," David said.

The embarrassment in Ricky Al-Amir's face showed that he wasn't happy about this conversation. Al-Amir sat silent, his face unreadable.

"This incident convinced me," Darius said. "We'll be some distance from the Yabrin settlement and quite a bit farther from Haradh, the nearest town. Being able to reach help in an emergency would make me feel better." He looked at his sister.

David knew that having her along had elevated his risk. A woman's needs would change the ways he was used to working in the desert.

"It's too bad you weren't able to bring in any radios," he said.

"We didn't even try. We were told before we came that they'd be confiscated at customs."

"Very likely. Saeed and I talked about your situation. He thinks he can locate some for you. If an antenna is installed on your vehicle, you'll probably be able to drive within range of Haradh fairly quickly. What have you done in the past?"

"I've never gone into an area like the Rub Al-Kahli. All of my fieldwork was in Yemen. Until the border troubles made it impossible for me to get in there again. Those observations were all with families who had been settled. Their days of nomadic herding are past."

Glowing with enthusiasm, he said, "That's what

makes this study so valuable. Mustafa's relatives are still taking their herds out for spring foraging. We're observing and participating in this vanishing way of life. An extraordinary opportunity!"

"We'll fix everything up," Ricky Al-Amir said, his cheeks flushed. "Nothing will stand in the way of this work. You may be certain of that."

David didn't think Darius blamed the trouble in Dhahran on the Al-Amirs, but the man must be touchy about it.

He and Darius went on talking, and David turned to the woman. "You've recovered from your shopping trip, Dr. Darius?"

"I didn't actually do any shopping."

"Oh? Then you were exploring the city?"

"I might have been."

"I'll be glad to drive you into town. Anytime. Please call me," he said.

Noticing that Al-Amir was still watching him, David said, "I suppose it's gratifying to you, sir, that knowledge of the traditional way of life is being preserved."

Al-Amir's lips twisted into a grimace of distaste, as if he were being forced to speak against his will. "It is, naturally, an admirable study. I could wish only that it were being done by those whose customs are being chronicled."

His tone sounded as if he had said all he intended to say, but David wasn't going to lose this chance to learn something that might explain why this man's name was in the message Saeed intercepted.

"You made that point quite convincingly in your last book, I believe. Still, isn't it better to have a record, even if outsiders have to write it?"

Al-Amir waved his hand impatiently. "Perhaps, as the product of a nation with only a brief history, you do not see the importance of holding one's past in one's own hands."

They stared at each other, the tension between them palpable. David tried to think of reasons for his hostility, but before he could say anything, Al-Amir leaned toward Hassan and said something in Arabic. Hassan rose immediately and Al-Amir got stiffly to his feet. He straightened to his full height.

"Mr. Hassan and I have some business matters to discuss. Good evening, Mr. Markam. Dr. Darius, Miss Darius, I hope you will be comfortable in my home." Without waiting for a reply, he and Hassan left.

David was disappointed, but he saw that Layne looked relieved.

Ricky Al-Amir still seemed uncomfortable. "My father tires easily," he said.

"We're indebted to him. I hope our being here isn't too much of a disruption," Darius said.

"On the contrary, he's delighted that you're here. This house is lonely for him. You see, my mother died many years ago, and his children do not make their homes with him. Our extended family—my uncles' and aunts' families, Rana and I, we all have our own houses."

"That's an unusual arrangement for your culture, isn't it?" Layne Darius said.

Her brother gave her a slanted glance, as if he were wondering why he'd brought her along.

Ricky Al-Amir said, "It's a break from traditions, yes, but my father was never a conformist. He was educated at Oxford and sent his children to school abroad. His father before him was the same. It must be in our blood to be dissenters. Also, we are not, in fact, people of this desert. Persian culture is quite different."

He passed on to another topic, but David kept thinking about what he'd said. Saeed mentioned that Darius was a Persian name, and the Al-Amirs were Persian. Was that a coincidence?

Did the messages intercepted by the technicians at the satellite station suggest a connection between the Darius family and the Al-Amirs that went beyond a mutual interest in anthropology?

As if she'd read his thoughts, Layne Darius said, "When I saw you at the hotel, you said you're worried about our safety, Mr. Markam. Do you really believe we're in some kind of danger?"

David made up his mind to go straight to the point.

"I'm concerned, yes. Bin Yousef has encountered something that's worrying. He spends a good bit of time at the satellite stations, especially the one near

Riyadh. A few days ago, he and I visited that one, and a technician there told us he'd picked up illegal side-band traffic from somewhere nearby.

"That was the first of a series of odd messages. At least three of the stations have intercepted them. They're in a code of sorts, but they seem to be hinting at a disruption of the government, if not an actual insurgence."

They all looked shocked. "Did Bin Yousef give them credence?" Darius said.

"He didn't take the early ones seriously, but the transmissions have continued. In any case, I'm telling you this to explain why I advise you to be especially cautious during your stay in country. If there is something brewing, you and your sister could be at risk."

"Something? You mean a rebellion, like the business last year at Mecca?" Darius said.

"But this is impossible," Ricky Al-Amir said. He looked more angry than alarmed. "This is a joke, bravado. The desert people are always spoiling for a conflict. They get bored and need excitement. They imagine they're still living in the old days of tribal warfare."

David wasn't surprised at the strength of his denial, but he didn't want to escalate the hostility by saying Al-Amir's name had been mentioned in at least one message. "In any case, we can't afford to dismiss it," he said. "Those Bedouin we saw today were heavily armed with guns that somebody supplied to them. And the transmissions picked up by the earth stations are real."

"What you say is unthinkable!" Ricky Al-Amir insisted. He looked as if he were squaring for rebuttal.

Just then, a servant came in to announce dinner, and David took the chance to head off an argument.

"I hope you're right," he said. "Saeed's trying to find out who's sending them."

He rose to go, and they all went with him into the entry hall.

As they shook hands at the door, David said, "How soon are you leaving for the Bedouin encampment, Dr. Darius?"

"A few days. We have more preparations to do, and the new vehicles won't arrive until next week. Last-minute problems always crop up.

"It'll be a push to get there by the end of the month, which is what we agreed to. Mustafa's uncle is headman of the extended family we'll be living with. We're obliged to abide by their preferences if we can."

"This time of year is not ideal," Ricky Al-Amir said. "I thought we'd have everything ready by early January. Unfortunately, there are no firm plans in the desert."

"Speaking of plans," David said. "Saeed Bin Yousef asked me to tell you he's hosting a party tomorrow night and would like you to be his special guests. He's anxious to hear about your work.

"If you're free, I hope you'll all come. His friends

are an eclectic group and always interesting. He has quite a reputation as a host."

"Most kind, but I'm afraid I am engaged," Ricky Al-Amir said quickly.

He and Darius exchanged a look, and David thought Darius wanted to refuse as well.

His sister, standing beside him, said, "I told Mr. Bin Yousef this afternoon that we'd love to come."

Ricky Al-Amir's expression stiffened. "Of course. Thomas, you and Layne should go. Excuse me. I must speak to the servant," he said and went down the hall.

"Can we talk with Bin Yousef about the radios tomorrow?" Darius said.

"I doubt he'll be free during the day. He's got a lot of projects going. You might bring it up at the party in the evening. Possibly arrange a meeting for the day after."

He held out his hand to Layne Darius. "Dr. Darius, I look forward to seeing you tomorrow."

She shook hands with him, and then she said in a low voice, "I wonder if Mr. Bin Yousef is interested in more than our research plans. How does he have radios that are illegal to own in this country? Why is he willing to help us?"

Her brother looked exasperated, but David admired her audacity.

"Saeed's got access to things most private citizens don't have. He's offered to help because he can get that equipment, and he's interested in your work.

He's a nice guy who likes to help people doing worthwhile things."

"What about you?" she said. "Why are you interested?"

David smiled. There was no coyness in her question. If she realized how she was affecting him, it must not matter.

"The company installing the satellite stations is American. Any threats to American enterprises overseas concern me. That's *my* job."

She held his gaze. Then, apparently making up her mind to trust him, she said, "In that case, I'd better tell you something. I saw that Land Rover on my way to the women's quarters. It was hidden behind the men's tent."

"You saw it? You're sure it was the same one?"

"The engine was still making popping noises. It had that whip antenna you were talking about, and radio transmitters were stashed in the back."

"You looked into it?" David said. "God! What would have happened if they'd caught you?"

He heard her brother groan, but Layne Darius smiled and said, "We'll see you tomorrow evening, Mr. Markam."

David gave her a look that meant, *I will definitely see you tomorrow.*

Chapter 9

Layne woke early and spent the morning nodding over a book on desert tribes, her senses dulled by jet lag and exhaustion. She'd gotten through the uncomfortable dinner last night and escaped as soon as she could, leaving her brother and Ricky at the table.

Al-Amir didn't appear at all, and she knew her effort to confront him about her mother was a clumsy mistake. If Katherine Darius was his guest, failing to protect her must be a source of embarrassment for him. Next time, she needed to be more careful. For now, he was giving her time to reflect. Aside from the sullen little maid who brought her meals, no one, not even her brother, bothered to speak to her.

At midafternoon, she went out without much enthusiasm for the tea party. In the hundred-degree heat, her long skirt and sleeves were a burden, and she was glad to see a white Mercedes, surely with air conditioning, waiting in front of the house.

The driver opened the door, and Layne slid into the cool interior. Rana Al-Amir grasped her hand.

"Such a pleasure to meet you, Layne. You won't mind my calling you Layne? I know you're officially Doctor Darius, but I hope we will be friends from the very beginning."

Rana was slim and beautiful, as one expected Ricky's wife to be, with large hazel eyes and the translucent skin of the fairest Persians. She was caped in a silk abaya with a matching scarf draped loosely over her dark hair.

"Women need women to talk to," she went on. "As fond as I am of Ricky's father, in his house I always feel I must speak in a hushed voice."

Her candidness made Layne relax a little. She glanced at the driver. He showed no interest in what they were saying, but every word would likely be reported to Al-Amir.

"Is your house nearby?"

Rana looked down at her lap. "We are not going to my house. Sahar asked me to bring you to her flat. She's anxious to meet you."

"Sahar?"

"The daughter of my husband's auntie. Asad Al-Amir is her uncle. Most of the year, she lives in France, near Paris. Now and then, she comes to stay in this country for several months. Perhaps she feels homesick."

Tension knotted Layne's shoulders. This invitation was arranged so the women of the family could get a look at her.

"What does she do? Does she have children?"

Rana laughed. "Sahar, children? She is a businesswoman. She has her own company. They harvest plants from the desert to make lovely creams and things, very expensive. We are all in awe of her."

So they were getting out the big guns, the power opinion in the family. She wondered if her mother had been invited to meet Sahar. If so, this tea party must be to size up Katherine Darius's daughter. In that case, she could do some sizing up of her own. At least they could answer her questions. Women knew more about what really went on in a family than men did.

The driver stopped in front of a high-rise apartment building in what Rana said was one of the newer areas of the city. They went in, shivering in the sudden chill. As they rode the elevator to the top of the building, Layne braced herself for whatever was coming. Care would be needed to avoid the mistake she made with Al-Amir.

Sahar opened her apartment door, and Layne saw the relationship at once. Her face had the angular, aloof features of the Al-Amir bloodline. She was willowy slim in a long blue dress that emphasized her height, and she greeted them without smiling.

Her living room, all plate glass, teak, and chrome, had a European modernity about it, serene and intimidating at once.

Instead of taking them to sit there, she led the way to an alcove, where a large table was laid with crystal plates of pastries and savories.

It was an English high tea, not a morsel of Middle Eastern food in sight.

As soon as they sat down, two servants, young women who looked to be from Sudan or Ethiopia, poured tea for them.

Sahar sat at the head of the table and studied Layne. "You are not like your mother," she said. "Except the eyes. You have her eyes."

Layne tasted the tea. "No, not much like her. I got my father's long bones." She paused and decided to be cautiously candid. "Since you know what she looked like, you must have met my mother during her stay here."

"My uncle was pleased to have a distinguished journalist visit him. He wanted our family to make her welcome."

And did you? Layne wondered. It hardly seemed likely. She reached for a raspberry tart, and the loose sleeve of her tunic fell back, exposing her elbow.

"Oh, you have a terrible bruise on your arm. How did it happen?" Rana said.

"Yesterday, in the city. I made the mistake of exploring by myself. Some young men harassed me a bit. My arm hit a wall as I was running from them."

"What? Men chased you? They attacked you in the city?" Rana said, horrified.

Sahar's eyes blazed, but she said nothing.

"Fortunately, I got into a shop, and they left soon after. I didn't see them again." The gunshot at the old fortress was still too vivid. She was not ready to tell anyone about that yet.

"You must never go out alone," Rana said. She began talking about the shops along King Faisal Road, doing her best to keep conversation going, without much help from Sahar.

Finally, Sahar told the servants to clear the table.

Sipping a glass of Perrier, she leaned back in her chair. "It's kind of you to visit me today."

Layne braced herself. Now, they'd get to the real reason she was here. "I appreciate the chance to talk with you. Anything you can tell me about your culture will be welcome. I didn't have much time to prepare before I came," she said.

"So I imagine." Sahar had her uncle's habit of tilting her head to look down in disdain.

"I have always considered cultures unique, defying generalizations. How are you, a woman from Western freedom, able to make judgments about our society?"

This was an unexpected tack. And it went directly to the heart of Layne's own doubts. "I'm trained to go into my research without forming opinions ahead of time. It's the basis of good science, to observe, not judge," she said.

"Desirable, but impossible! We all take our fears and prejudices with us."

In an effort to intervene, Rana said, "Sahar, I told Layne about your company."

Layne seized the distraction. "Yes, I want to hear about it. You make skin care products from desert plants?"

A light came into Sahar's face, transforming her. She called to one of the women who brought in a silver tray and put it on the table. Sahar pushed it closer to Layne. On it was a velvet box that looked like a jewel case. Layne opened it and saw pearlescent jars and bottles nestled in gold silk.

"You must take these with you," Sahar said. "I will have a larger jar of the moisturizer sent to you before you leave the city. Living outdoors in this climate will turn that lovely skin of yours into a prune."

Layne picked up one of the bottles. *Nectar of the Sands* swept across an image of golden dunes.

"Nigella sativa?" she said, looking at the ingredients.

"It's black cumin seed oil. The Bedouin have used it for hundreds of years. They believe it will cure almost any ailment."

"The women I lived with in India use oils and herbs. But I didn't know such plants grew here on the desert."

Sahar's expression took on its disdainful aspect again. "The desert is not barren. Sorrel, wild rapeseed, pimpernel, they all bloom in the season of spring forage. Bedouin women harvest and preserve them for medicines, for moisture and cosmetics. They make soap from goat and camel's milk.

"Our land is rich in these gifts. The elder women keep this knowledge from generation to generation."

She reached for one of the jars and showed the label. "You see, these are our ingredients. Chemicals cannot do what these plants have always done."

"You make the products here?" Layne said, searching for a way around the defensiveness she seemed to keep prompting in Sahar.

"We soon will. For now, women gather and process the plants to be sent to my laboratory in France. We are doing quite well in Europe. Next year, we will open markets in America."

"Don't Bedouin men object if their wives or daughters work outside of their homes?" Layne said, knowing it sounded like a challenge.

Sahar flushed and looked down at her hands, apparently regretting her enthusiasm. "For now, our workers are divorced wives, two who have chosen to defy their families and not marry. I set up a school to teach literacy and business skills to poor women. It is a gradual process, but it promises a future for them."

"Yes, I can see that," Layne said, trying to be careful. "In India some men are threatened if their wives earn money, even though the children are hungry and the need is great."

"It is no different here." Sahar's expression reflected anguish. "The women come to me full of hope. If their families want them to return home, they go."

"It must be very difficult for you," Layne said, embarrassed that she could think of nothing better to say.

"Difficult? Ha! We're climbing mountains with salad forks. Our male guardianship laws condemn us to be children our entire lives. Is that not appalling?" she demanded.

"Look at the way you were attacked on the street! No society should accept that as normal. Or worse, put blame on the woman."

"I've read about the male guardianship laws," Layne said. "It's hard to understand what it's like to live with that oppression."

"We are not waiting to be rescued from oppression!" Rana declared, her face pinched with distress. "I don't want to live as you do in America. Women expose their bodies to sell alcohol and cigarettes there. Here, I have dignity. I have respect for myself."

Layne held up her hands. "Please. There was so little time to prepare before I came here. I don't mean to offend you. Please excuse my ignorance."

Sahar sat up straighter as if she were starting a negotiation. "You want to understand us, but you offer us nothing in return?" she demanded.

Layne's throat tightened. Hedging, she said, "What do I have that you need?"

"You're a professor at university. You influence the attitudes of others. If a woman like you speaks for us, the rest of the world will know our complacency behind the veil is a myth, a lie. In America, the women's movement is changing everything. You could teach us how to do that here!"

"I wish that were true," Layne said. "I'm just an adjunct professor, with very little influence." She paused, trying to find words that wouldn't make things worse.

"I'd be happy to speak for your cause if my words could make any difference. We haven't solved all the problems in my country, either. The Equal Rights Amendment may never pass. We're changing out of necessity. Families need two incomes. Women have to work.

"Your country doesn't have that challenge. You're a small kingdom suddenly in possession of unimaginable wealth. There's no urgency for your social patterns to change."

Sahar crossed her arms, her mouth twisted in contempt. "It is not such a small country. It is quite large."

"Yes, of course. I meant in population. Your whole country has about as many people as our states of Michigan or Florida."

She looked incredulous. "What does population matter? Are not the women of this Michigan and Florida free?"

Wishing fervently that she'd kept her mouth shut, Layne said, "Most are, I guess. It depends. We have conservative communities with the same attitudes your people have."

They sat in pulsing silence. Not daring to look at Rana, Layne said, "What does Mr. Al-Amir say about these things? From what my brother tells me, he's in favor of equal rights for women."

"My uncle is a good man," Sahar said, sighing. "But he is a man after all. He has written about the need for these changes. I know he believes in equality. So I beg him to help our people who are working for this. Just moderation of archaic laws. That's all we ask.

"He is not against us. It is just—" She seemed reluctant to say what she really meant. "Every time we talk, he ends our conversation the same way. 'The time is not right. Be patient. It will come.'"

"That's probably true," Layne said. She'd spoken before she thought, and Sahar's reaction was explosive.

"You also tell us to wait? That's what you offer? Sit here in my marble cell until I am an old woman—waiting for someone to break our chains?

"So you are like your famous mother, after all! You come to me pretending interest in our cause. And in the end, you will betray us!"

She shot up from her chair, dashed across the living room, and disappeared through an arched doorway.

Layne sat, numb with chagrin and pity. One of her questions had been answered. Her mother had certainly been here.

She must have listened to Sahar's dreams of reform and heard her plea for help.

Did Katherine Darius, willing to do what was necessary to get a story, make herself an enemy by pretending sympathy? Did she really betray Sahar's trust?

Rana rose and called to the servants.

Having no choice, Layne left with her.

As they rode the elevator down, Rana tried to explain.

"Sahar's schooling in England and France gave her ideas that do not fit here. Please don't be offended. She has a good heart."

"I'm not offended. I sympathize with her frustration. I do understand."

Tension still lay between them in the car. Layne tried to think of a way to restore the feeling they'd started with, but Rana seemed seriously upset.

Glancing out the back window, Layne saw a black sedan with tinted windows pull away from the curb the moment after they left. Was someone following her? She wasn't sure whether to be afraid or grateful.

"You must be very tired," Rana said. "Perhaps you will rest tonight."

"I'd like to, but my brother and I have been invited to a dinner party this evening."

Rana raised her eyebrows. "Who has invited you to dinner?"

"One of the men we met yesterday. Our jeep broke down out on the desert, and they rescued us. His name is Saeed Bin Yousef."

"Yes. I know of him. An engineer. Very modern ideas. His behavior has made him quite controversial."

Her expression held the same look of hauteur that was on her husband's face when David Markam mentioned Bin Yousef's invitation yesterday. Here was a layer of social conflict Layne had never encountered.

They said little as they drove into Al-Amir's neighborhood in the subdued light of late afternoon.

Sahar's voice, the desperation of her appeals, kept stabbing at Layne's conscience. She thought about the women she'd passed on the city street yesterday. Laughing, yes. But not allowed even to lift their bare faces to the sun.

Regret made her feel inept and awkward. She'd offered Sahar nothing but platitudes.

So you are like your famous mother, after all!

Was that true? Was she like her mother? Katherine Darius made her reputation by telling the world about the Algerian women who fought as bravely as men, who took into their own hands the war of resistance against French colonial rule.

Sahar obviously expected her to speak for the women of this society in the same way. But Katherine did not espouse causes. If there were only ideals, no war, no struggle worth writing about, she wouldn't be interested. No wonder Sahar felt betrayed.

And now I've done the same thing, Layne thought. Declaring I'm a scientist, here to observe, not to take sides, I turned away from Sahar's appeal just as callously as my mother did.

"Rana," she said, "when my mother visited Mr. Al-Amir, did you meet her?"

Her lips thinned, as if she wanted nothing to do with this topic. "That was before Ricky and I were married."

"But the family, in general, didn't like her, did they?"

She hesitated, then lifted her hands in a gesture of helplessness. "I can't say."

They turned into the gates of Al-Amir's estate, and Layne glanced back. The black sedan had disappeared.

The dim entrance hall of the house was silent when she went in. She crossed to the library, hoping Al-Amir was there, working among those piles of books and papers on his desk.

Sahar had confirmed the first thing she needed to know. Katherine Darius was Al-Amir's guest. Now, she could face him and insist that he tell her the truth about her mother.

She tapped on the door and waited. Nothing.

Angry, she tried the knob. If he wasn't in there, she'd search his desk. He might have letters, notes, some hint of what happened those last days. The door was locked.

Turning to go, she heard a slight sound.

Nothing moved, but she knew that someone down that long, shadowed passageway was watching her.

Chapter 10

The moon hung like stage scenery above the sprawling opulence of Saeed Bin Yousef's mansion.

Mustafa eased Al-Amir's sedan around the circular drive and stopped at the foot of the marble stairs. Music and laughter floated down to them on the warm night air.

Layne got out and stood looking up at the lofty arches. No Cinderella ever arrived at a grander ball. She was glad Thomas had made her bring along a decent dress.

"Very big house," Mustafa said. "Make much party." He chuckled nervously. "I wait you."

"Thank you. We shouldn't be here very long, Mustafa. Unless the Doctor finds a good audience."

"At least I won't be alienating people every time I open my mouth," Thomas said. "You'd better behave yourself tonight."

Layne adjusted her shawl. "You've gotten bossy in your old age, Thomas."

As they reached the top of the stairs, Saeed Bin Yousef came through the crowd of people, the cream-colored silk *bisht* over his thob billowing around him.

"Dr. Darius #1 and Dr. Darius #2. You have arrived! I'm delighted you could come. We are all waiting to hear about your adventures!" He shook Thomas's hand and bowed to Layne.

Glancing down at Mustafa, still standing at the foot of the steps, Bin Yousef said, "There is no need for your driver to wait. I have a car available to take you whenever you are ready."

"That's very kind," Thomas said. "But I believe Mr. Al-Amir expects him to stay here."

Bin Yousef smiled. "Come, Dr. Darius #2," he said. "My friend David has been waiting like an impatient tiger for you, but I have something for you to see before he monopolizes you all to himself."

Layne found the prospect of talking to Markam again surprisingly pleasing.

They followed him down a wide hall into a brilliantly lighted *majlis* with brocaded couches around its walls, a gilded ceiling and massive chandeliers.

Overwhelmed by this luxury, Layne wondered if Bin Yousef was trying to impress them, show them his house was grander than Al-Amir's.

The impulse seemed childish, but thinking of Ricky's and Rana's disdainful expressions when Bin Yousef's name was mentioned, she remembered Thomas's warning about tension among these wealthy families. *Mistrust and loyalties run under every surface.*

The next room was a long gallery, displaying paintings and enough fighting hardware to arm a whole tribe. Gigantic scimitars hung on the walls, some that could lop off a person's head and others that might do in an elephant. The metal gleamed, and jewels shone in their carved handles. On another wall, swords, sabers, and pistols were clustered on either side of an antique rifle taller than a man.

The gruesome arsenal fascinated Thomas, and he went around touching the shining surfaces, muttering about tribal warfare. Layne doubted that he'd ever so much as held such a weapon, but under his scholarly reserve, he harbored the spirit of a buccaneer.

She bent over one of the glass display cases in the center of the room. Here were the jewels! She might not wear any herself, but she was not immune to the flash of real diamonds. Or a ruby the size of an egg. "These are beautiful, Mr. Bin Yousef," she said, admiring a necklace of square emeralds set in gold. "What wonderful taste you have."

He hurried to her side. "Please, you must call me Saeed."

Not expecting this informality, she said, "Thank you. And you will call me Layne?"

"I shall say, 'Dr. Layne.' A compromise." He smiled and peered into the case. "These are beautiful things, but it is not I who collected them. These are my family's treasures." Drawing a key from a pocket in his thob, he unlocked the case, lifted the emerald necklace, and held it in front of her neck appraisingly.

For one moment, she was afraid he meant to give it to her. But he drew back, looking startled. "No, not emeralds. Jade is the color of your eyes, Dr. Layne. Emeralds do no justice. I will find the right piece for you."

She laughed and shook her head. "I don't wear jewelry, Saeed. They'd be wasted on me." Bending over another case, she said, "Look at these Mogul miniatures! I saw tiny paintings like this in Delhi. But nothing of this quality. Your family must have been gathering these things for a long time."

A mix of pride and sadness in his expression, he said, "Many generations. We are an old family. From the north." He looked down at the emerald necklace in his hand and some strong emotion passed across his face. "A very old family. You see, after I am gone, this house will be a museum, open for everyone to see our cultural heritage."

Replacing the necklace in the case, he turned to her with his usual brightness. "I have been keeping you too long. The party's waiting."

Layne caught Thomas's sleeve and they followed Saeed back through the reception hall and out onto a crowded terrace. In the center was a spouting fountain that had a life of its own. Water from dozens of jets shot up through pink and purple lights, swaying and dipping in time with jazz music floating into the night from hidden speakers.

The people clustered in groups around the terrace were a variety of nationalities, most of their faces reflecting the ease and boredom of those who spend a lot of time at cocktail parties. They might have been in any large city in the world. A few men were in thob and bisht, but not a single abaya or veil in sight.

Saeed swept into a group and began introductions. Thomas loved talking to people interested in his work, and Layne was glad to listen while she looked for David Markam. If he was such an "impatient tiger" waiting for her to come, where was he?

Then, among the shifting clumps of faces, she saw him. In dark trousers and a white silk bush shirt that set off the richness of his olive skin, he looked at ease and far too attractive. He saw her and made his way through the crowd.

Stepping into the group, he greeted people, listened with interest to the conversation, and then deftly steered her away to the shelter of a potted palm.

"I've been waiting for you," he said.

"So I heard. We've had a tour of the museum." She looked at the fountain as the water dance changed in time to a new melody. "Everything in this house is enormous and amazing."

"Saeed's very proud of his fountain. He had it made by a designer in California. It was such a success that he bought the business."

A servant circled past with a tray of drinks.

"I thought drinking alcohol was forbidden in this society," Layne said.

"The rich do as they please everywhere."

Markam sounded distracted, and she could feel the energy he was suppressing. He definitely had something on his mind—probably something she didn't want to talk to him about. She headed him off.

"Why did you come to the Al-Amir's house last night?"

"As I said, I wanted to talk to your brother privately. I still do. There's something I just found out today that I'd like to discuss with him."

"The last time I saw him, he was lecturing a group of people over by the buffet tables. Good luck getting him to leave his audience. Can you call him tomorrow?"

"The phones aren't secure." He frowned. "Hell! One of Saeed's buddies is motioning for us to join him. Do you want to? If not, there's a garden on the other side of that wall, with benches where we can sit down."

"The garden. Yes."

His arm came around her lightly. It was an impersonal gesture; he was simply guiding her in the right direction, but it suggested that they'd passed into a new stage of familiarity. She was pleased with it, or at least cautiously comfortable.

They went through an archway into a walled courtyard and walked along a lighted path between square beds of rose trees. Unlike the fragrance in Al-Amir's garden, these flowers seemed bred for their huge blooms and exotic colors rather than scent.

Layne chose a wrought iron bench and they sat down. "What do you want to talk to Thomas about?" she said.

He glanced at her, his face tense as if he were making a decision. "I'll tell you, but I still want to talk to him directly. It's in regard to the illegal transmissions Saeed's technicians picked up. Several more have come through. They're referring to movement of items that could be weapons, and most of them include Al-Amir's name."

Layne didn't know what to say. "Al-Amir? He's planning some kind of political uprising?"

"We don't know. I'm just telling you that if some activity is underway, and he's either the instigator or the target, you and your brother may not be safe."

"Well, it will take more than a rumor to scare us into leaving. This fieldwork is the most important thing in Thomas's life. It's an opportunity he'll never have again. And I—well, I've got my reasons too," she said, less certain than ever whether she ought to trust him.

"But you do understand why I need to talk to your brother?" Markam said.

She looked at him, trying to read the intention in his dark eyes. His job was to protect Americans. Maybe he was overreacting.

"What does Saeed think about all of this?" she said.

"He's as baffled as I am about the transmissions. I told him you saw field radios hidden in that Land

Rover." He looked at her sharply. "Did you and your brother mention them to Ricky Al-Amir?"

"I didn't. And I doubt Thomas did. He seems to be discounting anything that could get in the way of this field study. He might even think I made up the radios in the back of the Land Rover."

"Did you talk to Mr. Al-Amir today?" he said.

"Haven't seen him since last night. Ricky and Thomas went to town this morning to order some new vehicles for us. Rana and I spent the afternoon having tea and somewhat prickly conversation."

"So, they packed you off to the hareem. Who's Rana?"

Ignoring his grin, she said, "Ricky's wife. But don't let the idea of afternoon tea fool you. She took me to meet Sahar. It was a case of looking me over to find out where I stand on some very volatile issues. It was more like an inquisition than a social hour."

"What does she look like?"

"Rana? She's around thirty, très chic. She went to school in Paris. But she's not likely to show up at any of Saeed's parties."

"What about Sahar?" he said easily.

She smiled at him. "Now, she's the one you might like to meet. Vehemently advocates for women's rights. Owns her own company and runs a program teaching Bedouin women literacy and job skills. She's Al-Amir's niece, by the way."

His reaction made her think she'd been right not to mention Sahar's possible link with her mother's disappearance.

"She's an activist?" he said. "Do you know whether she's involved with a particular group?"

"If she is, she didn't tell me who they are. I made her mad. I didn't mean to. The changes she wants are worth fighting for. She asked me to use my position at the university to advocate for their cause."

Remembering the despair in Sahar's face, she said, "I really felt bad. There's not much I can do. Adjunct professors have a very small circle of influence."

"I'll ask Saeed if he knows her. He's on the board of more than one human rights organization," Markam said.

For a while, he was silent and seemed to be mulling over what she'd told him.

She waited, hoping he didn't think she and Thomas had a political agenda themselves. He was probably suspicious of everybody. Was he paying attention to her just to find out what they were up to?

The idea hurt a little until she reminded herself that it didn't matter. They'd never see each other again after she left the city.

What she had to do was too vital to let distractions like David Markam get in the way. He probably had a wife somewhere, anyway. And two or three beautiful kids.

"Have you been in this country long?" she said, trying to realign herself as a disinterested acquaintance. "Your Arabic's very good. At least, I assume it is. I'm struggling myself."

He looked at her. "My vocabulary's still basic. Hindi is my primary foreign language."

"Hindi? Of course. You told me yesterday you were in the Peace Corps in India."

"I've also had a Foreign Service posting in Delhi. As hard as it is to live in that country, I miss it. Every time I go back I know part of me belongs there."

"*Mera dil bhee bhaarat mei hai*, My heart is in India, too," Layne said, slipping into Hindi before she was aware of it.

In an impulsive move Markam took her hand, brushed it with his lips, and put it back in her lap. "I don't want anything to happen to you, Layne Darius," he said.

Allowing the drift of an unaccustomed pleasure as delicate as a mist, she slid her palm under his. He curled his fingers between hers and they sat for a while, listening to the music and the rise and fall of voices on the other side of the garden wall.

"I'm trying to get back there to finish my study in Kasauli," she said, as if they'd been sharing their lives all along. That's partly why I'm here. Hoping my fieldwork with Thomas will boost my chance of getting permission to work in India again."

"I know."

"What? You know what?"

"That you've applied for a study visa three times. And the university in Chandigarh keeps rejecting your proposal. A pretty tough bureaucracy to deal with."

He let go of her hand and laid his arm across the back of the bench, his long fingers just touching her shoulder. "I wish you'd tell me about the other reason you're here."

She stiffened. "I have no idea what you're talking about."

He took a folded piece of paper from his shirt pocket and handed it to her.

Even before she opened it, she knew what it had to be. "Where did you get this?" she said, staring at a newspaper photo of Katherine Darius, running in a street riot somewhere in the Middle East.

"Our consulate has an archive of news stories involving Americans in this country."

"Did you find any other information, how she died, anything else?"

"I'm sorry. Nothing that would help you."

"That's the same thing the embassy in Jeddah told me. After my father died, I found the last two letters she wrote to him. He never told us he'd heard from her. It sort of renewed my hope of finding out what happened.

"I wrote to the embassy, made phone calls. The responses were phrased very courteously, but they all said that after so many years there was nothing to find. Katherine Darius simply vanished."

"Growing up with a parent who was that famous couldn't have been easy," Markam said.

Horrified to feel tears stinging her eyes, she said, "Everybody has something to live up to."

He brushed her cheek, smoothing back some stray hairs that had come loose from her braid.

"I think I understand how badly you want to know what happened to her, Layne. I'd feel that way if she were my mother. But I can't tell you how dangerous it could be to stir up secrets in this country."

"I'm not afraid." She stopped, hearing footsteps coming toward them.

A man emerged from the shadows farther down the path, and she recognized him immediately. It was Al-Amir's watchful friend, Hassan.

"Wonder what he's doing here," Markam said.

"I didn't think the Al-Amirs and their friends socialized with Saeed."

Hassan paused. "Good evening, Dr. Darius, Mr. Markam. I see you are enjoying Saeed Ben Yousef's beautiful garden."

Markam stood up. "Mr. Hassan. It's nice to see you. Is Mr. Al-Amir here as well?"

Hassan drew in a breath as if he were savoring the night air. "No, I am alone. I noticed Dr. Darius arriving, and I was hoping for a word with her."

"Would you like to sit down, Mr. Hassan?" Layne said to cover her alarm.

"Thank you, but I will be leaving in a moment."

Feeling at a disadvantage, she stood up and crossed her arms. "Is something wrong?"

He glanced toward the shadowed walkway he had just come along. "It occurred to me when I met you at Mr. Al-Amir's house that you might be in this country with an intention other than the work you are authorized to do here."

Listening to that smooth voice, she felt real alarm. Had he been standing in the shadows hearing what she and Markam were saying?

"I don't understand, Mr. Hassan. I'm here to help my brother with his research."

He was silent for a moment, and then he said, "A great deal is beyond your understanding, Dr. Darius. And many people engaged in activities you should wish to avoid."

She was afraid, now. Hassan must be responsible for the black sedan following her from Sahar's apartment building. How did he even know where she went? Did Al-Amir set a watch on her? She'd made it clear last night that she was determined to know why her mother vanished.

As if he'd read her mind, he said, "We would not wish for the tragedies of the past to be repeated."

Hassan wasn't just fishing. This little talk was a warning not to probe any secrets in his country. Did he know about the shot in the city yesterday? How could he? Unless he was responsible for that too.

Glancing at Markam, she wondered whether he would back her up if Hassan actually accused her of anything. His face was unreadable, but she could feel his tension, as if he were poised to handle whatever might happen.

"I thought it best to tell you now, before you make further plans," Hassan said. "You must not visit Asad

Al-Amir's niece again. Against all advice, she persists in activities that are dangerous for everyone."

"What dangerous activities? Harvesting desert plants, teaching poor women to read?" Layne said.

Hassan leveled his hawk's gaze at her. "I repeat, there is a great deal you do not know, Dr. Darius. A person determined to rush into the abyss will do so. Those who are helping her must take care not to follow her there as well."

Chapter 11

"David, where are you?" Saeed shouted from the other side of the courtyard. He came across the garden.

"So there you are. I've been looking all over. I knew you had Dr. Layne hidden somewhere. It's not fair to be so selfish, David."

Hassan murmured something to Markam and strolled back into the shadows before Saeed reached them.

"Dr. Layne," Saeed went on, seeming not to notice Hassan. "You have no less than a dozen admirers longing to meet you, and here David is keeping you all to himself."

"If her admirers are some of the bunch I think you mean, she's better off staying out of their way," Markam said.

Saeed laughed. "He is always serious. Never a time to relax."

"Speaking of serious," Layne said, "we've been talking to Mr. Hassan."

He flicked his hand in dismissal. "A civil servant.

You must know what they are—the same in any country." He glanced at Markam. "Except for those like my friend David here."

"Come now, Dr. Layne. A whole banquet of food is waiting. You have been captive long enough."

She picked up her purse. "Thomas and I should be going soon. We're still coping with jet lag, and I'm feeling its effects."

"That is no problem either. Many of my guests will be staying the night. Perhaps you and Dr. Darius would like rooms prepared for you?"

Layne glanced at Markam to see how he was taking this, but Saeed misinterpreted her look.

"You don't have to worry about David. He never stays the night. He disdains such frivolities. Poor man."

Markam shook his head indulgently. This was obviously a line he'd heard before. "Might as well humor him for a few minutes. Then you can round up your brother and make a break for it."

Saeed led the way, but Markam paused and said quickly, "Can you meet me tomorrow? We need to talk more than ever now. This visit from Hassan is something you can't ignore."

"I'm not sure what I'll be doing tomorrow," she said.

He seemed less than satisfied, but he motioned for her to go on ahead. When she reached the terrace and looked back, he had gone.

Saeed swept her into a group and introduced her.

She smiled and said appropriate things, but she kept looking for Markam, not willing to believe he'd simply lost interest and left.

Finally, Saeed's attention was distracted, and she went to stand next to her brother, who was explaining his work to the circle of people around him. As soon as he paused, she whispered, "Let's get out of here."

Thomas looked frazzled himself, but fatigue wouldn't prevent him from observing the courtesies. "We can't leave without saying goodnight," he insisted.

"Let's do it now. I can't take any more of this."

Saeed was in the foyer, apparently anticipating their effort to escape. "Oh, no! You're not going so soon," he said. But he gave in gracefully and walked with them to the top of the outside steps.

He told a servant to have their car brought around, and then he and Thomas went on with their conversation while they walked slowly down to the driveway.

Layne sat on the top step to wait. Below, there was a confusion of voices and car engine noise. After the closeness of the crowd, the air, though it was acrid with the odor of diesel fuel, seemed almost chilly. She pulled her shawl tighter and glanced up at the house, still hoping to see Markam.

In the center of the long driveway, a fountain sparkled in the moonlight, and she thought how much her mother would have enjoyed Saeed's fountains and the gaiety tonight. When she was at home, there were always parties, exciting people in the house. And Katherine Darius the center of it all.

In her last letter, she said her friend was giving a party for her. Layne couldn't imagine Al-Amir's quiet, orderly house filled with music and laughter like this one.

The sound of Saeed's voice shouting below shocked her to the present. From the agitated flow of Arabic between him and other men, she knew something was wrong. She heard Mustafa's name and saw men running toward a stand of trees on the far side of the circular drive.

"Something's happened to Mustafa," Thomas yelled up to her. "Stay there."

Ignoring him, she ran down the steps and followed them into the shadows.

In the deeper darkness under the trees, men stood in a circle, one of them shining a flashlight toward the ground. As she went closer, she saw the white mass of a thob stretched out on the ground and realized it was Mustafa. Pushing through, she dropped to her knees and touched his head. Her fingers met warm blood.

"Thomas!" she yelled.

"I'm here." He was kneeling beside her. "He's alive. I can feel his pulse," he said. He turned Mustafa's head slightly. "He's been hit by something."

"By some person," Layne said.

"This is terrible," Saeed said. He was standing just behind them. "How has he injured himself?"

"It looks like he's been hit. He needs emergency care," Thomas said briskly. "Has an ambulance been called?"

"My men will take him to the hospital where my staff is treated," Saeed said, his face flushed and grim.

Thomas discarded his usual reticence. "I want to go along with him."

"There is no need," Saeed said. "They will see to it."

"Mustafa's our guide, not a servant," Layne said. "We care about him." She heard her voice rising, but she couldn't help it. "He's essential to our work, not to mention the fact that he's a human being!"

Thomas laid a restraining hand on her arm. "It's all right. I'm going."

Layne stood up, aware that she'd insulted Saeed, who was clearly embarrassed by what had happened and trying his best to help.

Two men carefully picked up Mustafa and moved him to an SUV parked nearby.

Feeling helpless, Layne followed them. They eased him into the backseat and Thomas got into the passenger's side. She went to his window.

"I don't like to leave you here," he said. "No point in your going, either. You'd just have to sit in a waiting room alone. I'm sure Saeed will arrange a car to drive you to Al-Amir's house."

"I'll drive the car back there myself. It's not that far, and I can remember the way well enough."

"Don't even think about that, Layne!" he said, looking horrified. "You'd be arrested before you got two blocks from here. I mean it. You've got to be sensible about the laws of this country."

Saeed moved closer. "Don't worry, Dr. Darius. One of my men will drive your sister to Al-Amir's home immediately. Arrangements can be made tomorrow for the return of the car you came in."

Thomas thanked him and said, "I'll call you as soon as I know something, Layne."

She watched them drive through the gates and then turned to Saeed, who was looking at her solicitously. "Please forgive me for being so rude to you. I was afraid Mustafa was dead," she said.

"Don't worry yourself about me. It's a very upsetting thing to happen. Why not come into the house and have a cup of tea to make you feel better?"

"Thank you, but I can't face anyone else now. I was hoping to find David Markam."

"He must be close by. We'll look for him. Perhaps he'll drive you where you wish to go."

She nodded and he went up the stairs to his guests.

With no idea what else to do, she sat down on the steps. Just as she did, David Markam came out from the shadows between the trees a few feet from her, brushing leaves off his shirt.

"Mr. Markam—David," she said. "I thought you'd gone."

He sat down next to her. "I went after Hassan. He's with the national security police, you know. I wanted to find out why he confronted you here at Saeed's house."

"Did he tell you anything?"

"Not yet, but he agreed to talk to me tomorrow."

"Did you see what happened to Mustafa?"

"Saeed's security people are checking the car. They found blood on the back of the driver's seat where Mustafa's head would have been if he'd fallen asleep. Looks like somebody reached in through the open window and clobbered him with a rock."

"Oh, no!"

"He's lucky to be alive."

Layne shivered. "There are plenty of weapons in that museum in the house."

"That stuff's permanently mounted. Screwed into the walls. A rock is more likely here."

"I wish I hadn't made a fool of myself blaming Saeed for what happened. Do you think one of the other drivers did it?"

"I doubt it. As I was coming back along the walkway, I saw them sitting around their coffee fire on that lawn near the fountain. When someone yelled, they jumped up and ran toward the grove of trees."

"This wouldn't have happened if Mustafa had been with them instead of sitting in the car alone. He doesn't seem to fit in here in the city," Layne said sadly. "I mean, he isn't from this area. His people are desert herders. For some reason, he left them and came to the city. Thomas said the Al-Amir family hired him to work on their cars and sent him to school. But the kids in school treated him like an outsider. That's probably how he still feels. He's a proud man."

"This country is full of proud men," David said ruefully. "I doubt his background's a problem. Most of the drivers are Bedouin themselves."

"Could it have been an argument?"

"Possibly, but an open fight seems unlikely in a situation like this. We'd better go, if you're ready," he said.

She saw Saeed at the top of the steps, still surrounded by guests. He waved, and she thought he looked relieved that David was taking care of her.

They went down the driveway toward a row of sedans. David stopped beside one and opened the door for her. He got in behind the wheel but made no move to start the engine.

Adjusting to the intimate space, Layne said, "I was really glad to see you. I was afraid you'd left."

He turned so he could look at her. "You're kind of stuck with me now."

They stared, the need to touch each other as palpable as their habitual restraints. Layne knew her impulse to confide in him came from that desire, but she decided to trust it anyway.

She waited until he started the car and they were driving along a shadowed road, the streetlights muted by sandy haze.

"There's something I want to tell you, David. What happened to Mustafa worries me. You said violence isn't common here, but yesterday, downtown, somebody shot at me." Instantly, she regretted telling him.

He steered the car to the curb and yanked the emergency brake. "Where did this happen?" he said, turning to look straight at her.

"Some kind of abandoned ruin."

"The fortress in the Deira district, the old part of the city?"

"I guess. I'd have to look at the map again. I'm not sure."

"What were you doing there? Was Mustafa with you? Maybe they were shooting at him."

"I sort of ditched him for a while," she said, embarrassed. "I wanted to look around on my own."

"Are you sure it was a shot? Could someone have thrown a rock?"

"I know what a gunshot sounds like. And when I see a bullet lodged in a mud-brick wall a few inches from my head, I know it wasn't a rock."

His eyes narrowed. "What did you do? Did you see or hear anyone?"

"No. Total silence. No footsteps. Nothing. I just ran like crazy."

He grasped her hand. "This is serious, Layne. You were shot at before you got to Al-Amir's house. And you and your brother could have died out on the desert. Whoever tampered with your water and sent

SEE THE DESERT AND DIE

him to that Bedouin camp knew you were coming before you arrived. This attack on Mustafa has to be related. Why? Who wants to stop you?"

Hearing it said aloud was terrifying. "It's ridiculous. Nobody wants to stop us," she said. "Thomas has studied the Bedouin in Yemen for years. What could be wrong with studying a family on this desert?"

"Someone might think you've actually come to find out what happened to Katherine Darius," David said slowly.

"Thomas isn't part of that. He's absolutely opposed to it. I'm the only one who cares," she said.

They sat without speaking for a while. David began stroking the back of her hand with his thumb, and she felt soothed by it, wanting the peace it promised.

"Who knows you came to investigate your mother's death?" he said.

Layne sighed and moved her hand away. "Well, Mr. Al-Amir knows. I blurted it out the first night. He didn't deny she'd been in his house. But David, I just can't believe he'd bring us here and then try to scare us or kill us. Makes no sense."

"Unless there are things about her death that need to be kept hidden. Did you tell anyone else you're looking for your mother?"

"I wrote letters trying to get information after Dad died. Not just to the government. I wrote to the news services she worked for, groups that look for people who're missing for political reasons. I don't remember how many. A lot of them."

"Then any number of people might assume that's your reason for coming here."

She looked at him, realizing just how many people did know.

He reached for her and pulled her against his chest.

"Oh, Layne. How am I going to keep you safe from this?"

It was all she could do to handle the fire that shot through her when he touched her. She wanted badly to stay with him, not to think beyond this moment. But she moved back and stared at him in wonder. Two days ago, she didn't know this man. Yet, here she was, ready—to do what? Make love to him? Trust him with her life?

"I'm sorry. I shouldn't have done that," he said. He turned and stared out the window. "What the hell happened?"

Clearing his throat, he said, "We've got to talk. In the daylight. I'll find a way to see you tomorrow."

"David, I know you don't owe me anything, but I do need your help."

He took her hand, squeezing her fingers with his tension. "Something strange is gathering around you, Layne. We need to find out what it is. Just call me before you go anywhere by yourself!"

She shivered, hearing the echo of Hassan's words. *A great deal is beyond your understanding, Dr. Darius.*

Chapter 12

Layne woke too soon the next morning. Exhausted as she was last night, she hadn't slept well. Dreams of walking along a beach with David Markam suddenly gave way to rifle-wielding ghosts close behind in black sedans.

Wishing she'd never come to this hateful place, she sat up. Jet lag and culture shock, she assured herself, retreating into the comfort of reason as she always did. Her whole life she'd been trained to avoid feelings, to analyze them, think them into manageable size. Ethnographers observed. They did not judge.

Nor did they lose themselves in hopeless infatuations. Her face burned as she realized how much she already cared about David Markam. Was it reasonable to be obsessed by a man she barely knew? Maybe she was just afraid.

The danger he warned her about was real enough. Being shot at may have been an accident or a prank, but the sabotage of their water supply and the attack on Mustafa were deliberate malice.

Who was trying to scare her and Thomas? Al-Amir

came first to mind. As illogical as that was, she couldn't stop the suspicion from grinding away at her.

He told her the first night that he'd talk to her about her mother. So far, that hadn't happened. Well, today she'd make sure he did.

Flinging off the linen sheet, she swung her feet to the floor. Bright shafts of sunlight streaked the room. The paintings of London in the rain were no longer calming. What she'd learned about her mother here had given them a gray and alien look.

She came out of the bathroom just as the serving woman wheeled a teacart through the door. This tiny person, so silent and efficient, made her think of the mythological *jinn*.

Could she grant wishes? More likely, she put spells on visitors she disapproved of. Again today, her lips were pressed in mute resentment.

"As-Salaam-Alaikum," Layne said cheerfully, refusing to be intimidated.

"Good morning, madam," the woman said, her voice gravelly as if it were seldom used.

"Oh, you speak English. Thank you very much for taking care of my clothes yesterday. They've never been done so nicely."

The woman laced her fingers and stared.

"Will you help me with my Arabic? I'm not very good at it yet."

"I know much English," the woman countered.

Layne sat on the edge of the bed to be at eye level with her. "Good. Now we can talk. Will you tell me your name?"

Her lips clamped in a sour little knot, but her defiance showed that she understood.

"Have you been with the Al-Amir family long?"

"I come here young girl. My lady marry with Al-Amir. I coming with my lady."

"So, you helped raise the children."

"My lady here, this happy house. Much children. Much laugh."

"It's too bad they've all gone," Layne said, struck suddenly with awareness of how deeply sad this house felt.

"No good now," the woman said. Her face contorted in anger, or grief, she turned and went to the door, muttering. With her hand on the doorknob, she threw one last malevolent look. "Evil one come. Allah take her." She spat out the words like a bitter taste and slipped out.

Stunned, Layne stood up and went to look at the paintings, knowing without doubt that the "evil one" was her mother. And at least one person in this house hated Katherine Darius.

She opened her travel box and took out the two letters she kept in a little pouch under her clothes. Though she knew them by heart, she read her mother's last written words. Nothing in them suggested she'd encountered any hostility in this house.

One was dated a few days after she arrived here, and it told about a party and a camel race. The other, dated the following week, made it clear that something had caught her attention, and she knew it might be dangerous.

I've found something interesting. It's not really a story yet, but it could be big. I know who's running the show, so it's too late to walk away from it now.

My father might have known what the "show" was, Layne thought. Considering the stories she went after in the past, it might have been anything, from smuggling to plans for a coup. But since she was in this house, it seemed very possible that Al-Amir himself was the one running it. If so, he may have wanted to stop her from exposing his secrets.

Then why risk bringing her daughter and stepson here? Even if Ricky arranged the permission for Thomas's fieldwork, it would never have been granted without Al-Amir's approval.

Hearing a scraping noise from outside, she opened the French doors and stepped onto a wide balcony that extended around the back of the U-shaped house.

Her door, in the right wing, was partially screened by a huge cascade of dark red bougainvillea. Putting on a robe, she went out and peered through the lush branches of the sweet vine.

The garden below her was laid out in freeform beds of rose trees, brick pathways meandering among them. Large oaks and shrubbery all around the walls shaded this precious oasis. A gardener with a rake in his hand was just going through a door in the other wing of the house.

Strolling back into her room, she poured a cup of tea and went outside to sit in a wicker chair shaded by the vine. She took a few sips of the strong black brew. Footsteps sounded on the pavement below. Through the vine tendrils, she caught a glimpse of Asad Al-Amir moving slowly among his roses.

He bent to examine a blossom and lifted it to inhale its scent. He seemed lost in his thoughts. At the sound of other footsteps on the flagstone, he straightened. A man came around the tall hedge.

Seeing Al-Amir, David Markam stopped. They both looked shocked.

Al-Amir recovered quickly. His voice was composed. "Mr. Markam. So you found your way back to my house."

David matched his control. "I beg your pardon for intruding, sir. I came to see Dr. Thomas Darius, and your servant told me the garden would be a suitable place to wait for him. Is he here?"

Al-Amir seemed to struggle between his instincts as a host and his reluctance to be disturbed. The host won out. "He may have gone to the hospital to inquire about his guide."

"That's partly why I'm here. After the attack on the man last night, I'm concerned about the safety of Dr. Darius and his sister."

Al-Amir frowned. "They have come to do research in the desert. There are many risks inherent in that venture. But perhaps you fear danger comes from some other quarter."

"Didn't your son tell you about the messages intercepted by the technicians at the satellite station? If these illegal transmissions signal a political insurgence of some sort, the danger to foreign visitors would certainly be greater."

Al-Amir motioned toward a wooden bench in a recess farther along the path. "Shall we sit down, Mr. Markam?"

"Damn," Layne whispered. Straining to hear what they were saying as they moved away, she leaned into the bougainvillea branches. A thorn jabbed her scalp, and she barely stifled a cry.

The two men sat without speaking for a few moments. Al-Amir caught the blossom of a yellow rose at his side and drew in its scent. Releasing it, he turned to Markam. "I have been told of this rumor."

Layne couldn't hear the rest of his sentence, but she saw David tense, on his guard. "Your name was mentioned in one of the transmissions. Do you know who these people might be?" he said.

Al-Amir's control was not quite perfect. There was a twitch of shock before his face became neutral again. His lips curled in disdain. "You could not possibly be suggesting I am engineering a conspiracy against my government."

"No, sir, I'm not. Nor am I suggesting that *my* government has anything but respect for you. My concern is the Americans staying in your house and under your sponsorship. Hostilities toward you might well put Thomas and Layne Darius in harm's way."

Amused, Al-Amir shifted to the side, crossing his legs. "Let me assure you, Mr. Markam, that I am not engaged in subversive activity of any sort. Further, no one of my acquaintance is either so stupid or so bored with his life as to be plotting against our government. I wouldn't be overly worried about this rumor."

Markam seemed to be deciding how to counter. "Are there any arrangements in place to protect the Darius team while they're traveling or living out in the desert?"

Al-Amir looked up, staring directly at Layne's camouflage. She froze, but he didn't seem to see her. In the brightness of the morning sun, he looked fully his age. There were hollows under the sharp cheekbones and bitterness etched around his mouth.

"Protection is a meaningless concept, Mr. Markam. Which of us can truly keep those we love safe from 'the slings and arrows' of life? I've done what I could to make Thomas Darius's research possible. Beyond that, what else do you suggest?"

Markam said something in a low voice.

The old man shook his head, annoyed.

"You let her come here knowing what she wanted to find," Markam insisted.

Grasping the side of the bench, Al-Amir pulled himself up unsteadily. His body shook with the intensity of his emotion. "This insinuation in my own home is hardly a worthy strategy, Mr. Markam."

Markam rose. He said gravely, "My apologies, sir."

He left quickly, his footsteps echoing along the terrace, the set of his shoulders angry and determined.

Al-Amir stood looking after him. Finally, he came slowly toward the house.

Layne hurried into her room and threw on clothes. This opportunity to talk with Al-Amir alone was what she'd been waiting for. He was probably on his way to his study. Once he was in there with the door closed, she might not be able to get to him for the rest of the day.

Downstairs in the entry hall, she could see that he was still out in the garden, walking slowly along a pathway.

He saw her coming and straightened as if he anticipated another challenge.

To give herself time to think about what she wanted to say, she bent to smell the velvet sweetness of a burgundy rose. Smiling at Al-Amir, she said, "I hope I'm not disturbing you."

He still had his diplomat's ability to turn on charm at will. "On the contrary. I've been hoping we might have a talk about so many things. Come and sit with me." He led the way to the same bench. "Tell me, are you comfortable here? Is there anything you require?"

Just the truth, she wanted to say, but she made an effort. "Everything's fine. The maid is very efficient.

Though I had to find out her name from the butler. Puja. She's originally from South India, isn't she?"

His heavy brows lifted. "The woman has been rude to you?"

"No. Of course not!" she said quickly. The last thing she wanted was to alienate anybody else. "I think she's connected me with something that happened in the past."

"Puja was my wife's nurse and has grown eccentric after so many years. But you must tell me if there is anything in this house that disturbs you."

She hesitated, sorting her words. "I think you know what I want to ask you. My mother was your guest when she died. Can you tell me what happened to her?"

He was so still that she was afraid he might leave without a word. Pressing him for answers was risky. With one motion of those long, sensitive fingers, he could dismiss her, just as he'd done to David. Or even end her stay in the country.

"I'm sorry if my questions are impertinent, Mr. Al-Amir," she said. "You've been very generous to us. I didn't mean to impose on your kindness. But I need so badly to know why my mother vanished from my life. What happened to her? Please."

"There was no generosity in my arranging for you to come here," he said. "I brought you here for indefensibly selfish reasons."

Hardly believing what she heard, Layne waited.

Finally, he said, "Very well. I shall answer your questions." He touched her arm gently. "But I warn you, my dear, you will not be happy with what I tell you."

He said nothing for a long while, as if composing his thoughts. Then, he looked at her with a hint of a smile. "You have difficulty with patience, I perceive. Just as your mother had."

"I've waited a long time for an answer."

He said nothing, and she went on, trying to keep anger from her voice. "My father spent the last years of his life hoping to find out what happened to her. After he died, I came across two letters she wrote to him. She told him she was the guest of an important man. But she did not say who that man was.

"I wrote to the American Embassy in Jeddah," she went on, "to the news agency she worked for, everywhere I could think of. Nobody would tell me anything. It was as if my mother never existed."

Without looking at her, Al-Amir said, "One of your letters was passed on to me by a friend in your embassy. It disturbed me." He sighed deeply.

"Life has held many things for me—duty, triumph, failure, despair. And love. Much love, as well as pain. I was reluctant to respond to your questions because they meant delving into that past I no longer wished to examine."

"So you chose to ignore me."

"I knew you could not reach me here."

The candor of this comment astonished her. In the fortress of his estate, buttressed by an implacable government and an insular society, what he said was true. If he had not willed it, she wouldn't be sitting here now.

"Why did you change your mind?"

Gazing over his garden, he said, "I am becoming an old man. It is time to put my life into order."

Suspicious of this sentiment coming from the Quiet Lion, she said, "But you could easily have written to me to explain the circumstances of her death. That's all I want. The truth about how she died. You didn't have to go to the trouble and expense of sponsoring Thomas's study."

He shrugged, and she wanted to shake him. "Don't you see how this is for me, Mr. Al-Amir? Why won't you tell me?"

The parchment colored skin grew taut over his jutting cheekbones as his features worked with emotion. "You cannot know what you are demanding of me." He pressed his fingers against his forehead.

Layne waited in an anguish of impatience. She had come all this way, lived with her own grief so long. Her hands ached to shake the truth out of him. Watching him struggle to master himself, she tried to ignore the compassion that threatened to overwhelm her.

Stripped of arrogance and charm, of intellectual power, he was just a sad old man.

Tentatively, she said, "I'm sorry to cause you pain. That's not what I wanted."

For a full minute, he didn't speak. Then he raised his head, and the lion had returned. "It is only justice that you should know."

After another pause, he cleared his throat and began to speak dispassionately. "Katherine was following reports of some activities by dissidents who were after political and economic upheaval, urging radical social changes that conflict with this society's fundamental principles. That sort of dissent is intolerable in such a system as ours.

"It is difficult to estimate the consequences that might have resulted if she had written of what she found. At the least, there would have been arrests, executions. The stakes were very high. And the potential danger to her was great. That did not dissuade her."

Layne shook her head, knowing very well her mother's ambition and her courage. The promise of breaking a story like that would have been irresistible.

"I did all I could to stop this headlong plunge into disaster," he went on. "Once, I even threatened to have her expelled from the country. She knew I would never do it. Several days after she came here, she told me she had an appointment to meet with one of the higher people in the group. Foolishly, I forbade her to go." His lips lifted in a nostalgic smile.

"The following day, she seemed content. After breakfast, she came down with her camera strung round her neck and said she wished to take pictures of Al-Diriyah. It is a ruin, a town with historic significance. Perhaps I knew she was not really interested in the photography, but I allowed myself to believe her.

"My driver took her there. She told him to wait with the car while she walked up into the ruined town. After a few minutes, he began searching for her. Nothing. Always nothing."

Layne felt a new empathy. Having misled Mustafa to get some time on her own, she had an unnerving awareness of the ruthlessness she and her mother shared.

"There must have been a means of keeping her from going," Al-Amir said.

"Probably not. I know how single-minded she was," Layne said.

She waited for him to go on, but he sat staring at his garden, the secluded domain in which he had tried and failed to shelter Katherine Darius.

"She must have met someone there who killed her," Layne said, squeezing her eyes shut. "I don't suppose there was any evidence."

Al-Amir's lips twisted in a grimace. "If there was, I could not find it. That is the intolerable part. I do not even know how she died or who killed her." In his face was an anguish and frustration that Layne understood very well.

"How far away is this ruin, this town she went to?" she demanded, needing to know every detail.

"It is near the western side of the city, the royal family's ancestral home. These days, the site is being restored, but then it was nearly abandoned, the mud-brick buildings falling into rubble."

"You really tried to find out what happened?" she said.

Indignation flashed in his eyes. "I set the police and my own people looking. Every means I had. For months, years, I searched. It became my mission to find her killer. And still I failed."

"But there must have been people who knew. Who were the dissidents she was trying to expose?"

"Of course, someone knew. Someone knows, even now. There were rumors, hints. Many times I suspected one man or another. I shall never be satisfied until I look into the face of the man who killed Katherine."

Shocked by his vehemence, Layne didn't know what to say.

She thought about Saeed's concern after Mustafa was attacked. Al-Amir's reaction was so much greater than the embarrassment of a host who could not protect his guest. Once again, she felt overwhelmed by her ignorance of this culture, these people.

After a while, he held out his hand, palm open. "So you see, my dear Layne, I had little to tell you after all. Our most important questions have no answers."

They sat in silence.

Finally, clinging to the resolve that brought her here, she stood up and faced him. "I just can't accept that this is the end of it. There must be a way. After this much time has passed, someone will have relaxed his guard. If you would only help me."

Al-Amir's look was fierce. "No! That is the reason I avoided telling you. In my heart, I knew it might be a mistake to bring you here. Not for myself. You have more than fulfilled my desire to know the woman who was Katherine's child. But I should have known how much you would be like her. If harm should come to you—"

"I have to try. Can't you see that?"

"I see only your determination to put yourself into danger. I shall not allow it."

So that was that. It would be useless to argue with him. She sat down again, staring at nothing, deciding what to do.

He went on in a milder tone. "In a few days, your time will be fully taken by other matters. Living with Bedouin in the desert will require all of your attention. For these few days before you embark on your work, we may talk of Katherine again."

Getting to his feet, he said, "Now, you must excuse me. I have business waiting."

Layne nodded and managed to find the words to leave him courteously.

Upstairs, she paced the length of her room several times, trying to ease the disappointment. Al-Amir was the only real resource she had. Without his help, how would she ever find anything in this country of stone walls and barred doors?

Even as she admitted how naïve her ideas had been, her determination grew. Since Mustafa was hurt, transportation would be a problem. Thomas wouldn't help with anything that interfered with his work. Still, there must be some way.

She gazed at the sumptuous ceiling and imagined her mother standing in this spot, looking for ways to overcome these same barriers. Well, she was Katherine Darius's daughter. The same will lived in them both. She would make a better plan.

Chapter 13

Layne circled her bedroom practicing a dialogue in Arabic. Though words with Persian roots were close to Hindi and a little easier, she'd never be fluent in this language.

A new servant, a younger woman, appeared at lunchtime with a tray of sandwiches and fruit and a pot of tea and left as quickly as she could. By midafternoon, Layne was dozing over an article on family relationships in Bedouin tribes. The younger maid came again to say she had a call from David Markam.

"Can you spare some time to go for a drive today? I really want to see you," he said.

Layne was not prepared for the rush of emotion she felt. "When can you be here?"

"I doubt Al-Amir's people will let me into the grounds," David said.

She knew what he was talking about, but she was not going to admit she'd heard his confrontation with Al-Amir in the garden. "I'll try to get someone to drive me. Where should I meet you?"

"Isn't your brother there? I actually need to talk to both of you."

"Oh," she said, disconcerted that he didn't want to see her alone. "He went to the hospital to check on Mustafa. He should be back soon."

"Saeed found some field radios stored at the satellite station near here. He arranged for your brother to visit the site. One of the technicians agreed to show him how they work."

He paused. "No reason you can't come along if you like. I'll drive the two of you out there this afternoon if you have the time."

"I thought those places were high security. Aren't they afraid we'll see something secret?"

"You won't see anything Saeed doesn't want you to see," he said smoothly. "And the technicians are foreigners, so they won't be shocked by the sight of a lady's face."

"I'll tell Thomas. He'll be thrilled. We can come to the consulate as soon as he gets back."

"Good. Call me before you leave there and I'll be waiting outside the gate. Be sure you both have the ID and papers from the Foreign Ministry." He hung up before she had a chance to ask why.

She heard the front door close and went to the foyer. Thomas, sweaty and looking tired, greeted her with his usual cheerfulness.

"Mustafa's better today. They're saying he'll probably be able to leave the hospital tomorrow or the day after."

134

"Did he tell you what happened to him?"

"It's as much a mystery to him as it is to us."

"Well, I have good news," Layne said. "David Markam called. Saeed's got some field radios for you. He invited us to come to a satellite station outside the city so the technician can be sure you know how to use them."

"You said 'us.' Saeed invited you too, or was that Markam's idea?"

"Either way, I'm going. How soon will you be ready to leave?"

Thomas rubbed his hands together in satisfaction. "Just let me change my shirt and have a cup of tea first."

They went into the dining room, helped themselves from the teapot keeping hot on top of the Russian samovar, and carried their cups into the library. Thomas sat in Al-Amir's big chair, and she sat across from him on the sofa so she could see his face.

He took off his glasses and cleaned them with a napkin, his eyes defenseless without them.

"The attack on Mustafa disturbs me, Layne," he said. "The blow was savage. It's miraculous that it didn't kill him." He put his glasses back on and reached wearily for his tea.

She knew how disturbed he was. In his sheltered academic world, human passions were dealt with in orderly discourse, not carried close to the thigh like polished steel or clasped in the fist like a cudgel.

But her brother didn't lack courage, or common

sense in dealing with problems. He'd been calm and efficient after Mustafa was injured. She'd lost her head and insulted Saeed. That still made her feel guilty.

"Does the doctor think Mustafa will be able to travel soon?"

"Mustafa insists he'll be ready to start the end of this week."

"I hope he's well enough. That desert drive's going to be hard even for a healthy person."

"Yes, it will be. I told him we could postpone our start."

"As stubborn as he is, he'd probably insist on leaving tomorrow if that was the plan," Layne said.

"He knows better than that. He's no martyr. We'll take it easy, and he knows what he needs to survive out there."

Thomas sipped his tea, absently replacing the cup crookedly in the saucer.

"These delays are tedious, but we've really needed this extra time. The new Land Cruisers may not be delivered for a few days. Being able to get used to the climate is a good thing, too."

"I hope we don't wear out our welcome while we're waiting," Layne said.

He looked at her suspiciously. "Ricky keeps saying he'd like to have us stay at his house. If one of us is getting in Mr. Al-Amir's way, we'll move over there. You haven't been behaving badly, have you?"

"What makes you think that?"

He waved his hand vaguely and hit the cup, sending hot tea across the surface of the rosewood table.

"Oh, no!" He jumped to his feet. Jerking his handkerchief from his pocket, he slapped it down on the spreading puddle and knocked off the carved box that Al-Amir had touched so fondly the night they arrived.

The box hit the carpet with a muted thump and fell open. A revolver slipped from its black velvet interior. Thomas paused in his frantic mopping efforts to gawk at it. It was a gleaming weapon, made even more threatening by the swirl of blood red rubies set in its silver handle.

Layne handed him her napkin and picked up the gun. "What do you suppose he uses this for?"

"It's probably an heirloom of some sort, Layne. Put it back."

"Why does he keep it in that box, close at hand?" Checking the cylinder, she said, "This thing is loaded." She wished she knew what kind of bullet was fired at her downtown.

"Put it away!"

She was still holding the box when the servant came in with a cloth and a can of furniture polish. Once again, she was aware that everything they did in this house was observed.

Thomas apologized for spilling his tea, but the man just nodded. He finished cleaning, put the box in its place on the table, and left.

Looking harassed, Thomas said, "Give me a minute to change my shirt, and then we can go."

She followed him up the stairs. At his bedroom, he stopped. "Make sure you're covered up. That skirt's fine, but you need a scarf. We've got to get you an abaya as soon as possible."

Half an hour later, as they drove to the consulate in one of Al-Amir's sedans, Layne said, "Thomas, whose idea was it for us to come to this country? I mean, who really decided to make it happen?"

"I don't know why you're asking me that. Ricky and I have been talking about this research for years. It's always seemed to be a monumental undertaking. The expense, the logistics, not to mention the political machinations. It's been a game of waiting, watching for the right moment, until the government's attitude was favorable to foreigners doing this kind of work here."

"Why was it suddenly possible?"

He glanced at her, and she knew he didn't want to answer. Finally, he said, "Ricky was aware that I had a sabbatical coming up."

"Why was I allowed to be part of the study? Was bringing me along a condition of the arrangement?"

"The family thought you should be included," he said lamely.

"Ha. I knew it! Ricky made the arrangements, but his father put up the money and moved the wheels of government to make it happen. He as much as admitted that to me."

"What are you saying? You're suggesting Al-Amir had a nefarious motive for sponsoring my study? I hardly think so!"

He pulled to the curb to read a street sign. After making a turn, he said, "There's no need to imagine anything sinister in Al-Amir's decision to help us. Your ability to talk to the women in the tribe is an asset to the work. You know all of this."

"My room upstairs is the same one my mother slept in. There's an old servant who talks about an 'evil one' coming here, and she looks at me as if she'd like to boil me in oil."

Smiling, he said, "With your imagination, you ought to be writing screenplays."

"Even if you think everything's fine, you can't dismiss the fact that somebody sabotaged our vehicles and water supply and sent us into the desert to die. Then they tried to kill Mustafa. Somebody doesn't want us here, Thomas!"

As mad as she was, she rejected the impulse to add one more point. If he knew about the shot fired at her, he'd probably tell Al-Amir's guards to keep her from leaving the house.

After an angry silence, Thomas said, "The consulate's in the next block. I don't want you to bring this up with Markam or anybody else. I'll explain what I can to you later."

She stared at him. For the first time she could remember, she did not know whether she could trust her brother.

David Markam was waiting for them, and Layne sighed as she climbed into his hot, dusty backseat. How many more hours was she going to spend riding around in sweatboxes?

They drove without much conversation through narrow, congested streets, past dingy storefronts, warehouses, and a vast outdoor produce market. Brown dust rose in clouds around them as they neared the edge of the city.

The highway, when they finally reached it, was a wide strip that passed between a gauntlet of power line towers and finally became a shoulderless paved line running through the scrub desert.

David turned on the air conditioner and accelerated, trying to get ahead of a line of hulking Mercedes trucks that were spewing diesel exhaust. Most of the traffic was trucks, each decorated with an expression of its driver's personality—bright flags, streamers, black feather duster plumes, and across the front of the cab, an Arabic inscription exhorting Allah's protection. The drivers had lost none of the daring of their Bedouin roots. They roared along with ghotras flapping in the wind and apparently little regard for danger.

This was perilous driving. She could see in the rearview mirror the concentration in David's face and admired his nerve facing a truck roaring at them head-on. After a while, the traffic thinned, and the ride became monotonous. The sky, paled by its haze of sand, emphasized the emptiness around them.

"Is your guide Mustafa recovering?" David said to Thomas.

"The doctors don't seem worried, but he still can't tell us what happened to him."

"They may never find that out. I went back to Saeed's house after I left you, Layne. He had his security people investigating the grounds."

"I thought they might not do anything since Mustafa was just a driver," she said.

"Saeed has very democratic ideas about most things. And the attack happened on his property. He felt responsible."

"What did the security people think?" Thomas said.

"They decided it was a robbery attempt. All the drivers knew he worked for the Al-Amir family. Someone may have thought he had money."

Going into a curve that rounded a low hill, David had to brake hard to keep from running into a line of trucks slowing down.

Ahead, they could see a small guardhouse on the left of the road. Several soldiers with rifles were lined up on either side of the roadway—the unmistakable signs of a military checkpoint. Nobody was getting through without being stopped.

"Hand me the manila envelope in there, will you?" David said, indicating the glove compartment. "You'll need to get your IDs out."

Thomas handed him the envelope and took out his own papers. He glanced at Layne. "Put your scarf over your head."

"What's this for?" she said, apprehensively.

"It's usually routine. Didn't you encounter any of these checkpoints on the way from the east coast?" David said.

"We did have to stop a couple of times," Thomas said.

Layne handed her papers to her brother. "There weren't so many soldiers at those points. This makes me nervous."

"The satellite station is out this way and some other areas the government needs to control access to," David said.

They eased forward, and as they reached the guardhouse, soldiers cradling M-16s closed in on both sides, the barrels of their rifles inches from the windows.

She tried to follow what David was saying to the soldier in Arabic, but her mind refused to recognize meaning in the sounds. The man scrutinizing their papers took his time. Then, he looked at her and asked a question.

Glibly, David began what sounded like an explanation. She caught the words "brother" and "sister." Thomas leaned over and said a few words in his rapid, colloquial Arabic. With an indifferent jerk of his head, the soldier handed the papers back and waved them on.

"They know how to stretch that out for maximum effect," David said.

Layne glanced back at the guardhouse.

"These checkpoints were a constant in Yemen a few years ago," Thomas said.

"They're on most of the major highways here now. You'll encounter some on your way to the Bedouin camp, so it's a good idea to have a plan for dealing with them. I'm sorry to say we've had reports of people being dragged out of their vehicles, even arrested, if there was anything suspicious."

"If you meant to scare us, you've done your duty," Layne said.

His response was an irritating grin.

Chapter 14

Glancing at Layne in the rearview mirror, David could see that the checkpoint had upset her more than he anticipated. He'd hoped a drive out to the dunes would give them time to talk privately. And help her relax enough to tell him why she was so frightened.

Rounding a range of hills, they came suddenly upon the huge white satellite dishes, poised like giant UFOs inside a chain-link fence.

At the gate, he honked the horn and recognized the man in T-shirt and jeans coming out of one of the prefab buildings clustered at the base of the tracking dishes. Jenkins opened the gate and waved them through.

David parked in a few feet of shade at the edge of the office building and got out.

"Saeed is trying to reach you on the order wire," Jenkins said.

"I thought he was going to be here."

"He got delayed at Ha'il. Flew up there this morning. Are these the folks he told me about?"

Thomas and Layne got out and David introduced them.

"They're going out to the Empty Quarter to study a Bedouin family," he said.

"Yeah, we heard about you," Jenkins said to Thomas. "Living out there with the camels. Better you than me." He turned to look Layne over. "Well, this is a pleasure," he drawled.

"When did you last hear from Saeed?" David said sharply.

Jenkins sniffed and raked his fingers through his gray-streaked beard. "First time around noon and again an hour ago. Wants you to call him."

"Can Dr. Darius and his sister go in there?"

The technician indicated with a sweep of his arm that they were welcome and led them to the central equipment building, emitting the labored sounds of the large air-conditioning system. They stepped inside into cold so intense it made their breaths catch.

"Keeping this stuff cool must be a big priority," Thomas said.

"We'd be out of business in minutes without it," Jenkins said. "I'll be in the office when you're ready to look at the radios."

He left and Thomas wandered along the gray metal banks of knobs and dials, his hands clasped behind his back.

Layne was still shivering, and David said, "Come and sit here. I won't be long." He pulled out the chair from the battered wooden desk at the far end of the room and reached for a telephone receiver hanging from a hook on the wall.

Perched on a high stool beside her, he shouted, "Ha'il," into the receiver. "Riyadh calling Saeed at Ha'il." A crackle of static came through. Then a voice yelled, "Saeed here. That's you David? You have Dr. Thomas and Layne with you?"

"They're here."

"Give my kind regards to them. Jenkins knows what to do about the radios." His voice dropped a few decibels. "Our mysterious talkers are on the side-band again. They must have shifted up to this area. Let me ring you on the secure line."

David replaced the receiver and turned to the phone on the desk. It rang, and he picked it up. "What've you got?"

Wedging the receiver between his shoulder and ear, he took a clipboard and pen from the desk drawer. "Okay, go."

Saeed read in Arabic, and David did his best to write down what he said. "That's it? Nothing more? How did you translate it?" He jotted down the English words:

Little brown fox echoes on the wind.

Four times three he dances down.

Watch him. 478. 739. 436.

"There's that fox again," he said. "The rest of it's different from the others you showed me. What time did you pick it up?" He looked at his watch. "I'll be back in my office in a couple of hours." Glancing at Layne, he said, "Maybe by six. I'll call you."

He hung up and stared at the scribbled message. "Code, wouldn't you say?"

"Or pretty meaningless poetry," Layne said. "I thought the messages said something about Al-Amir and shipments of military equipment."

"Some did. There's not much consistency. Saeed keeps insisting they're nonsense, but he is worried about them. If the transmissions are just a joke, they may be thumbing their noses, saying, 'We know you've intercepted us.'"

"Why did Saeed tell you about all of this?"

"Don't you think I'm trustworthy?" he said.

He could see she was trying not to smile. "How would I know? I haven't a clue who's telling the truth in this place. Even my own brother tells me only what he has to."

"I heard that," Thomas said from the other side of a circuit bank.

"You can trust me. On most topics," David said.

He reached for her hand, but the door opened, and Jenkins came in. "Dr. Darius, I've got the radios set up. If you want to come on over to the office, I'll give you the rundown on what they'll do for you. Should take an hour or so." He glanced doubtfully at Layne.

"We're going to drive out to see the dunes," David said. "It's not far. Only a few minutes." He saw a smirk on Jenkins' face and threw him a warning look.

The shock of stepping into the heat was less severe than going into the cold. They climbed into the truck, and Layne winced, feeling the burn of the leather seat through her heavy skirt.

David switched on the air conditioner as soon as they cleared the gate. "This was the only way I could think of to have a little time alone with you," he said.

She smiled at him. "I'm glad you did. I really want to talk to you. I found out some things from Al-Amir that I think are important. My brother doesn't want to hear it. You're the only one who's willing to listen to me."

"I'll do my best," he said. This was not the conversation he'd hoped to have with her, but he did want her to trust him.

In a few minutes they reached the line of hills where the hard plain gave way to undulating waves of sand.

He found a narrow track between two dunes and went slowly along until they were out of sight of the highway. At the V-shaped bowl formed by the sloping sides of the dunes, he stopped and turned off the engine. They rolled down the windows and sat looking at the shadows in the hollows on the left side and the opposite slope glistening reddish gold in the late afternoon sun.

"Now that you have my full attention, what do you want to tell me?" he said, settling his back against the door.

He watched her face, drawn with tension, as she recounted her meeting with Al-Amir. She finished and looked at him as if she were willing him to understand.

He wanted to put his arms around her, but he made himself sort through the rush of words. "So he confirmed that your mother was investigating a potentially dangerous group. And the people she was tracking eight years ago could be linked in some way with the messages Saeed's picking up?" he said, trying to keep incredulity out of his voice.

"That last part is my idea. I'm sure those people are still around. Even Al-Amir believes they are." Her eyes narrowed. "You don't think I'm just making this up to create drama, do you? That's what Thomas said."

David searched for words. "You're not making it up. These things did happen. But, Layne, they may have been coincidences. It's plausible that the crooked garage owner sabotaged the water supply to cover his theft of your trucks. He could have set up the invitation to visit the Bedouin camp, too, assuming you'd break down on the way. I don't know what to think about that business in the city."

"I knew it! You don't believe me any more than my brother did." She glared at him.

"He even threatened to have me deported if I keep searching."

"That's the same thing I'd say if you were my responsibility. If you stir up a hornet's nest, the security police may do worse than deport you. Long before your brother can get you out of the country."

She didn't answer and he said, "Why don't we walk around a bit? The dunes always give me a little serenity. I hoped they'd do the same for you."

At first, she seemed reluctant to let go of her anger. Then she sighed. "I do need that."

Pointing at the dune on the right, still bright with sun, she said, "Let's climb that one."

Without waiting for him, she jumped out, shed her sandals, and started up the slope. The sand sucked at every step, making her leap more than run toward the sharp-edged crest.

David leaned against the fender, his arms folded, watching her. Every move she made was fascinating. He knew now why Arab poets compared women to gazelles. But that would not do for her. Layne was like an energy rising from the sand itself. She filled him with a deeper longing than he'd ever known.

At the crest of the dune, she balanced with one foot on either side and shouted, "Come on up. It's great!"

He began to climb toward her.

Turning, she ran along the crest until her skirt tangled between her legs, and she fell backward, sliding down the slope, powerless to stop. Her hair came loose from its braid, and her skirt rode up, baring exquisite long legs.

Just before she reached him, she managed to dig in her heels and stop, sprawled at his feet, helpless with laughter.

He dropped down beside her.

"You are the most beautiful wild person I've ever met," he said.

He brushed sand from her face and traced the line of her jaw with his finger.

"This is the first time I've felt free since I got to this country," she said. "It's infinite. Like we're all—you and me, this universe of sand—we're all there is."

"We are all there is," he said. Slowly, he touched her lips with his and circled the rim of her mouth with his tongue.

She put her arms around his neck, and he moved over her, hungrily, as she molded her body to his.

In a moment, he would have been unaware of sound or motion beyond the need for her, but the raucous blare of a truck horn on the highway wrenched him away.

Stunned, he rolled over, feeling as if he'd lost a layer of skin.

"God! Every time I get near you—" He stood up.

Layne lay still, her eyes closed. "This place does strange things to me. It's bewitching," she said. She sat up and tossed back her hair.

David understood. He felt the same way. But it wasn't the desert that bewitched him. From now on, wherever he was, it was going to be a struggle to care about anything more than being with her.

"I didn't intend for this to happen," he said. "I'm sorry." Reaching for her hand, he pulled her up.

"I'm not sorry," she said.

He lifted her chin, and this kiss was far from gentle.

She gasped when he stepped back from her.

"I've got to stop, Layne," he said.

Looking at him, her eyes dazed, she moved away and began to shake sand from her skirt.

David took a jug of ice water from the truck and poured cups for them both. They sat on the hood, not talking or touching, but peaceful together.

"We'd better get back," he said finally.

"Just one more minute. I want to see what that soft-looking sand around those bushes feels like." She jumped down.

He caught her arm. "No, Layne. Look at the holes, by the side of that bush."

"What's in them?" she said, more alarmed than he expected.

"Most likely scorpions. They come out after the shadows cool things off."

She leaped into the truck, and David got in beside her.

Covering her face with trembling hands, she said, "It was hard enough dealing with spiders and snakes in India. How am I going to live in this desert?"

He rubbed her arm, trying to soothe her. "The Bedouin will help you. They know what to look for. Last spring, I went into the western desert with some friends and a couple of Bedouin guides.

"The first evening, we embassy *wallas* picked out a stretch of fine sand at the base of a hill to put up the tents. The guides vetoed it immediately. That's how I learned to look for scorpion holes.

"I've seen giant black things, straight out of a horror movie, but the little green ones are the most deadly. You start being more careful once you know what's there."

She said nothing, and he started the truck.

He drove back to the satellite station slowly, wishing they had time and freedom to be alone, to know and love each other.

Layne stared out the window as she braided her hair.

"I shouldn't have gone out there with you," she said suddenly.

"Why not? You looked like you were having fun running up that dune."

"It was fun, but I—I just don't want you to think that what happened—that I'm easy."

Realizing what she meant, he said, "I didn't bring you out here hoping to get lucky, if that's what you mean."

He glanced at her and saw how troubled she was.

"Why did you say that?" he said.

"The feelings I had today—I never felt like that before. I know a lot about human behavior from my research, but in a situation like this—in my own life— I'm not sure what's right."

"We didn't break any rules," David said.

"That's just it! I don't know what my rules are. Living in other cultures, watching people conform to different traditions and attitudes, I guess rules seem relative to me. I'm never sure exactly what I'm supposed to do. That sounds ridiculous at my age, but my mother didn't give me much guidance when I was young. I probably shouldn't be here alone with you."

She turned back to the window, her cheeks flushed.

David doubted any reassurances would make her feel better. Sensing how badly she needed to talk, he said, "Tell me about your mother. What was Katherine Darius like?"

She glanced at him suspiciously.

He waited, and after a while, she said, "Nobody's asked me that for a long time. Most people have forgotten her. She really was a great journalist, you know. The strongest woman I've ever known.

"She was traveling for wire services most of my life. Reporting from all over. Algeria, Lebanon. In Vietnam while I was in high school. Any place people were resisting a French colonial government.

"She spoke fluent French, and she loved France. We spent a few weeks there in a country inn when I was about twelve, just the two of us. That was right after the Algerian War of Independence. She made her reputation during that war, mostly reporting on the efforts of women in the Resistance, the work male reporters ignored. But after it was over, she wanted to be in France again. She was very conflicted about that war."

"I imagine a lot of people were," David said.

"Then she went to Vietnam and reported on another group of women who were trying to throw off French colonial rule. I never understood how she felt about that."

Smiling, she said, "I remember mostly the times when she was home. People were always in the house for parties. We were all so happy. Especially my father. Then she'd leave and the house was empty again."

After a pause, she said sadly, but without self-pity, "People expected me to be like her, full of talent, beautiful. All of that. Of course, I wasn't any of those things.

"I got my degrees and did my work in India. That's where I realized I could be somebody other than Katherine Darius's daughter. So you see why my work is so important to me. It's all I have to prove my own worth."

"You don't have to prove anything to me," David said.

She shook her head, and he knew she regretted the impulse to tell him so much.

He said, "In the newspaper article, your father claimed Katherine Darius didn't come to this country to investigate a story."

"Maybe he wanted to think that, but it wasn't true," Layne said.

"In the letters I found after Dad died, my mother said she was on to something but wasn't sure it was a story she could report. She knew who was 'running the show' and it was 'too late to walk away' for some reason."

Turning to him, she said, "She was in danger, David. Who it was from, or why, I don't know but I intend to find out."

David felt real concern. Layne's efforts to dig into that past might prod secrets more sensitive than any of them realized.

"Were there any names? What did she mean by the *show*?" he said.

"I haven't had a chance to find out. When I visited Sahar, she accused me of being unsympathetic to the struggles of women in this country. 'Just like your mother,' she said. She even said Katherine Darius betrayed them."

"It sounds like Sahar might be part of the 'show' your mother mentioned," David said. "Maybe a group that's engaged in subversive activity?"

"I have no idea. She obviously told my mother about the work she's doing and asked her to let the rest of the world know what they're struggling against. Sahar said she turned her down."

"Does that seem likely?" David said. "Wasn't Katherine Darius's main intention to show the world the contributions women in Algeria and Vietnam made during those wars? She must have been an advocate for women's rights."

Layne sighed. "If she didn't think there was a story worth telling, or she couldn't verify facts—that's what really mattered to her. She could be callous, terribly selfish. I know that.

"But—oh, David. Don't you see? No matter what my mother did, I'll always keep thinking, if I try harder I'll find out, I'll know for *sure* that she's dead or alive. It's irrational, but I can't help it. I owe it to her, to myself!"

Her hands were tensed into fists, waiting for his argument. He searched for a response to comfort her.

Finding none, he said, "What are you planning to do?"

"I'm not sure," she said. "I'll find more people to talk to. I have to go to Al-Diriyah, that old town where she was last seen."

"How will you do that? Will your brother take you? Maybe Al-Amir will let his driver do it."

"I doubt it. Thomas doesn't even want me to talk about it. And Al-Amir told me nothing else could be done."

She thought for a while and then said, "I could call a taxi. It isn't very far, is it?"

He shook his head. "No. You can't take a taxi anywhere, Layne. Don't you know women alone are in danger of being assaulted here? Especially if they're unveiled. And it's automatically assumed to be their fault. In a taxi, outside the city—"

"Okay, I won't take a taxi. I don't even know how to find one."

"I'll drive you there."

"You have a job. I can't depend on you for

157

everything. This is *my* problem."

"And I'm going to help you. Promise me you won't do anything—I mean anything—until I get back."

"You're *leaving*? Where are you going?"

"I've got to fly to Jeddah tomorrow morning. As soon as I get back, I'll drive you to Al-Diriyah."

She crossed her arms, looking belligerent.

"You might not be able to get into the site, anyway," he said. "The ruins are being reconstructed, and it may be closed to visitors. I'll have to check on it."

"If I need permission, Al-Amir would have to get it for me?"

"Probably, since he's your sponsor. Do you think he will?" David said.

"No."

The misery in her voice pulled at him. "Maybe Saeed can help," he said. "He likes you and your brother. We'll find some way to do it," he said, hoping that was true.

Chapter 15

It took Saeed two days to arrange the visit to Al-Diriyah. He called Thomas to let him know he'd persuaded the architect in charge to give them a tour on Friday, the Islamic Sabbath, since workers wouldn't be on the site.

While she waited, Layne read the books her brother had brought and listened to his explanations. She practiced Arabic with him but liked talking with Al-Amir's gardeners, who corrected her errors more kindly.

In the other hours of the long days, she walked among the roses alone, planned what she'd do in the old city, and wished she could talk to David Markam.

She hadn't expected him to call while he was in Jeddah. He said he had meetings with his boss at the embassy. And there really wasn't any reason for him to call. Except that she missed him and wanted him to be missing her.

Al-Amir seldom appeared. Every time they met, Katherine's death hung between them like sheets of tattered silk that neither would touch.

Still, she never felt free of his presence. Every few hours, Puja opened the bedroom door and stared at her, as if she were making sure the prisoner was still where she belonged.

The old lion's aloofness was an advantage in a way. She didn't have to explain what she intended to do. He would certainly prevent it if he knew.

Friday morning, she woke with a mingling of excitement and dread, unable to let go of a sense of momentous occasion. This day was not going to end without change.

She came out of the bathroom to find her breakfast tray waiting. Spearing a piece of ripe mango, she sucked it into her mouth, loving its tang on her tongue. On the veranda, a tiny breeze caressed her skin. Invisible birds chirped in the trees.

As anxious as she was to go to Al-Diriyah, she wanted to see David Markam even more. Once or twice in her life, she'd been infatuated, perhaps in love. But those times she felt no fearful urgency, no longing for something she couldn't even name.

A burst of dramatic piano music broke into her reverie. Chopin's *Heroic Polonaise* poured from an open door farther along the balcony. Her brother must be responsible. It was the only music he knew by heart, the one he played when he was full of energy.

She strolled along the balcony and stood outside the French doors of the music room.

"Good morning," Thomas said, without looking up.

Layne sat in a gilded chair next to the grand piano and watched his fingers fly over the keys.

Pounding out the last notes, he swirled around on the stool and reached, carefully, for his teacup on top of the piano.

"So, you're all set for our excursion today," he said. His eyes gleamed, but there were dark circles under them, and she guessed his restlessness was keeping him from sleeping. The delay caused by Mustafa's injury and the delivery of new trucks was taking its toll on him.

He glanced at his watch. "What's on your mind, little sis?"

"Have you talked with Mr. Al-Amir recently?"

"Not since the day before yesterday. Ricky told me not to expect him to be sociable. He's been living alone for the past few years."

"He must have gone into seclusion after my mother was killed."

"Oh, Layne, I wish you'd stop harping on this theory of yours. It comes up in every conversation."

"That's because it's important to me. But if it bothers you, I won't mention it. For a while, anyway." With this attitude, he wouldn't be sympathetic to anything she said.

"You've got plenty of other things to think about. We ought to discuss the kinship patterns you'll be recording. And your Arabic needs work."

He turned back to the piano and played a few notes. "Of course, all of this must pale in comparison to spending time with your handsome diplomat."

"What makes you think he belongs to me? It's you he's doing favors for."

"Certainly true. But my main interest in the man is that you're interested in him. I've never seen you react to anyone the way you do every time he's around."

"All right. I'm not going to deny that I'm attracted to him," she said. "I didn't think you even noticed how I felt."

"I notice. Actually, I was teasing you, but it looks like I hit the mark."

"I'm not sure how I feel. I just met the man. I really don't know him at all. Besides, there's no future in a relationship with him. I mean, in a few days, we'll be gone. With his job and mine, we might live on opposite sides of the world. He may not even be the type who gets serious. If there is such a type."

Thomas sighed. "That's too bad. I was hoping you'd settle down someday."

"I don't see you breaking any speed records to the altar."

"What I've seen of connubial bliss has convinced me its rewards are far fewer than its pains, my dear."

"Does Barbara feel that way, too?"

Thomas and Dr. Barbara Davis, a colleague of his, had been unacknowledged lovers for years, and appeared to be content to keep it that way.

"She agrees with me entirely. After all, she's been tested in the matrimonial fires herself and found them grossly overrated.

"But Markam, now, that's a different matter. I wouldn't be too quick to dismiss him as a prospect. He's intelligent, ambitious. Altogether, not a bad catch. He's quite fit, too. Probably spends his time walking everywhere like you do."

"It wouldn't hurt you to walk a little more."

She got up. In this mood, Thomas was frustrating to talk to. Real emotions were relegated to an out-of-service-for-the-duration drawer.

"I'll be ready in ten minutes," she said over her shoulder.

She'd been so afraid that David wouldn't be back from Jeddah that she had to take a calming breath when she reached the stairs and looked down.

There he was, standing with Thomas and Saeed in the entrance hall.

He glanced up as she rounded the curve in the staircase, and the spark that leapt between them was like an electric shock. She walked down slowly, letting it dissipate.

"Layne, you have arrived," Saeed said in a ringing voice.

He was wearing a thob and ghotra today, and his silver Mercedes stood outside the open doorway. They were going to make a proper impression in the old town. His face beamed with the good will of a man who loves to be generous and has the means to do it.

"We should start now if you're ready."

He pulled out a handkerchief and mopped his forehead. "Every year I vow to escape in the summer. Here we are at eight in the morning, and the temperature is already at thirty-eight degrees—one hundred in Fahrenheit."

The library door opened, and they all turned to stare at the tall form framed in the doorway.

Al-Amir seemed surprised, as if he'd been lost in his own thoughts. His hair was ruffled, and he wore a dark silk dressing gown over shirt and trousers. He looked as though he'd been awake all night.

Recovering himself, he assumed his habitually imperious expression, and Layne felt the panic of a child caught breaking a rule.

He came toward them, his mouth twisting into a line of mild amusement.

"I hardly expected to find your party up and about at such an hour, but it is well to make an early start," he said.

Amazed, Layne stared at him. He knew where they were going! The question of who had told him seemed less important than the fact that he apparently didn't care! Was it because he was sure they wouldn't find anything important in the old city?

No one spoke as his gaze traveled benignly from one to another.

Emotion suffused his cheeks when he looked at David.

David's jaw clenched, his expression hardening into resistance. After that scene in the rose garden, he was openly defying the old lion by being here.

Al-Amir's eyes narrowed, but he said conversationally, "I had the pleasure of meeting one of the young men directing the restoration of Al-Diriyah not long ago. You will find the visit interesting."

Thomas surged into the silence that followed. "I hope my piano playing didn't disturb you."

Al-Amir shook his head. "No, no. I sleep very little these days. One finds the mind less willing to relent with passing time."

He lifted a hand in farewell and went back into the library.

With a general sense of relief, they hurried down the stairs.

Layne slid gratefully into the plush backseat of Saeed's car, and David Markam got in beside her.

He squeezed her hand. "I missed you."

As soon as the gates of Al-Amir's compound closed behind them, they settled into the cool comfort of the big car.

"Your host is quite a personage," Saeed said. "His family has been in the middle of politics here for generations."

Ricky's told me a little about their history," Thomas said. "They have no relationship with the royal family, but they seem well-regarded here."

"Oh, no. By all means, no! Al-Amirs have no connection with the desert tribes. They came, originally, from Persia. From what I've heard, they were influential there until a change of power put them in opposition to the government. Then, they escaped here, bringing their fortunes and skill as diplomats with them. They are a shrewd bunch of fellows, let me tell you."

Layne glanced at David to see what he thought of Saeed's frankness. He seemed preoccupied, staring out the window. Remembering his anger when he left Al-Amir's garden, she wondered again what he wasn't telling her.

They went along a broad road, nearly empty of traffic, that ran past a huge Arabian horse stable and a line of four identical palaces before the buildings gave way to the scrub desert.

As they got closer to the place where her mother died, Layne felt her anxiety growing. Her expectations were too high, her need to know too great.

At the first sight of the mud-brick ruins perched on top of a hill, her excitement and dread were hard to control.

Saeed parked the car under a stand of dusty trees about fifty yards from the graded roadway that led up to the site, and they got out, lethargic immediately in the heat.

"Walk carefully in these ruins," he said. "The

desert has an impassive face but a treacherous heart."

Layne said nothing. It was that treacherous heart she had come to find.

To her troubled mind, the parched bushes, the fragments of walls rising above rubble, looked barren and desiccated, as if human life had never been welcome. The thought of her mother dying in this forsaken place nearly unnerved her.

She and David fell behind the others as they trudged up the slope.

He put his arm around her and said, "I know a guided tour isn't what you were hoping for, but at least you'll get to see it."

From the top, they looked out over an ancient riverbed. On the far side of the wadi lay a cultivated grove of date palms and a village of mud-brick houses, silent in the bright morning.

Saeed made a sweeping gesture. "History is all around us. You must picture, Layne, that on this hill these were palaces and government buildings, houses, stables, and a great fortification wall just along there, you see?"

He pointed at a low wall of stones between the hill and the date grove.

"Once that wall was seven kilometers long. Think of that! This was an old city even before its glory days in the eighteenth century when it was the ancestral home of the royal family."

He turned and shouted, "There you are!"

A tall, red-haired man was climbing up to meet them.

"This is the architect overseeing the work," Saeed said.

The man's first words identified him as a Scotsman, and Thomas plunged eagerly into a conversation with him, spouting questions about what they had found in their excavations.

The man led them through the portion of the city he and his team were working on, obviously proud of their efforts to restore crenellated walls and towers that had stood for centuries against the unrelenting desert wind and sand.

Layne followed the men around, listening with half of her attention to the architect. Her frustration grew as she waited for a moment to talk to him alone.

Finally, he led them along a line of carved wooden doors opening into restored rooms, and she seized her chance.

He paused outside a doorway to let them file into one of the rooms, and she said, "Can I ask you a question?"

Without waiting for his answer, she said, "You've excavated the floors of all the houses. Have you found any human remains buried there or anywhere on the site? A makeshift grave or something under the rubble?"

The man looked puzzled. "We've identified a burial area at the base of the hill. We won't be excavating there."

"No, I don't mean a burial; I mean a body of a person killed and hidden."

His expression became wary. "I'm not certain what you want to know. Do you have something specific in mind?"

David, Thomas, and Saeed had come out of the room and were all staring at her.

"I—I'm sorry. Forgive me," she said. "Please excuse me. I need to go back down. I'm a little tired."

David touched her arm. "I'll go with you."

When they reached the bottom of the sloping roadway, she said, "I'm going to sit on the wall over there next to the date palm grove. I just need a few minutes of quiet."

He left her sitting there, and she looked up at the ruined town, imagining her mother waiting for a stranger among the rubble.

The grief easing gradually, she looked at the rows of trees in the grove. If no body was buried in the ruins, this grove could have offered a way to dispose of a woman quickly.

Of course, Thomas and David were right. Finding anything was unlikely after all this time. Still, she couldn't resist the compulsion to search. At least it was doing something.

The bare ground between the orderly rows of trees was packed hard, but a wide strip of lumpy dirt and grass lay along the inside of the wall. Dropping to her knees, she plunged her fingers into the rocky sand. It would be easy to dig here. A few feet away, under the shade of a scraggly clump of bushes, she saw a low mound.

Before she could stand up, she heard the clank of metal on stone and looked up to see David with a large thermos.

"Checking for scorpion holes?" he said.

"I learn fast about things that bite." She sat on the wall and took the cup of cold water he gave her.

He sat beside her and put his arm around her. "Why don't we go to the car? It's in the shade. More comfortable."

"I need fresh air. Do you think anybody would care if we walked around this grove?"

"If somebody objects, they'll let us know soon enough."

They walked along rows of trees with orange-brown fruit growing like grapes at the base of the fronds. All of it carefully maintained, innocent of any possibility of evil.

"Do you want to see the rest of the town?" he said, finally.

"I don't think so. There's nothing there."

He looked at her. "Nothing there? You asked the architect if they'd found human remains. You were really hoping to find a grave?"

She saw his compassion, but hearing him say it made the absurdity clear. "I had to try, David."

"I know. I just don't think there's anything to find." He looked up at the hill of ruins.

"This site must have been more or less abandoned when your mother was here."

"That's what doesn't make sense. Why did she even come to this place? She didn't care about old ruins, not even much about history."

"Must have been to meet someone," David said.

After a pause, he said, "What if she *didn't* die here? That story may have been invented."

She stared at him. "By Al-Amir? You're suggesting he killed her and made up the story about her coming here?"

"No, I'm not. But from what I've heard, he isn't reluctant to take action if he wants things to happen."

Layne knew that was true. "You didn't accuse him of that, did you? The day you confronted him in his garden."

He was good at hiding surprise. "Not directly," he said. "I knew he made the arrangements for you to get into the country."

"I wish you'd told me you were going to talk to him, David. I appreciate your help, but I don't want my problems to interfere with your life."

His voice suddenly hard, he said, "There isn't a single aspect of my life you haven't interfered with, Layne."

They glared at each other, and she felt a barrier solidifying between them, becoming as tangible as the stone and mortar wall surrounding the grove.

A sense of finality, like another kind of grief, took hold of her. This morning she told Thomas she had no future with David Markam. Was that the truth after all?

"Let's go back to the car," David said, impatience and frustration clear in his voice.

Too angry to be reasonable, she said, "Go if you want. I'm not sitting in that hot car until my brother and Saeed decide to leave."

"Damn it, Layne. You can't stay here alone."

"Yes, I can. There's nobody else around."

He hesitated, and looked for a moment as if he might pick her up and carry her to the car. Instead, he swore and strode away.

As soon as he was out of sight, she went back to the shaded area next to the bushes and knelt down on a patch of tough-bladed grass. She ran her hand over the top of the raised mound and reached across it, trying to gauge whether it was wide enough to be a grave.

The breeze rustled the leaves of the bush next to her, and she thought she heard a scraping of rock on the other side of it.

She sensed movement, but before she could turn, a blow struck her left shoulder and slammed her to the ground.

Chapter 16

Layne got to her knees and looked around. Not even the fronds of the palm trees stirred overhead now. On the hill, the eroded towers and walls of the ruin stood stark and forbidding, shapes blended by the sun's glare.

How was it possible for someone to do this without her seeing him? Just like the day in the city. The silent ruin, single shot, then nothing.

This time, there were running feet afterward. She'd heard them, shoes pounding toward the village.

A chunk of rock was lying in the grass nearby as if it had fallen from the wall. Lifting it, she knew it was the thing that hit her.

She reached under her collar and touched her throbbing back, not sure whether the clamminess she felt was sweat or blood until her fingers found the wound.

Slipping down, she huddled against the wall. This was how easily Katherine Darius could have died here. Her eyes stung with tears that would not come.

"Layne, where are you?" David shouted.

Before she could sit up again, he leaned over the wall. "What're you doing down there?"

She didn't answer him.

He vaulted over and squatted beside her. "Have you been rolling in the dirt?"

Trying to stand, she fell backward. He caught and held her. "You're hurt! You're bleeding. My God, what happened?"

She rested her head against his chest, waiting for dizziness to pass.

"Tell me what happened, Layne. How badly are you hurt?" His voice was tight with alarm.

"I'm all right."

"Let me get you to the car. We'll take you to the hospital."

"Wait a minute. I don't want to go anywhere. I told you, I'm okay. See?" She raised her arm and winced.

He opened the thermos he'd dropped as he jumped over the wall and handed her a cup of cold water.

After she drank a few gulps, he wiped the dirt and sweat from her face with a wet handkerchief.

"At least let me see the wound. Take off your shirt," he said.

"Not very subtle, are you?"

"I'm not kidding, either. Turn around."

She let him lift her shirt. He poured cold water over the wound and cleaned it gently.

"The skin is broken, but it's mainly going to be a bad bruise. I still think a doctor should look at it."

"No. It's okay." She pulled her shirt down.

He waited until she looked at him. "Why won't you tell me what happened? I can see something hit you," he said.

"There's nothing to tell."

She knew searching for a grave was a ridiculous, desperate thing to do. It wasn't necessary to hear him say that.

How could she explain the disappointment, the frustration she felt? She'd been so sure some evidence would be here. Something she could touch with her hand and *know*.

David was obviously making an effort to control his temper.

"Okay, let's go back to the car," Layne said.

When they reached the car, she said, "I'll probably get blood on Saeed's upholstery."

David opened the trunk, took out a cotton blanket, and folded it behind her back. He got in and, resting his arm along the top of the seat, he gripped her as if to keep her from bolting out the door.

"Now, let's have it," he said. "This is the second time you've been attacked in four days. I want to know what the hell's going on."

"I didn't say anybody attacked me."

His hold tightened. "Then what did happen?"

Sighing, she leaned her head back.

"I was looking around. And thinking. Then, something hit me. I heard a scraping against rock, but

I never saw anything. It was like that day in the city. This time I did hear feet."

"You heard someone running? Inside the grove or along the track outside the wall?"

"Outside. It was hard, like shoes, not sandals." She paused. "We should have looked for him. The people in that farm village might have seen a stranger around."

"If they did, somebody else will find him," David said. He moved his arm away and stared at her, his face tense.

"Were you looking for a grave?" he said.

Layne rubbed her eyes. "I don't want to talk about that."

Before he could say anything else, they saw Thomas and Saeed coming toward the car.

"You have to tell your brother about these attacks," David said.

She nodded. "I will. But not right this minute."

Saeed opened the door and beamed at them. "See, Thomas, I told you they were together. I knew David wouldn't pass up an occasion to be alone with your beautiful sister."

He and Thomas both gazed at them indulgently.

If Thomas noticed anything unusual about her appearance, he probably assumed it was the result of what she'd been doing with David.

David gave her a prodding look.

"Later," she said.

On the way back to the city, Thomas and Saeed

tried to outdo each other in praising the restoration work.

Layne was glad to let them talk. Her shoulder throbbed, and she was preparing herself for Thomas's reaction when she did tell him about the attack.

On one hand, he might throw a fit and insist that she go home. Even more likely, and more galling, he'd probably make sure she wasn't allowed to leave Al-Amir's house again.

At Saeed's estate, servants met them in the foyer. Layne had draped her long scarf around her back to cover any bloodstains, but Saeed looked at her with concern.

"Layne, I fear you've suffered from the heat. Perhaps seeing that place was more difficult than you anticipated. Please use one of my guest bedrooms upstairs. You can refresh yourself, even have a lie-down if you like. There's plenty of time before lunch."

He said something to a servant, who went away and came back immediately with a middle-aged Yemeni woman.

Layne followed her upstairs to a bedroom fully as luxurious as she'd expected. The woman showed her the bathroom, gave her towels, and hung a robe on the door hook.

Stripping off her filthy shirt, Layne looked in the mirror and cringed at the size of the bruise spreading down her back.

As bad as it was, at least the blow missed her head. It might have killed her or left her unconscious.

Like Mustafa.

Neither of these attacks seemed to have been planned ahead of time. A rock was convenient and it didn't make noise like the gunshot in the city.

Was it reasonable to believe some person randomly attacked them both on impulse? If they wanted to stop Thomas's work, it made sense to attack Mustafa.

But if they wanted to stop her from finding out what happened to her mother, why try to kill Mustafa?

And who was there both times? The man who hit Mustafa had to be inside Saeed's compound, very likely one of the drivers. No one like that was with them at Al-Diriyah.

The question seemed too big to think about right now. She spent a long time bathing, letting the warm water soothe the pain in her muscles and soften her fears, at least for a while.

The Yemini woman was waiting when she came out of the bathroom. She held up her clothes. "I clean for you. You put on, please," she said, pointing to silk underwear and a kaftan she had laid out on the bed. Layne dressed, grateful for the delicacy of the silk against her skin.

Looking for toiletries and a hairbrush, she opened a drawer. Then, out of curiosity she opened all of them. If this woman managed Saeed's home, she had thought of everything a guest might need. Hairdryer, cosmetics, toiletries—even condoms.

Among several bottles of lotions, she recognized

the image of golden dunes and the name *Nectar of the Sands*. Sahar's company.

So they were marketed in this country, not just in Europe. Or Saeed might have them imported. The guests who stayed the night after his parties were well provided for.

Had David ever been one of them? Saeed said he "disdained such frivolities." Of course, David wouldn't need a bedroom here. He had an apartment of his own.

She brushed her hair as energetically as she could. Why was she even thinking about that? Her life had no room for a complication like David Markam.

The thought of leaving him already hurt too much, anyway.

Armored with fatalism and determined not to let the pain in her shoulder show, she went downstairs to the terrace.

Today, the jets of the pool fountain swayed in sync with "Somewhere Over the Rainbow," and the air felt moist and cool. A buffet was spread out on a long table, grilled fish, lamb, salads and fruit.

As soon as she saw the three men standing beside the fountain with glasses of beer in their hands, she knew they knew what had happened.

David looked concerned, Saeed distressed, and her brother angry.

"David's told us of this horrible attack on you," Saeed said. "We must take you to a doctor."

Her brother said, "Are you really hurt? Why didn't you tell us this happened?"

"There really wasn't any point. I'm all right, and I didn't see anybody. Not a single person. What could we do?" she said.

"We will make inquiries," Saeed said. "Even now, it's not too late to question the villagers. Someone will know who has done this."

Layne wished she could believe in his optimism. Feeling lightheaded, she sat down. "I don't need to see a doctor, and I doubt a search would find anything. Please, let's just forget about this."

"We can't forget it. If Al-Amir had anything to do with it, I don't want you to go back to his house," David said.

"That's absurd," Thomas said. "Was that your idea, Layne? Ridiculous! I thought we'd settled that."

"What makes you think of Al-Amir?" Saeed said.

"It's all this secrecy," Layne said. "Strange things happening. Our equipment sabotaged." She stopped herself from blurting out, *and somebody shot at me.* "Then there were those illegal messages with his name mentioned."

"Ridiculous!" Thomas insisted.

"No, no. That part is quite true," Saeed said, looking worried. "We must not discount what Layne is telling us. Didn't I say Al-Amir is a mysterious fellow?

"They are controversial for many reasons—their origins, their interests abroad. And, of course, the

Quiet Lion's diplomatic career is regarded by some as brilliant and by others as traitorous. It depends on whom you ask."

"We don't have evidence of radical associations," David said. "Is he involved in any activist groups here?"

"Not that I've heard in this country. But he spent many years in Europe and the States. Two of his sons live abroad still. Who knows what goes on there? And what of his private life?" Saeed said.

Thomas's face was flushed with anger. "The whole thing's fantastic. If it weren't for the attacks on you and Mustafa, I'd suspect you'd been indulging in some ill-advised histrionics, Layne."

"I've been expecting you to say that! You ignore anything that threatens your work."

"There was nothing imaginary about the attack on her today," David said.

Saeed sailed into the fray. "You must be fair, Thomas. Your sister is no ordinary woman. The motives of courageous people are often misunderstood."

He smiled at her. "Since you came here, Layne, I have read about your illustrious mother, Katherine Darius. What a glorious legacy to inherit."

"I'm afraid I didn't inherit much glory," she said. "And I didn't mean Mr. Al-Amir actually brought us here to harm us. I don't believe that at all. It's just unnerving to know somebody is going to a lot of trouble to scare us."

"I shall find who's behind these things, no matter who ordered them," Saeed said. "As to your safety in Al-Amir's house, you are both welcome to be my guests."

"Thank you, Saeed, but no," Thomas said quickly. "We are perfectly safe and comfortable with the Al-Amirs. And I wouldn't dream of offending him or his family."

Saeed shrugged and looked inquiringly at Layne.

She knew what her brother had *not* said, that without Al-Amir's support, there wouldn't be any research, or even permission to stay in this country.

"I'm sure he takes his obligation as a host seriously," she said.

"That must be true. Not even a madman would harm a guest in his house," Saeed agreed.

"So, if we have settled things for now, let's eat this food my chef has prepared. He will be outraged if we don't enjoy it."

In spite of his efforts, the lunch was subdued. Layne forced herself to eat, but she said little. From time to time, she saw David watching her.

While they were drinking coffee, Saeed said, "Thomas, I have a collection of antiquities from various sites in our area. We didn't have time for them the other night. Perhaps you'd like to see them now."

Thomas looked delighted, but Layne shook her head. "Please excuse me, Saeed. I'm a little tired. I'd like to retrieve my clothes and go."

"So you have grown weary of me already? No, I'm joking," he said, laughing. "You're welcome to rest here, or my car will take you to Al-Amir's house immediately if you wish to go."

David stood up and tossed his napkin on the table. "I'll drive you," he said.

Layne nodded, relieved.

She went upstairs to change, and when she came down in her own clothes that the Yemini woman had cleaned and ironed, Layne tried to tell Saeed how grateful she was for his help.

"It is nothing; nothing. In fact, I'm hoping you will let me give you a much more pleasant time tomorrow evening. A few friends you will enjoy, I promise," he said.

"Thank you, but I'm afraid I can't," she said. "I'm invited to a ladies party tomorrow night."

"Well, we leave her in your hands, David. You must take good care of this lady," Saeed said.

In David's car, she pressed her spine against the seat, trying to ease the ache in her back.

He got in and looked at her. "Do you really want to go to Al-Amir's house or was that an excuse to get out of seeing another one of Saeed's collections?"

"I really am tired."

"And obviously in pain. I wish you'd let me get you some medical help."

"I'm not a martyr, David. I'd go if I needed to. Right now, I just want to be quiet and to think for a while."

They drove in silence through the hazy afternoon sunshine. When they reached the streets of Al-Amir's neighborhood, Layne glanced at him, liking the familiarity of his profile in the shadows of the old oaks. Liking everything about him.

It was sorrow, almost mourning, to know she didn't dare to love this man. No matter how much they wanted each other, the differences in their lives could never be reconciled. One day, he would leave her, just as her mother did.

Chapter 17

Once again, Al-Amir did not appear for dinner, and Layne and Thomas ate a nearly silent meal and went to their rooms. She slept little that night. Her muscles ached, and her mind roiled with the day's adrenaline.

Puja's knock the next morning jerked her back to the concerns she wasn't ready to face. Looking more disagreeable than usual, the woman busied herself moving dishes around on the breakfast tray as if she were composing a speech she could hardly wait to deliver.

"Thank you. I'll eat later, Puja," Layne said.

"Must say message," she announced. "Son of Al-Amir say you go wife house today. Say you ready eight o'clock."

She waited, pleased to be giving an order that couldn't be refused.

"I know about this, but thank you for reminding me," Layne said.

Puja's disappointment showed only in a tightening of her mouth. She pulled a folded piece of paper out of the waistband of her sari, and put it on the tray.

"Other message," she said triumphantly. Her smug look guaranteed this one was news. And Layne wasn't going to like it.

Having scored her victory, she went out the door, skinny hips swinging belligerently.

Layne picked up the paper, actually two notes. The first, from Asad Al-Amir, asked her to come to his library to talk to him. This must be the one Puja was so smug about. A summons from the master would hardly be a friendly chat.

The other was unsigned, but she knew her brother's scribbled writing.

Ricky and I leaving at dawn to see a B. settlement village outside the city. I trust you're feeling well enough to finish reading the chapters we discussed. Pay attention at the ladies party tonight. We need to make the most of every opportunity to observe. Stay out of trouble!

In a last line, he proposed that they drive into the desert tomorrow. *A break from all the distractions will be good for you.*

"A break for me?" she said, crumpling the note. It wasn't she who needed distractions. He was the one fretting over the forced delay. And he was probably intending to lecture her again about antagonizing Al-Amir.

A bath did little to improve her mood. The bruise had spread into an ugly purple splotch across her upper back, painful when she tried to prop herself up on pillows to read.

She resented being ordered around by every male that came along. It was as if, little by little, they were shrinking her into some kind of apprentice adult.

Deciding it wasn't yet convenient to respond to Al-Amir's summons, she opened one of the books from the pile on the bed. Not fascinating, but it kept her from being sucked into one of the twin rabbit holes of worry and euphoria that her mind kept slipping into. After rereading the same passage four times, she finished dressing and went downstairs.

Outside the library door, she hesitated. Someone had undoubtedly told him about the attack at Al-Diriyah. Was he going to put even more restrictions on her now?

A low voice sounded through the thick wood in response to her knock. Assuming she'd been given permission to enter, she opened the door.

Behind his desk, Al-Amir sat engrossed in reading what looked like a manuscript. The disheveled appearance of yesterday was gone. He was immaculate in a pearl gray shirt, open at the throat, but his skin was still sallow, the folds deeply etched. A breakfast tray lay barely touched on a side table. He gazed at her impassively.

"*Salaam.* I'm not sure what the Farsi word is," she said, hoping he would be surprised that she knew he was Persian.

"Salaam will do well enough." He waited, making no move to lay his work aside or invite her to sit down.

She eased into one of the big leather chairs, feeling awkward and hoping he couldn't see she was in pain. "You want to talk to me?"

He put the manuscript on the desk. "Merely to inquire about your visit to Al-Diriyah. Did it meet your expectations?"

She studied his face, trying to read whether he knew what happened.

"The ruin is interesting. My mother disappeared before the restoration work began. The architect claims his team excavated the floors of all the houses. They didn't find any bodies." She held his gaze.

"How can you be sure that's where she died?" she said when he didn't respond. "Your driver wasn't with her when she walked into the ruin. She might have gone into that village nearby. Why wasn't any trace of her ever found? What about her camera? She went there to take photographs."

Al-Amir drew in and let out a breath, as if he accepted the inevitable. "Her camera was found at the base of the ruined tower. No photographs were on the film. Nothing else."

"I know she came here to investigate a rebellion or something like that. Did anybody outside of your family know why she was here? Did people ask questions about why she was staying with you?"

"You cannot imagine I compromised her reputation."

"She didn't need any help doing that."

He smiled patiently as if interpreting her cynicism as a judgment of her mother. "One day, you will understand these things. Love chooses us without regard to logic or circumstance."

Closing his eyes, he said softly,

I marveled as she came darkling to me
and entered free,
Then she rose and bade farewell,
And when she turned, my life well-nigh
went forth with her.

Layne struggled to deflect the pull on her emotions. Of course she understood. Wasn't she already over her head in a love with no future, no logical reason to exist?

"It's odd how the past holds onto the present, because we won't let go of it," she said.

Al-Amir's expression grew severe. "If you allude to my error in bringing you here, I admit that is true. But you are here. I see no purpose in discussing it."

"Well I do. Too many things have happened to us—to me—that I can't ignore. I don't have to tell you what they are. You know everything that goes on.

"It isn't reasonable to believe these things are meant to stop Thomas's work," she said. "They must be related to the past. To your past and my mother's.

"You owe me the truth, Asad Al-Amir. I am Katherine's child. I need to know why she never came home."

He shook his head as if he were amazed. "Oh, how you are like her," he murmured.

"Never for a moment could I evade her questions." He gazed at her wistfully. "So like her."

When she didn't respond, he said, "Very well. It is more than curiosity that impels you. You are struggling to find your own place in this life, are you not? To grow up the child of an extraordinary parent is inevitably difficult, but to be deprived of the years during which you might learn to know each other. That is a tragedy."

He spoke gently, meaning to be kind, she was sure. But even so, it was an invasion. He saw what she'd longed for all her life.

"To the world," he went on, "Katherine Darius was a daring adventurer. To me, she was a spring of clear water in this desert.

"She came late into my life, after my wife had died and my children had children of their own. I was content. I wrote my books, I had a few friends. Occasionally, I went to London to renew my memories of those days. It was into this peaceful, insouciant life that Katherine Darius came.

"My eldest son and his family were living here with me at that time, and I could, with propriety, invite Katherine to be our guest. Two weeks after her letter telling me she wished to come, she was here.

"We sat in this library that first night and talked hour upon hour. By the light of dawn, I knew I could no longer live without her. When she came to me, it was the beginning of a new life. She gave me the only completeness I have ever known."

"She left people who loved her," Layne said.

He looked disconcerted for an instant. Then he said, "Her marriage with your father had ended. She did not intend to return to him."

"She was going to divorce him and marry you?" His words horrified her, but she knew they might be true.

A spasm of pain distorted his features. "I cannot say what she would have done. I wished to marry her. It was more than a wish. I did not believe my life could go on without her. She was unlike any woman I have ever known."

"She wouldn't have put up with the traditions of this society," Layne said bitterly.

"We would not have made our home here. Perhaps in Greece."

"I just can't believe she was willing to give up everything, leave her family after a few of days of knowing you."

"My dear Layne, I told you the last time we talked that what I had to say would be difficult for you. Katherine and I knew each other for many years. Her coming here was the culmination of a long friendship and the beginning of our lives together.

"I met her the year after my wife died, at a diplomatic reception in London. I was ambassador to the U.K. then and Katherine just starting to make her reputation in journalism."

He flung his head back, laughing. "She was tenacious. Always a story she must have, anywhere in the world she would go!"

His eyes still shining, he said, "I was called home from that post, and perhaps six months passed before I saw her again. I went to New York and then Washington on a rather excruciating speaking tour for my book *Arab Modernization*.

"There, I saw her in a television interview. She said she loved her family and regretted that she had to be away from them often. I did not dare to call her again.

"Some time later, we both happened to be in Cairo, and I did call her. From there, we met whenever we could. London, Madrid. One glorious time, just for a holiday, in Santorini."

When he paused, Layne watched him, torn between a desire to get away and an even stronger one to hear everything he would tell her. "Why did she come here?" she said.

He rubbed his jaw, reflecting. "I wanted to believe it was only to visit me, but she never went to any country unless a story drew her there. She heard rumors of a rebellion brewing here.

"In the beginning, her intention may have been simply to gather information. Of course, I was opposed to her plan to pursue that investigation. It was best left alone."

"If you'd really objected, she couldn't have gotten into the country," Layne said.

"My motives were never noble. I made no effort to keep her from coming. Just to have her with me, to touch her again, gave my life significance, a sweetness for which there are no words."

Layne listened, feeling a humiliating confirmation. She and Thomas had always feared Katherine didn't love their father, that her work held more of her attention than anything else. Even suspecting she'd had affairs, they never imagined a great passion like the one she must have had with this man.

"So, she came here to spend the rest of her life with you," she said.

"Yes." The word was barely a whisper.

Layne waited, but he sat gazing out the window as if he were still seeing the past.

She wasn't sure she believed him. His was the only version of events she'd heard. How much was interpretation? How much a cover for guilt of his own?

"Did you send for me because you wanted to tell me this?" she said.

Al-Amir's expression was more serious than she'd ever seen it. "I asked you to come for another reason. To caution you not to become entangled with the activities of my niece Sahar. I did not know you had visited her until after it had happened."

So he had set Hassan on her trail sooner than she realized.

"It was arranged for me, Mr. Al-Amir," she said. "I didn't even know she existed until I went to her apartment with Rana. There weren't any sinister motives for it. Wasn't it appropriate for me to do that?"

"Despite my council, my niece is seldom restrained in expressing her views. Nor is she prudent in choosing friends who come into conflict with the lawful government."

"A government whose laws are unjust, immoral by my standards," Layne said. Confronting him was foolish, she knew, but she couldn't stop herself.

"How can you justify treating women like children? Keeping them under a male guardian's control their whole lives? Forcing them into marriages, denying their talents and their dreams!"

Leaning back in his chair, he crossed his arms, his head tilted to the side, a half smile on his face. He shook his head. "You do have Katherine's fire."

"I'm not sure how my mother felt about these issues. But I thought you were in favor of reform. You say in your books that women should be educated and given the same rights men have. How can you modernize this country if women don't have freedom?"

Sighing, he shook his head. "My opinions have little effect on that process. Of course I support Sahar's desire for reform. It is just. But I tell you now, as I have told her many times, radical political activities, extreme behavior, will only push her cause further from its goals. What she is doing is perilous."

"So you're telling me not to visit Sahar again? I can't see how teaching poor women to read and training them in skills for a trade is radical behavior."

"She hasn't told you all she is doing. Even she may not understand the risk of it," he said. His face was stern. "Our government is intolerant of dissent. Vengeful execution, imprisonment without hope of appeal. These are commonplace. The peril cannot be overstated. You must not be caught in this maelstrom. Your friend Mr. Markam knows something of this. He, too, has warned you, has he not?"

"He thinks *you* might be leading the activists," she said and then regretted the words. Was she betraying David, turning this powerful man against him?

Al-Amir sat very still. Finally, he said, "I will not give you another warning."

Chapter 18

Layne closed the front doors of Al-Amir's house and stepped into still, hot air that felt like invisible thorns pricking her skin. She needed to walk, anywhere, to get as far from this house as she could.

Two men in thobs were sitting near the bottom of the steps, and her anger gave way to relief. One of them was Mustafa. Her impulse was to hug him, but she knew he'd be embarrassed. "Allah be praised. You are here, Mustafa," she said.

Mustafa blushed, a wide grin making him look like a boy, too young to have such a dark bushy beard. His ghotra covered most of the bandaged area of his head, but a yellowish-purple bruise spread down to his cheek.

"Are you sure you're all right?"

"Doctor say I new man."

"Do you know what happened at Mr. Bin Yousef's house?"

He shrugged, his eyes shifting uneasily to the other driver. "Somebody mistake me different one. No sweat." Tilting his head, he said, "You go shop?"

"Yes, I do need to shop for something." She hadn't thought of a reason. But there was always the damned abaya. She might as well get it over with.

Mustafa pointed at the Mercedes parked just beyond the steps. "I take you." She followed him to the car. He opened the door for her and said, "You no get lost today."

Glancing back as the gates opened, she saw the other driver, still nonchalantly lounging on the steps, but watching them. He was the same man who drove her and Rana to Sahar's apartment, undoubtedly part of Al-Amir's surveillance team.

The compound gates closed behind them, and they moved sedately through the dappled sunshine under the old oaks. What deceptive calm there was on the surface of this place. A placid order that defied the wasteland around it.

Mustafa stopped the car in front of a cluster of small neighborhood shops. Layne glanced into a tailor's shop, and saw a few readymade abayas on display. Finding one long enough to fit her took a little time, but she left with the entire outfit of cape, veil, and two yards of black gauzy material to cover her head.

Afterward, she looked into other shops, delaying the drive back to Al-Amir's house as long as possible. Mustafa stood on the sidewalk in front of each one, making no secret of his intention. He would not be fooled this time.

Accepting the inevitable, she went back to the house and quickly upstairs, relieved not to see anyone. In her room, she put on the black cape, pinned the veil over her face and covered her head with the gauzy scarf. Feeling smothered, physically and emotionally, she jerked the pieces off and stuffed them into a drawer. The rest of the afternoon, she spent pacing the floor, memorizing Arabic nouns and wishing she could talk to David Markam.

Thomas sailed in, dusty and reeking of sweat, just as she finished dressing for the evening.

"Be sure you're ready early for our trip tomorrow," he said. "We've got to leave before nine. So don't party too much tonight." He was smirking, but she knew he'd lick the ground for a chance to see what went on in a women's party.

It was dark by the time Mustafa dropped her at the front of the Mediterranean villa Ricky and Rana shared with their three children and an assortment of relatives and servants. Built in the center of an acre or so of garden, the blue tile roof and whitewashed walls gave an impression of tradition enlivened by vines in late summer bloom. Unlike Sahar's cold marble penthouse or Al-Amir's country estate, this was a home. On this warm, still night, the whole place was alight, and guests were coming in, laughing and chatting.

Rana, dressed in emerald silk, met her in the foyer, beaming. She kissed Layne's cheeks in the French way. "We're so happy you came," she said. "I have been longing to see you."

She led the way into a huge majlis already filled with perhaps fifty women, some talking in groups, some sitting on the divans that lined the walls, others reclining Bedouin-style on tapestry pillows.

But these were not Bedouin women. Diamonds flashed on manicured fingers, and French perfume drifted through the leisurely conversation and soft laughter. Layne tried not to feel dowdy as sophisticated eyes appraised her embroidered skirt and blouse.

"You have lots of friends," she said.

Rana squeezed her arm as if she sensed her discomfort. "This isn't really my party. My mother invited most of these people. Some of them I don't even know." Layne braced herself for a round of introductions, but Rana led her to a spot where two oversized pillows and a low, glass table were set up as if for a special guest.

They sat down, and Rana waved to someone across the room. "That's one of my friends from the Sorbonne. I haven't seen her for years!"

Layne tried to spot the schoolmate, but Rana nudged her attention toward the door.

"Look, there's Sahar. I wasn't sure she would come. The lady with her is her mother, my husband's Auntie Nayam."

Layne watched the mother, a small person with a sweet, patient face, who seemed incapable of having borne the tall, angular woman by her side. Sahar, her features set in bitter lines, urged her mother to find a seat.

"Nayam is Mr. Al-Amir's sister?"

"Yes. A charming lady."

Thinking of the marriage traditions in this culture, she said, "Is Sahar's father a cousin of Mr. Al-Amir's?"

Rana nodded, distracted as everyone started clapping. A door opened on the far side of the room and five women in black dresses came in carrying small drums, tambourines, and a kind of flute.

Applause stopped and the musicians settled themselves cross-legged on a raised dais in the corner. The oldest woman, her gray hair confined in a massive bun, sat in the center on a cushion. She held a beautiful oud, like a pear-shaped guitar. The audience went quiet and she began to pluck strange, minor key notes.

Gentle music went on for a while and a few women began chatting. Then, the lights dimmed and conversation stopped. A young woman rose and went to stand in front of the dais. One of the musicians tossed bits of incense into a brazier at the edge of the stage and the scent of sandalwood pervaded the room. The woman tensed, her body seized by passion. Her voice rose in a melancholy tonal melody.

Layne tried to observe, to record the experience, but the music lulled, the fragrance intoxicated. Her mind succumbed to a kind of drowsy peace, the perfect harmony of women in the company of women.

Silence at the end of the song was broken by staccato drumbeats that quickened her pulse. A young woman squealed and leapt to her feet. Two more followed her and began to dance, swaying awkwardly at first and giggling. Others joined them, twisting, swaying as the drums beat faster.

The music ended, and the dancers sat down, laughing and wiping sweat from their faces. For a few minutes, they all waited in the darkness. Then suddenly the women sitting near the dais slid back, clearing a circle in the center of the room. Light from a single beam shone on a beautiful woman who stepped into the cleared space.

She had a narrow, sensuous face and a body a man might kill to embrace. With a defiant gesture, she bent her head, jerked loose the ribbon that bound her hair, and tossed free the cascade of dark waves.

The musicians began a slow, jerky kind of rhythm. Her body undulated to the pulse of the drums, the folds of her red silk gown caressing her as she moved. The music rose into a heart-stirring whine and her dance became a frenzy.

Here, in the voluptuous flesh, was a sultan's dancing girl, her hair flying in wild arcs, her body promising unspeakable pleasure. It was a practiced ritual of allure, danced with compelling abandon.

Layne watched her, fascinated, her senses suffused with desire to be with David.

She heard again Al-Amir's expression of love. And now she believed her mother loved him, too. Whatever Katherine Darius wanted, she was as vulnerable to bewitchment as her daughter was.

The music ended, the room erupted in applause, and doors were flung open, letting in merciful drafts of fresh air. Bright lights came on, and Layne was again in a room of talking, laughing women, though the spell of excitement lingered.

She staggered to her feet, dazed and drenched with sweat, and reached to help Rana up.

"Ah, that was fun," Rana murmured, a dreamy look on her flushed face.

"I never knew anything like this really happened. Do you have these parties all the time?" Layne said.

Tossing her hair back and fanning herself, Rana said, "Oh, yes. We have parties often. Sometimes they're fun and other times, deadly dull. It depends on who comes and how everyone feels. My mother wanted this one to be special. Did you enjoy the dancing?"

"It was overwhelming," Layne said. "Who are these musicians? And that dancer, she's like dancing girls in a Hollywood movie."

Rana looked shocked. "You are not thinking these are street women who dance for men in coffeehouses? These are not *ahira*, Layne. These women are professional musicians. No man ever looks at them."

"I'm sorry. I didn't mean— There's so much I don't know."

Across the room, Sahar was looking at her thoughtfully.

Layne dreaded having to talk to the woman again, to lose this wonderful sense of pleasure and peace.

"Come!" Rana said, leading her by the hand. "My mother is trying to get everyone into the dining room. Our food is ready."

Outside the door to the dining room were servants holding steel basins and towels. Layne liked this custom of washing before a meal. She'd discovered it when she visited a friend's home in India, and she dipped her hands gratefully in warm, perfumed water and held them out to be dried.

The dining room, paneled in white and gold and lighted by crystal chandeliers, was fragrant with the aromas of coriander and cumin, cinnamon and the smell of grilled meat.

In the center of a huge round table was a tray holding a whole roasted lamb on a bed of pilaf, ringed by roasted chickens. Towers of fruit were surrounded by plates of savory pastries, stuffed vine leaves, tabouli, vegetable dishes, and on a side table, cakes and tarts.

They filled their plates and stood in small groups eating, chatting, and assessing each other.

"Prepare yourself," Rana whispered. "Auntie Nayam and Sahar are coming this way."

"Sahar doesn't look happy," Layne said.

Patting her arm, Rana said, "Don't mind Sahar. She's the eldest cousin, and she fancies herself guardian of the family's affairs."

Layne swallowed a bite of chicken and waited while the women made their way through the crowd.

"My daughter has been telling me about the illustrious professors," Nayam said when Rana introduced her.

"You must be very brave to accompany your brother into the desert. Such a difficult life for a young woman. My Sahar believes the only way to cross the desert is by airplane." She smiled indulgently at her daughter.

"I go to the desert every spring to look at the forage or visit the farm growing our herbs," Sahar said. "I don't have to live in a tent to appreciate its value."

"Did you enjoy the dancing?" Nayam said.

"Yes, very much," Layne said. "In fact, I'm enjoying the whole party. It's wonderful to be around women for a change. I'm outnumbered in Mr. Al-Amir's house."

Nayam sipped the sparkling juice she was holding. "It is sad, really. My brother has been a lonely man for many years now. What a pity you did not see his house in the old days. He was ambassador then. There were always parties. Even the ladies would attend. We were very free and Western in that house." She flushed and smiled. "Such memories. I was sure we would have that again when the American came to stay—"

"Mother!" Sahar said.

In the charged silence, Layne waited, hoping she would go on, tell her about those days when her mother was here. But Sahar's grim face made it clear the family had drawn its armor around itself.

"It is very late," Nayam murmured, and they moved away.

"Why did Sahar stop her?" Layne said.

Rana leaned closer and spoke in a low, sharp voice. "We do not discuss your mother, Layne. It is better to let things be."

"But Sahar talked about her the other day." She stopped, aware she was on the verge of alienating the only friend she had here.

Forcing a brittle smile, Rana put her plate on a side table. "Your culture is very different from ours. You must think us quite strange."

"Not strange. Just more mysterious than seems necessary," Layne said, astute enough to know she'd been rebuked, gracefully but firmly.

She made an excuse to leave, hoping to get out of the house without another encounter, but in the foyer, Sahar was waiting for her.

"Dr. Darius—Layne," she said, looking oddly uncertain. "I have stayed to apologize to you for my discourtesy when you visited me."

She twirled her fingers as if she were trying to summon words that wouldn't come. "It's one of my faults that I say the wrong things to people I most want to know as friends."

Layne was astonished. The arrogance in the woman's expression had melted into anxiety.

"I understand, Sahar. If I sounded like I didn't care about your work, that's not what I meant. The cause you're striving for is worthy, and I admire you. I, well, I suppose I was feeling defensive. None of my academic training, not even my fieldwork in India, prepared me for coming here. Believing I can study Bedouin people now seems presumptuous at best. What do I know about being a woman in this society?"

Sahar shook her head. "You are sincerely trying. I'm sure of that. But you see only the surface of our lives. For all their excitement and freedom tonight, these women must go home to families where they are forever restrained by the will of a father, a husband, a brother."

"I'd like to talk with you more, Sahar. I truly want to learn from you."

"Then you will come to see me again? Tomorrow, perhaps?"

Layne knew she should refuse. The warnings from both Hassan and Al-Amir resounded in her mind.

"My brother arranged a trip for us in the morning," she said. "It will probably be afternoon before we get back. May I call you?"

"Yes. Please ring me as soon as you can," Sahar said, looking relieved.

Outside, beyond the lights of the house and driveway, the sky was deeply black. A smell of hosed down pavement mingled with the scent of geraniums in the dry, warm air.

Mustafa, as usual, was not among the other drivers sitting around a brazier in a grassy area just inside the gates. When she asked for him, the men pointed to a line of cars parked along the roadway.

Al-Amir's gray Mercedes was several yards away under a streetlamp. Walking toward it, she passed a black sedan. The driver's door opened, and a large man stepped out.

With the streetlight behind him, she couldn't see his face, but the authority of his manner sent fear through her. She stopped and waited.

"Good evening, Dr. Darius," he said. His voice was level, nothing more than a polite greeting.

She tried to match his tone. "Mr. Hassan. I seem to be running into you every time I go out on my own."

He moved closer, planting himself in her path. "I have made it my mission to know of your comings and goings." His tone didn't change, but she felt menace behind its courtesy.

"Would you mind telling me why?"

"Let us say, we would not wish you to experience a repetition of the incident at Al-Diriyah."

She stepped to the side, maneuvering to see his face.

"There's no danger here. Who would try to harm me with all these people around?"

"People were present at Al-Diriyah. Mr. Markam, the American, was with you, was he not?"

"Well, he wasn't the one who hit me."

"But you cannot say who did. Is that not so?"

Anger—fear—made her challenge him. "Did Mr. Al-Amir tell you to follow me here?"

He was silent except for his slow, heavy breathing.

She started to walk past him, but his hand shot out, holding without touching her.

"Perhaps your friends have convinced you that you may behave as you wish in this country. That is a mistake."

Which friends? Did he know she talked to Sahar? Were there microphones planted in Ricky and Rana's house, spies among the women at the party?

"I don't understand why you're here, Mr. Hassan. What have I done?"

"Were you not advised that a visit to Al-Diriyah was unwise?"

So that was it. She'd ignored Al-Amir's wishes, and Hassan was here to be sure she didn't do it again.

"You don't have to keep a watch on me. I'm not going anywhere until we leave the city. But you might as well know I'm planning to visit Sahar's school. She's doing important work, and I have a right to see it. Mr. Al-Amir can't object to that, can he?"

"I urge you not to do it. As I told you earlier, she participates in dangerous activity. Despite her family's efforts, she persists. If she continues, we will inevitably step in."

He paused. Then, in a harsher voice, he said, "It is

most important that you understand this. Your stay in this country is entirely dependent upon Asad Al-Amir's good will. If you choose to defy him again, you are not immune from that same consequence."

He glared but motioned for her to go.

She hurried to the car, and Mustafa woke with a jerk when she tapped on the glass. Before he could get out, she slipped into the back seat, still shaken.

"Sorry it's so late," she said, regretting that his wait had been long. He must still be weak from his injury. Once again she wondered why he didn't sit with the other drivers. And whether he'd told Thomas what was bothering him.

As they moved down the road, she looked back. The black sedan pulled away from the curb and was prowling behind, keeping half a block's distance. Hassan was going out of his way to make her aware he was watching her.

More angry than afraid, she sat fuming for a few minutes. Then a sound penetrated her thoughts. Mustafa was humming. It was bits of the tonal melodies the musicians played during the dancing. How tantalizing that music must be to the men waiting outside. Hearing and imagining, but forbidden to see. How did relationships in this society work at all?

She saw again Sahar's look of desperation. For women who chafed under its repressions, the system did not work.

Gradually, she made up her mind. Katherine

Darius may have rejected Sahar's plea for help, "But I am not my mother," she whispered to herself.

Here in this country, there was little she could do. Defying Al-Amir's orders would force him to withdraw his support, cancel the work that meant so much to Thomas.

But Al-Amir's influence could not touch her when she was back in Washington, D.C. There, she was free to advocate in her classes, write articles to make other people aware that there were women here longing for freedom.

In Al-Amir's house, she hurried through the dim entry hall. Upstairs, she considered knocking on Thomas's door to tell him Hassan had followed her again. But even if he were still awake, he'd be tired. And just as unlikely to tell her what was going on.

Undressing, she smelled the heavy scent of incense clinging to her clothes and hair. She took a long shower and fell asleep quickly, but it was a troubled night. Dreams of small black cars creeping after her were interwoven with longing for David and fear that losing him was already inevitable.

Chapter 19

Layne groaned when she woke early the next morning. She was still groggy from breathing incense smoke, and her back was stiff and sore. Whatever Thomas's reason for taking a drive today, it couldn't be worth spending hours in a hot truck.

She pretended to be asleep when Puja swung the door open and pushed the breakfast cart into the room. Waiting until the woman had gone, she poured a cup of tea and got back under the sheet to meditate over the rising steam. Rest was what she really needed.

Thomas's knock on the door radiated enthusiasm.

"I'm not here," Layne shouted.

He tapped again and opened the door, looking as disgustingly cheerful as he sounded. "We have to be on the road while it's still cool. Let's go. I've got something to show you."

After the luxury of Al-Amir's car, the SUV seat felt like a hard bench. It wasn't even eight o'clock in the morning, already over ninety degrees, and of course, her brother refused to use the air conditioning.

Deciding to make the best use she could of the day, she said, "While we're out of Al-Amir's house, I've got to talk to you. It's important."

Thomas sighed. "I knew you would."

"I think it's time you leveled with me, Thomas. Every day, I find out something you haven't told me."

"Go ahead. What do you want to know?" he said.

"I suppose you're aware that Hassan and Al-Amir have warned me not to see Sahar again."

"More or less. Ricky said they were worried that she might involve you in her radical politics."

"Did you tell Al-Amir I was attacked at Al-Diriyah?"

"No, but Ricky must have. Not the kind of thing you can hide."

"That's not all you can't hide," she said, hoping to shock him into being honest. "I found out yesterday that Al-Amir and my mother were lovers."

Thomas blinked several times, as if he were resisting a painful thought. "So he told you."

"You knew?"

Thomas negotiated a traffic circle and drove another block before he said, "Ricky told me a year or so after she was killed. He was in the States on a business trip and he came to see me. His father's relationship with Katherine embarrassed him."

"How do you think I felt when I heard my mother had an affair with Al-Amir? And realized why he arranged this field study for you? Was he curious about what Katherine's daughter would look like?

Bringing me along was a condition of his support, wasn't it? What else have you kept secret from me, Thomas?"

"Your reaction answers your question. I knew it would upset you."

"I don't understand how you can be so unemotional. Weren't you angry for Dad's sake?"

"Dad didn't know. Would he have been any less miserable if I had told him?"

Layne felt deep sorrow for their father. In the last years, his shoulders stooped under his tweed jackets, a look of resignation on his face. Lecturing about ancient Greece was the only thing he seemed to enjoy. Did he believe his wife died loving him?

She felt fresh anger at Al-Amir—the great man who could move people around the world on a whim. What kind of compromise did her brother make with his conscience to accept the patronage of this man, aware of what he was?

Thomas glanced at her. "I know you're hurt, confused, and I'm sorry, Layne. You may not believe this, but I honestly thought I was doing the right thing for you."

His attention shifted to the trucks slowing down ahead of them, and Layne's anger slid into fear as they rounded the hill and saw the guard hut and lines of soldiers on either side of the highway.

At the checkpoint, Thomas spoke to the sergeant casually and handed him the papers. This time the man seemed almost indifferent. With only a glance at their documents, he waved them through.

Layne looked back, baffled. Why did everything change each time they encountered it? Nothing seemed predictable in this place. It was like wandering through a maze of dunes that kept reshaping when she turned her head.

On the other side of the hills, the big white tracking dishes of the satellite station came suddenly into view, standing hard and bright against the sun.

Thomas said, "Too bad your friend Markam isn't with us. If he were here, we might get another tour of the facilities."

She knew he was trying to ease the mood between them. "One time was enough for me. I nearly froze in that building."

He glanced at her sideways, and she could see the knowing look on his face.

Turning to feel the wind whipping through her hair, she watched the desert spread out before them, desolate and austere. Its monotony was beginning to comfort her. Even the scrub bushes clinging to the sand here and there seemed courageous, as if they meant to hold on until they dried into brittle sticks.

In the distance, dunes came into sight and with them, the memory of that sudden, beautiful time out here with David. She willed herself to push it away.

"Is there really something to see out here, Thomas? You didn't make that up, did you?" she said.

"I do. Be patient. After that, we'll look for fossils. This area was once an inland sea."

Layne sighed. He'd fabricated this trip to keep her away from the city and out of trouble. She might as well humor him.

"By 'once,' you mean thousands of years ago? Wouldn't shells and things be buried under miles of sand by now?"

"You never know," he said. "Layers alternately cover and uncover. Ricky found some marine fossils in this area, so we'll see. By the way, has your friend Saeed heard any more from the revolutionaries?"

Thomas could be sarcastic when he felt like it. "You still think he and David are being paranoid?"

"I've been discussing it with Ricky. What it comes down to, in our opinion, is misinterpretation. Bin Yousef intercepted some messages he and Markam projected into an incipient uprising. And, of course, you were eager to believe it. No, I don't think there's any revolution underway."

"You're wrong about the messages, Thomas! You know they're real. We were there. You heard David read the one Saeed picked up."

"Where's your objectivity, Layne? Those transmissions could have dozens of explanations. I've been in countries on the brink of an uprising. They have a definite atmosphere."

He shook his head. "No, it just doesn't feel right. You've been downtown. Did you sense any tension there? Insurgencies don't happen in a vacuum. In cities where unrest is building up to a riot, you can feel the tension in the air. Streets are deserted or

215

thronged with people milling around. Anticipation and fear are palpable."

She had to admit she hadn't seen anything like that in Riyadh. Except for the shot fired at her, which was likely more personal than random.

"Markam's suspicions of the Bedouin we met the first day aren't very convincing either," he went on. "I talked to the headman while we were there. In fact, I asked him if he knew of any troubles stirring among the tribes. Do you know what he said?"

"That he'd never heard of such a thing? And he was insulted that you suggested it?"

"He said, 'There is always talk. Men do not stay contented like women or goats. There is always talk.'"

"Like women? Or goats? What does that prove? Aside from the fact that he's a chauvinist pig? He's probably the head of a gang of terrorists himself. The Land Rover was hidden behind his tent."

"Peace. I know how you feel. But there must be an explanation for these things." He pointed into the distance. "I think we've come far enough. If you look carefully at that hill over there, you can see the trail worn by camels crossing it. I've seen them in the south. They're traditional routes, followed for hundreds of years. The Bedouins' skill at finding direction still amazes me."

He turned off the highway, and went over a bump that threw them up, their heads nearly hitting the roof.

"This is only marginally more comfortable than that jeep was the first day," she said.

Thomas didn't answer, and they bounced over rutted sand, heading toward a semicircle of yellowish limestone hills. Finding shade of a sort under a parched, twisted tree, he stopped, wiped dust from his glasses, and jumped out.

"We drove this far to look at old hills?" Layne said.

"Just wait. All along this part of the desert are ancient limestone caves called *dahls*. I've been wanting to see one for years."

"Caves? In the desert? This is a joke, right?"

"Come on. You'll see. The Bedouin have known about these underground lakes as long as they've herded in this area."

The track curved down a steep slope between mounds of boulders.

"It's like a giant landslide," Layne said.

"All that was left after this hill collapsed and exposed the cave."

At the bottom of the hollow was a crescent-shaped opening in the base of the hill.

It took some effort to climb over and around the massive boulders, but finally they stood inside the entrance.

"Here we are in a dahl," Thomas said, and his voice echoed down a shaft of rocks into the darkness.

"You're not really going down in there, are you?" Layne said. "We don't have ropes or anything. We'll never get down that passage without falling."

Thomas looked disappointed. "I should have brought some gear. This is a bit rougher than I expected. Too bad. I wanted you to see the underground pool at the bottom. Ricky says the water's so clear, it's like green glass."

He stepped closer to the shaft. "I'm going down a little way. Maybe we can make it."

"No. It's not worth that much effort," she said. "Please don't go far."

Climbing back over the boulders, she sat on one to drink from her water jug. She could see Thomas gradually going down and hear the rocks he dislodged, rattling into blackness.

The hills above the cave, with their crevices shadowed by morning light, looked very old. They might once have been imposing monoliths, ridged and pointed like naked stone spearheads. But the desert has no sharp lines. Time had rounded them into crumbled, disorderly mounds.

What if she and Thomas were obliterated here, too?

Finally, she saw the top of his head as he trudged up the steep slope of the cave.

After a drink of water, he said, "Let's find fossils," and went down to the flat ground.

He began walking around, peering at the crusty sand littered with small stones. Every now and then, he turned over a stone with his toe, as if he expected to find a prize under it.

Layne had started down when she heard him shout, "Ha! Here's one."

Irritated but curious, she went to see what he'd found. Ten feet from him, she froze, registering all at once the stillness around them, the glint in Thomas's eyes, and the yellowish-green scorpion that sidled away from a rock near his foot.

She stared at the thing, horror prickling her arms and legs as it always did when insects or snakes roused the sensation from deep in her memory of tiny, wriggling bodies crawling all over her.

Of the time her mother was at home for the Christmas vacation and they rented a cabin in the woods. Of waking that night with earwigs swarming over her, dozens of them, in her bed, in her hair.

The scorpion lifted its arcing tail and scuttled under a cluster of stones. Again, she heard David's words, *The little green ones are the most dangerous.*

Shivering, she glared at her brother.

"Come on. They won't hurt you," he said. "Just don't get near the tails."

"So, leave them alone! I thought we were looking for fossils."

Ignoring her, he squatted down and lifted another rock gingerly.

Layne left him to it. This childish side of her brother asserted itself so seldom that she'd almost forgotten how infuriating he could be.

She wandered in a circle, searching the ground, and after a few minutes, found a flat piece of rock with the outline of a worm-like creature embedded in its surface.

Thomas gave her a wave when she held it up. He came over and showed her a handful of snail and shell fossils he'd found. Then, he sauntered toward the hills, turning over rocks again.

"I wish you'd stop that. This isn't fun if you behave like a brat."

For an answer, he held up a clamshell fossil as large as his hand.

"It's beautiful. Can we keep it?" Layne said.

He shrugged and stowed it in the pouch he had strapped to his belt. "Let's work our way around to the other side of this hill," he said.

Layne knew he'd be kicking every rock he saw to scare scorpions out of hiding.

"Go by yourself," she said. Her nerves were still raw from the shock of seeing the first one and the tormenting memories it dredged up. After some halfhearted searching, she went back to the truck for another jug of water.

Just opening the bottle, she heard Thomas scream.

The single, horrible sound was followed by an agonized effort to yell her name. Clutching the water bottle, she ran without seeing the ground.

He was on his knees, hunched over in obvious agony. Grasping the loose material of her pant leg, he raised his stricken face. "I never saw it," he gasped.

"Why didn't you listen to me, Thomas?"

She took his arm and pulling with all her strength, got him to his feet, sweat from his face dripping onto hers.

"Damn, it hurts. It's like—" His mouth contorted in pain.

They staggered together to the truck. She got him into the backseat and poured a little water into his mouth. Her mind worked frantically. Should she slice the skin and suck out the venom? Another look at his hand, bloated like a blown-up rubber glove, quelled the idea.

"Do we have any first aid stuff?" she said.

He didn't answer. Rummaging through the gear in the back, she heard his hoarse breathing stop. "No!" she screamed. Grabbing his uninjured hand, she felt for a pulse. It was there, throbbing. But he was unconscious.

She fastened the seatbelt around him and got behind the wheel. Law or no law, she had to drive somewhere to get help. Cursing the stick shift, she jerked the lever, grinding metal until she got it into gear, and careened toward the highway, bucking over potholes and throwing up a storm of dust.

Lurching onto the highway, she accelerated. A tingle of fear rose above her anxiety for Thomas. Those soldiers at the checkpoint would stop her. What if they dragged her out and arrested her like David said might happen? Even if they did, surely they would take Thomas to a hospital, too.

Swerving around a curve, she caught sight of the satellite station in the distance and felt a spurt of hope. The technicians would help her. They must have emergency medical equipment. And they had a phone.

At the gate, she blew the horn and jumped out. Opening the back door, she listened to Thomas's shallow, rapid breath. He was still unconscious, his face and chest coated with sweat. "It's going to be okay," she said, stroking his forehead.

Hearing the clang of metal, she looked up and a sob of relief caught in her throat. Two men were opening the gate, and one of them was Saeed. He hurried toward her.

"Layne! What's going on? Why are you driving this truck? Do you not know you'll be arrested for this?" His dark glasses didn't hide his shock and alarm.

"Thomas has been bitten—stung. By a scorpion. He's unconscious. Please help him," she said.

Saeed leaned over Thomas and felt his pulse. Raising up, he shouted to the other man. "Do you have an antivenin kit?"

"We've got one. We never had to use it."

"Let's take him inside."

"No! I think it's too serious. We need to get him to a hospital," Layne pleaded.

Saeed dropped Thomas's swollen hand and turned back to the technician. "Help me transfer him. Then, call the hospital and tell them we're coming."

They picked Thomas up, carried him to the big SUV parked inside the fence, and laid him on the seat. Layne got in beside him.

Saeed handed her a blanket "Wrap him up. I'll get you there as quickly as I can."

She had no words that were adequate.

He swung into the driver's seat and roared toward the city while she clung to her brother, willing him to stay alive.

An Australian nurse met them at the entrance of the hospital, and Saeed negotiated Thomas's admittance with terse efficiency.

Thomas was wheeled away, still barely conscious, and Layne stood in the empty waiting room, staring at the green, unadorned walls, the rows of steel and vinyl chairs. Ivy, running limp and scraggly from ceramic pots in the corners, did nothing to mitigate the room's indifference to the human pain that came and went every day. But it was clean and modern, and that reassured her a little.

She and Saeed had barely spoken on the way to the hospital, his attention focused on the tense driving and hers on her brother's shallow breathing. Now, there seemed to be even less need to talk. She'd thanked him so many times the words sounded meaningless.

He looked at her with concern. "Shall I get you some water, Layne? Or tea? You are very pale."

"Yes—No. Thank you. I can't drink anything right now. I'm just so worried."

"The doctor said Thomas isn't in grave danger."

"He also said he wasn't sure."

He touched her arm gently. "It's a dreadful time for you."

"Please forgive my rudeness, Saeed. I'll always be grateful to you for saving my brother's life."

They both turned when the doctor, a Pakistani with tired eyes and gray-streaked hair, came through the door.

"Miss Darius," he said, glancing at her and then fixing his gaze on a pot of ivy in the corner. "Your brother will be settled in his room in a few minutes. He is conscious. You may look in on him, but he will need to sleep. Rest will be important for a few days."

He left, and Saeed said, "I shall go, Layne. You have my number. Call anytime you're ready. My driver will come to take you where you wish to go."

He hesitated and then said with a teasing smile, "Don't worry. I'll let David know what's happened."

Thomas looked small and ill in the hospital bed. His dark hair was damp and plastered back from the receding hairline he always tried to keep covered. He peered nearsightedly at her, and she went to the bed and bent to kiss his cheek.

"Layne, you're here." His voice was a weak imitation of his usual heartiness. "Don't say I'm a fool. That's all too apparent.

The last word was a whisper, and she leaned closer to hear. "I'm not calling you any names. Not for a long time, anyway. I'm just glad you're alive."

His lips moved in an effort to smile. "This is very unlike me . . . to be so irresponsible. I can't imagine why."

"It was an accident, Thomas. You didn't have any business taunting scorpions, though."

"I've let everyone down. Delayed our start even further," he said miserably.

"It probably won't make much difference. And we still have to be sure Mustafa's recovered before we travel."

His eyelids flickered. "They might keep me here for a while. They're consulting with a doctor on the west coast, a tropical medicine specialist."

"Tropical medicine? For a scorpion sting?"

"No, the malaria. The sting must have triggered it again. It recurred after I fractured my arm in that accident in Yemen. Five years ago. Trauma, you know." His voice trailed off, and he drifted into a doze, looking pathetic.

She pulled a chair close to the bed and sat holding his moist, limp hand, needing to be connected with him.

This helpless feeling was new to her. As long as she could remember, she'd been responsible only for herself. Now, she was sitting here with control over nothing. Relying on every man she met.

Thomas continued to sleep, and she sat with him for an hour or so, until hunger and the need to wash off sand and sweat couldn't be ignored. The doctor came in again to check on him and insisted there was no reason for her to stay.

She allowed herself to be ushered out of the room, planning to come back as soon as she'd cleaned up and gotten something to eat.

When she stepped into the waiting room, tears stung her eyes. There, reading a magazine, his long legs stretched out in front of his chair, was David Markam.

Chapter 20

Before he'd taken two steps toward her, she was in his arms. She was trembling, and he held her as long as he dared.

"How is your brother?" he said, letting her go.

"The doctor says it's malaria. Thomas has had it off and on for years. The scorpion sting triggered it again."

"Is he going to be all right?"

"I think so, but I want to be here. I just need to go to Al-Amir's to change clothes and get something to eat. I'd better let Ricky know, too. Then I'll come back."

David opened the door of his car for her.

"Saeed offered a room at his house," he said.

"I can't impose any longer. I've already taken up too much of his time."

He got into the driver's seat and waited.

"Could you drop me off at Al-Amir's house? I'll get Mustafa to drive me back to the hospital later," she said.

"Leave you there? No. I'd rather wait while you

get what you need. We'll go to Saeed's house for dinner."

"I have to face Al-Amir, David. Explain what happened to Thomas. We're his guests."

He understood how uncertain and afraid she must be, and he didn't argue.

Smells of hot concrete and dust blew in the open windows as they drove out of the parking area, and it wasn't until they reached streets with trees that the air softened.

The twilight prayer call began from a nearby mosque, and its haunting chant filled David with peace. Glancing at Layne, he saw her relax as well.

He wished, as he had before, that he could take her to his apartment. Each day that passed, he wanted that more. Though it would entangle them in a situation he had no idea how to handle. And letting her go afterward would be torment.

"I'm grateful you came to help me, David," she said.

He lifted her hand to his lips. "Nowhere I'd rather be. Besides, somebody has to keep watch over you. I never knew one woman could get into so much trouble."

"This wasn't my fault. I'm not the one who played with scorpions and nearly got myself killed."

"No, your scorpions use bullets and stones. But you do keep turning over rocks that ought to be left alone."

"I guess you're right," she said sadly. "Every time I

SEE THE DESERT AND DIE

think I'm close to finding out about my mother I run into a wall. One I can't even see, much less get over.

"The important thing now is for Thomas to be okay. If something else goes wrong, we might lose our chance to do the study."

David considered not telling her what *could* go wrong. Maybe sooner than he expected. But he knew she'd resent his effort to shield her from it.

"Saeed intercepted another message last night," he said. "He thinks they've got a start date. Possibly before the end of the week."

For a moment, she didn't move. Then she looked at him with disbelief. "A coup? A rebellion? It's *real*? What should we do?"

"I don't know what to tell you, Layne. We're doing all we can to find out who these people are and what they're planning."

"Was the message in code like before?"

"No. Plain Arabic. No silly stuff this time. It confirmed our assumption that they're likely to move fast."

Layne frowned. "You're awfully calm about this."

"There's not a lot we know yet. I finally got somebody in the Ministry to talk to me. We have the impression the key people are aware of the conspiracy. But nobody's saying much, as usual."

"Does that mean it won't actually happen?"

"No. I think there will be an attempt. The integrity of the government depends on its ability to invalidate any threat to its authority, so things are usually denied until after they happen."

Wishing he could ease the alarm he saw in her face, he said, "I'm reasonably sure the security people can handle it. But things might get rough around here for a while."

She looked away.

"This is definitely a good time to stop digging into the past," he said. "Security will be on high alert and even more suspicious of foreigners."

"Why foreigners? We aren't threatening the government."

He waited, deciding what he could tell her.

Finally, he said, "Foreign nationals are always under suspicion. That's true in any country. Especially if there's a perceived threat and nobody's sure where it's coming from.

"A force, possibly more than one, is building up to a crisis here. We think they're activists agitating for social reform, but we don't know for sure what's driving them because we don't know where the power base is. It's hard to judge the tenor of things right after Ramadan ends.

"Usually, it settles down in a few days, but my boss in Jeddah tells me this year feels different. He thinks something's brewing. By the way, he's flying here tomorrow. That, as you might imagine, is significant too."

She sighed. "It's hard to tell the difference between what matters here and what doesn't."

"You're still in touch with Al-Amir's niece? Do you think the activists she's involved with could be planning something?"

"I don't think so, but her uncle and Hassan both warned me not to see her again. So I suppose I'll have to comply if I don't want to be deported. It makes me feel bad that I can't help her now. When I get home, I'm going to do everything I can to support her struggle for the rights of women in this country!"

Hearing the passion in her voice, David had no doubt she would do that. She'd probably always be an advocate for beleaguered causes, always throw herself wholeheartedly into whatever she believed was right. He was also certain he wanted to be there when she did.

As they approached Al-Amir's house, the headlights cut into the shadows along the stone wall. Nothing seemed unusual until he rounded the corner. The front gates stood open, and a line of parked cars stretched around the circular drive. A black sedan was parked in front of the steps.

Layne clutched his arm. "Wait. Don't drive through the gate. Something's happening."

"Looks like they're having a party.

"Let's go around to the back," she insisted. "There's a little door in the wall. If I can get in there, I can make it up to my room without any of those people seeing me."

Exasperated, David wheeled the car around and drove slowly along the wall until she told him to stop under the shadows of the trees.

She started to get out, but he said, "Tell me what's going on, Layne. What are you really afraid of?"

"Hassan's there. I don't feel like dealing with him tonight."

"Why not?"

"I think he came to arrest me. He's been following me. He was waiting for me outside of Rana's party last night."

"Why would Hassan be here to arrest you? Don't tell me you've done another crazy thing."

"How do I know?"

"Damn, I wish I could put you on a plane and send you out of this mess."

"I thought about going, David. But I won't leave Thomas! Why should I? I haven't broken any laws. Hassan's just bullying me."

"Whatever Hassan's up to, he's not acting on his own. He has to be following Al-Amir's direction, if not his orders. I don't think they'll arrest you unless you do something that forces them to."

She pressed her hands over her face.

"I expect they'll put a tighter rein on you when Al-Amir hears your brother's been injured," he said. "You might not be permitted to leave the compound. I know they won't let me in to see you."

Before she could answer, David saw a figure emerge from the darkness.

"You go from here," the voice hissed outside Layne's open window.

"Mustafa! What're you doing?" she said.

"Police in house. I wait you, tell you no go inside."

"I have to get my clothes."

He raised his arm, displaying a bulging nylon shopping bag. "Here cloths. I tell woman you need. She say 'no.' I say must do." He pushed the bag in through the window.

"You told Puja to pack my clothes? Why?" Layne said, reaching to open the door.

"You go now!" Mustafa insisted.

"We're leaving," David said, starting the engine.

"Wait a minute, please! I need to think," Layne said.

"You can think somewhere else." He wheeled onto the roadway and accelerated, leaving Mustafa standing by the road, a faint paleness in the deep shadow.

Layne sat clutching the bag for several blocks. He knew she was shocked and terrified, but he didn't know what to say to help her.

Finally, she let the bag slide to the floor.

"God knows what Puja packed for me," she said. "I'll bet she didn't put my traveler's checks in there."

"They won't do you any good in prison," David said. "I'll give you money, and Saeed's housekeeper will have anything else you need."

"Saeed? We're going there?"

"I think it's best. I could take you to the consulate, but as I said before, that creates more complications than solutions. My apartment's not safe. If the police really are after you, they'll check there. Saeed has a pretty well-fortified compound."

He was trying to reassure her, and himself, too. It still worried him that Hassan was able to get into Saeed's compound the other night. And that Saeed didn't seem to be bothered by it.

Most of all, David feared that he'd misjudged Al-Amir. If he was willing to let the police arrest Layne, maybe his whole take on the old lion had been wrong. In that case, he needed to rethink it, and fast!

Saeed greeted them as if he'd been waiting all day to entertain someone. They told him what happened at Al-Amir's house, and he laughed.

"I expect Mustafa got hold of the wrong end of the stick," he said. "But let's not worry about that tonight. Whatever the problem, it's brought you two to me. I'm delighted to have you as my guests for as long as you wish."

He paused and his expression changed. "Forgive me, Layne. I know this has been a terrible day for you. First, the anxiety for your brother, and now this business."

"I should go back to the hospital and stay with him," Layne said.

"Perhaps that's not a wise thing to do tonight. I've been in touch with the doctor myself. He assured me Thomas is not in danger and will have the best of care. You can call the hospital and talk to the nurse now if you wish. When you're ready, the room you used before is waiting for you upstairs."

Surprisingly, she agreed.

When she left with the Yemeni housekeeper, Saeed said, "She'll have to stay here tonight, David."

"I appreciate your saying that, Saeed. I can't think of any better place to take her."

Saeed looked at him with a slight grin. "Perhaps you'll bend your own rules and be my guest as well. The bedroom across from hers is prepared."

David knew what he was suggesting, but he didn't dare let himself think about being alone with Layne right now.

"If the police do show up, I want to be here," he said.

When Layne came back, her skin glowing, her hair brushed into soft waves, he found it hard to think about anything other than being with her.

Saeed had dinner served on the terrace. They ate slowly, talking about neutral things, the dancing fountain soothing raw nerves.

Afterward, while they were drinking coffee and cognac, Layne leaned back and crossed her arms.

"Why do you think Mr. Hassan is hounding me, Saeed? It started the first time I went out, but he was even waiting for me after the party at Rana's house."

He seemed surprised by the question. "What did he say to you?"

"He warned me not to visit Sahar again."

"Why? She is a respectable person, is she not?"

Layne shook her head, looking frustrated. "She doesn't hide the fact that she's actively advocating for women's rights. I think she's doing admirable work. I wanted to see her school and help in some way with her cause. Now, I don't know what to do. Hassan really scared me last night. And now that he's at Mr. Al-Amir's house—"

"I will find out the whole story first thing tomorrow," Saeed said.

As if she hadn't heard him, she went on. "I don't understand why he's treating me like a criminal. All I've done is ask questions about my mother's last days here. After eight years, who'd be threatened by that? I've never seen Mustafa so upset. Hassan must have come to Al-Amir's house to arrest me. But why were all the other cars there?"

"It may not be as dire as Mustafa thinks," David said. "Maybe he misunderstood. At least, he was trying to help you."

Layne was silent for a while. Finally, she said, "I have to go to sleep. It's all closing in on me, and I can hardly think."

"You must rest," Saeed said. "I promise, tomorrow we will see a clearer path."

David took Layne's hand when they left the terrace. He shook his head at the satisfied matchmaker smile he got from Saeed.

In the doorway of Layne's bedroom, he said, "I hope you can get some rest. You look about ready to fall down."

"I don't think sleep will be a problem," she said. "Are you going to stay here tonight?"

"Yes, Saeed gave me the bedroom across the hall. I'll be close by," he said.

Gathering her in his arms, he intended to kiss her gently, but she pressed against him, ready to give herself absolutely.

He looked at her face, her eyes half-closed, her lips parted. His need for her was acute, yet she was so worn out, so vulnerable. Dragging in a painful breath, he let her go.

"I'd better talk to Saeed about plans for tomorrow," he said.

For a moment, she stared at him, her eyes large and troubled. Then, she nodded and turned away.

When he went back downstairs, Saeed was still sitting on the terrace with a glass of cognac, watching his fountain sway to a Mozart melody. He looked up in surprise.

"What are you doing here, my good friend? I imagined you'd be comforting the beautiful lady by now."

David stopped at the drinks cart, splashed scotch into a glass, and sat down wearily across the table from him. "We don't always get what we want," he said.

"Ah, you Americans with your masterful restraint."

"She's exhausted, emotionally and physically."

Sipping his drink, Saeed said, "And you are worried about the trouble gathering around her, are you not?"

"Yes, I am. I don't know where the danger is or why it's aimed at her, but I know it's there. Twice she's been attacked."

"Twice? Something else has happened? Today?"

"The day she and her brother got here. She went off on her own while she was downtown with Mustafa, and somebody took a shot at her."

Saeed looked shocked. "This is much more serious, David." He was silent, his brow wrinkled in thought.

"You must insist that she give up this search of hers," he said finally. "She has been quite outspoken about it. Who knows what ears she has reached?"

"She doesn't take suggestions well, you know," David said. "Now that she's aligned herself with Sahar's cause, she may be in danger from more than one source."

"Tell me, is it revenge she's seeking for her mother's death?" Saeed said.

"She doesn't seem to be. Knowing what happened is all she wants. But who can say what she'll do if she finds out?"

"Yes, David, you people do breed difficult women," Saeed said, shaking his head.

David got up and poured himself a glass of water. He thought again about the line of cars in front of Al-Amir's house.

"I'm beginning to believe we need to get her out of the country," he said.

"If she has done something to bring herself into conflict with the police, it may be too late for that."

Hearing his own fears spoken aloud, David said, "She just doesn't understand what she's up against here. Even if she did, she's not likely to let it stop her."

"I see how worried you are. This woman is different from the other Americans you've protected, is she not?" Saeed said.

"She's different, yes." He swallowed the water and put the glass down.

"I think she's really in danger. If I had my way, I'd put her on a plane tomorrow. Though she'd probably refuse to go. She's so invested in this search for her mother. It's more important than anything else in her life. Except her brother. She won't leave him. That might be a moot question anyway. If he can't give her written permission, she won't be able to board a plane."

"You've talked to Al-Amir about this?"

"I tried to. Took the wrong tack with him, but Hassan's been more communicative. I'm going to see him in the morning. Maybe I can persuade him to tell me what was going on at Al-Amir's place tonight."

"Hmm," Saeed said. He leaned back. "If, by chance, it should be advisable for Layne Darius to leave the country quickly, you know I can help."

David looked at him sharply. "You mean you'd fly her out in your plane? That would be a hell of a risk for you."

Saeed shrugged. "What is life if not an adventure?"

Chapter 21

Layne lay in the darkness listening. Through a haze of dreams, she had heard the roar of engines, loud enough to penetrate the tall casement windows.

Turning in her cocoon of linen sheets, she heard it again. The unmistakable sound of cars starting. One after another, they gunned to life, five of them.

Panic held her rigid, waiting for the sound of footsteps, of police banging on the door. Hassan, with his hawk's glare, leading the pack.

He must not find her naked like this. Untangling herself, she groped for the robe on the foot of the bed and moved across to a window. Only a soft glow shone from the garden lights, and beyond them, darkness.

As she scanned the shadows outside, her fear rose to confusion. Where were David and Saeed? Why hadn't she heard any voices? Surely by now Saeed would be shouting orders or protests. And David would have come to see if she was safe.

She went back to the nightstand, switched on the light, and looked at her watch. It was three thirty. The sounds were cars starting and going away, not arriving. Relief made her mad at rich men in general, with nothing better to do than party all night. She sat on the bed to think.

Suppose this was more important than a late-night party? What if these people were leaving a meeting, a planning session for some sort of conspiracy? A secret group working for its own goals, good or bad?

Terror began to creep over her, as if she were mouse-sized and seeing for the first time how huge and menacing the world around her had grown.

She could think of nothing to calm her fear but to go downstairs and see what was happening.

The hallway, in this house of marble, was so quiet she could hear the whispering gushes of her bare feet on the thick carpet.

Passing David's room she paused, craving the comfort he might give her. She wanted so badly to trust him, to believe he loved her and would go on loving her.

But he left so abruptly tonight. She must have misinterpreted his kindness, misunderstood what he felt, like she had so many things here.

Her thoughts bitter, she kept walking. How could she have been so wrong? Falling in love with him, thinking he cared about her. None of it mattered anyway. In a few days, she'd be gone. Carrying a little bundle of "if onlys" away from this desert.

Dim wall sconces lit the way to the staircase that led down to the central part of the house. Passing the corridor to Saeed's personal quarters, she stopped and listened, then went on. An army of people could be asleep behind these doors. Though it wasn't likely. Saeed seemed to live alone in this splendor when he didn't have guests.

Momentarily, she pitied him. He'd lost one wife and divorced another. And there were no children. In his culture, the lack of children was a tragedy of epic size. No wonder he spent his life working, traveling, and giving parties. It must help him forget that the people who filled his house were no more than guests or servants. Even the glory of his family name was only collections in a museum.

The curving staircase led down to the foyer, where the glass wall gave a view of the deserted terrace. Tiny lights cast a cold glitter onto the still surface of the fountain pool.

Crossing the foyer, she went along the passage to the majlis and saw a shaft of light coming from an open door at the far end. She hurried across the vastness and peered around the doorjamb into a smaller room.

Through a haze of cigarette smoke, she saw metal weapons glinting on the walls. This was an extension of the treasure room, a smaller version of the majlis. It was furnished with couches grouped around a gigantic coffee table, littered with glasses, cups, and full ashtrays.

She was right. A meeting was held here tonight. And abruptly disbanded. It must have excluded servants, who would have cleaned up the mess and turned out the lights.

Easing into the room, she caught the stench of a smoldering cigarette filter in one of the ashtrays. Judging by the debris, there might have been a dozen or more men here, meeting secretly in the night.

A sandaled footstep sounded somewhere nearby. She waited, feeling cornered and defenseless. Only silence.

Her impulse was to run back through the hall and up the stairs to her room. But in the foyer, instead of going up the stairs, she pushed open the heavy glass doors to the terrace. The sky was just beginning to lighten. She stood for a moment, breathing in the fragrance of a night-blooming vine.

What was going on in this house? Were those men meeting to plan an uprising, a rebellion? How could it be? Wasn't Saeed doing all he could to stop such a thing from happening? These men might be a counterforce, committed to helping him. And David might be one of them.

Alarm tightened in her chest. If David were part of something like that, everything she believed about him was a lie. Had she really been such a fool? Without another thought, she ran up the stairs.

Stopping outside his door, she turned the cold brass knob and pushed the door open. She heard him move in the darkness.

He switched on the bedside light. "Layne! What's wrong?"

His hair tousled from sleep, he looked young and wary as he sat up. He was wearing only pajama pants, and she could see the long hard muscles she had imagined were there.

She sat in a chair beside the bed, hugging herself defensively. "David, I need to hear the truth from you."

Leaning back against the headboard, he said, "Which particular truth? What's happened?"

His eyes didn't leave her face as she told him about the cars and the remains of the meeting downstairs.

When she finished, he said, "So, you think Saeed is conspiring either for or against some insurgents. Is this the truth you're talking about? And I'm one of them, too?"

"How do I know? I want to believe every word you've told me."

"Why shouldn't you? I never said anything that wasn't true."

"Doesn't it bother you that there was a secret meeting here tonight?"

He didn't answer, and she began to be more afraid. He wasn't denying that he was at that meeting. Maybe he'd never lied to her, but had he thought it necessary *not* to tell her everything, just like her brother did?

"A late-night meeting puzzles me, yes," he said finally. "But in this house, it doesn't alarm me. Layne, my job—once in a while, my life—depends on judging who I can trust. I do trust Saeed."

He held her gaze, but his eyes were worried.

"He's helped me ever since I came here," he said. "My work would be infinitely harder without his influence. And he's a friend."

Layne said nothing. It would take time to think, to find a way to be sure what was real. She got up to go.

He swung out of the bed and stood there waiting, as if her trust mattered a great deal to him.

So close, she could feel the heat of his body. She wanted him desperately. Still, she was afraid.

Grieving for her mother all these years, she'd grown a scar in her heart, a protective barrier. No feeling had touched that place for eight years.

How had David Markam broken it open, roused love so deep that it made her vulnerable again, nearly willing to bear the pain that would come if she lost him?

Torn between wonder and the fears that had followed her into the room, she turned away.

"Stay with me, Layne," he said softly.

"Now? For a couple of hours?" she demanded, swinging around.

"Yes, now. And for the rest of our lives."

She looked up at him. A conviction stronger than any she'd ever known settled over her. Even if they never met again, and these few hours were the only ones they had, she wanted David Markam with her whole heart.

Loosening the sash of the robe, she let it fall and stepped into his arms.

Chapter 22

Full daylight streamed through the windows by the time Layne went back to her room to shower. Strange, new feelings surged in her, giddiness, then an aching longing she did not know how to bear.

Apprehensive as she went downstairs, she found David and Saeed sitting at the table on the terrace. She tried to look at ease, but the effort made her even more self-conscious.

David smiled. "Good morning," he said gently and brushed her hand as she passed him. He looked relaxed and happy, as if he'd run a marathon and was worried about nothing.

She sat down next to him, wondering what he had told Saeed.

If Saeed knew they were together, he made no sign. He was dressed in khaki trousers and shirt today, as he was the first time they met. His face was haggard, and he was more subdued than usual as he poured cups of strong coffee for them.

"Good news of your brother, Layne," he said. "I telephoned the hospital this morning. He's feeling well enough to be released. I was told Mr. Al-Amir's car will fetch him. It's a relief. I was truly worried about him yesterday."

"So was I. Thank you for doing that, Saeed. Did my brother seem upset that I was here?"

"He is surely worried about you and wishes to reassure you that Mustafa was mistaken about danger at the Al-Amir house."

Layne nodded and sipped her coffee, wondering whether she should mention the visitors last night.

Before she made up her mind, David said, "What the hell was going on here last night, Saeed? Have you started hosting an after-hours club?"

Saeed looked blank. "How do you mean? Something disturbed you?"

"The sound of car engines woke me about three thirty this morning," Layne said. "I was afraid the police might be here."

"Ah, that! Nothing so official." He looked embarrassed. "A few of my friends did arrive rather noisily last night, wanting to carry on their party. It was a job to get them to go home. I'm sorry they woke you.

"My friends are no matter," he went on, "but something else I must tell you, Layne. I had two calls very early this morning. One from Asad Al-Amir and the other from his son Ricky.

"They were alarmed when you and Thomas did not return from the desert. They somehow knew that your brother is in the hospital, but Asad Al-Amir was quite anxious about you."

"Oh, no! I should have called them last night," Layne said. "I meant to do it. I need to apologize."

She glanced at him, aware that he had something else to tell her. "You said he was anxious about me. How anxious? Do you mean angry? Should I be worried?" Layne said.

Saeed looked at her with compassion in his eyes. "Whatever Al-Amir has in mind, it cannot be to harm you. There was distress in his voice."

David put his hand over hers and said, "I don't see any reason to be worried. You haven't broken any laws. I know Mustafa made it sound like Hassan was there to arrest you, but Hassan obviously knows where you are. If he meant to do that, he'd be here now."

Saeed said, "No one comes through my gates without my permission. Not even Hassan, unless I allow him. You are safe here."

"I didn't intend to bring either of you into my mess. I shouldn't have come here," Layne said.

"David, can I ask for asylum at the consulate if something happens?"

Saeed waved aside her fear. "Truly, it is no matter."

"Asylum's granted only in the U.S.," David said. "Refuge might be possible. But the process isn't automatic. It always has political ramifications."

He squeezed her hand. "Look, I have to get to my

office. I'm late for a meeting and my boss is here from Jeddah. Saeed is probably right, but why don't you come with me? At least if you're inside the consulate, you might feel safer. And I can find out what's really going on."

She shook her head. "No, I'd better stay here. I just need to rest until I can figure out what to do. I should call Sahar today, too. She invited me to see her school, and I said I'd let her know yesterday. Now I have to tell her I don't dare see her at all. Damn this country!

"I'm sorry, Saeed. It's just so frustrating. Not being able to drive is like lifelong house arrest."

"My dear lady, you never offend me," Saeed said. "You're welcome to stay. Go for a swim, if you wish. Or, I have a marvelous library. All sorts of books in many languages."

Glancing at David, he said, "Don't worry, Layne will not even have to talk to me after you leave. I'm on my way to the satellite station this morning, so she'll be mistress of the whole house!"

He gulped his coffee and rose. "If you wish to see Sahar, ask her to come here. It will be better than going to her apartment. I'll leave word with my guards so she'll be allowed to come in."

"You know where Sahar lives?" Layne said.

After a pause, he said, "I know her, though we must remain strangers here. In Paris we have many friends in common. She's a good woman who wages a valiant battle against impossible odds." He shook his head.

On his way out, he turned back. "Next to the telephone just inside the foyer there is a number where you can reach the phone in my truck. Any problem comes, Layne, you must ring me."

When he was gone, David stood up and pulled her into his arms. He kissed her, and she clung to him, loving him more than she ever imagined possible. If he loved her the same way, wouldn't this be enough for a whole life?

He let her go and looked at her intently. "It hurts to leave you for even a minute. I'll be back as soon as I possibly can. Then I'll go with you to talk to Al-Amir."

"What if that's not the right thing to do? I don't know who to trust. If I'm arrested, Thomas will be in danger, too."

"He should be all right at Al-Amir's place. You know how seriously people in this culture take their responsibility for a guest under their protection."

"I could just leave," she said. "I thought about it. I've got my passport."

He held her gaze as if trying to read her intention. "You can't board a plane unless Thomas gives you written permission."

Throwing up her hands, she said, "I know. It's ridiculous!"

"Where would you go? Most countries won't let you in without a visa. If you leave here, I doubt you'll be allowed to come back."

"Maybe I should just go home," she said. But I

don't even have a job."

"If you're willing to do that, it might be the best choice. At least you'd be safe."

Safe. There was that word again. In her anxious state of mind what he said sounded like a negation of her work, her dreams, all that mattered to her.

"That's not what I want, David. I'm scared right now, but I'll never settle for a life that's just safe."

His lips compressed into a thin line. He glared at the fountain, trickling serenely into the pool. "You're certainly Katherine Darius's daughter."

Anger didn't come. Instead, she felt a kind of sad chagrin, knowing how right he was. She'd heard her mother say her home and children were her "safe haven." Then restlessness always returned, and she left behind a house that was desolate and still.

The same drive was in her. But David was not a man who would wait at home patiently like her father did.

"Things could change," she said.

"Things maybe. I'm not so sure about people." He looked at his watch. "I've got to go, Layne."

She was suddenly afraid again. "David, if something happens to me, will you be sure Thomas is okay? I know you don't have any obligation to us."

"I'll take care of him," he said brusquely. "And I'm doing my damnedest to keep anything from happening to you. Just stay here, Layne. I'll be back in a few hours."

She watched David's car drive through the gates and then went upstairs to the bedroom, suddenly exhausted. Dozing for what seemed like five minutes, she heard a knock on the door. The housekeeper told her she had a call. Reluctantly, she went downstairs.

Sahar's voice came rushing through the phone. "Layne, you are there. Such a relief! I've been trying to reach you. Please, please will you help me?"

"Sahar, what's wrong?" Layne said.

"Will you come to my apartment? Please, Layne, it is most important. I must see you at once."

"I'm afraid I won't be able to visit your school today. I've been warned not to see you at all."

Sahar was silent. Then she said, "There is no time for visiting the school. I must talk with you this morning."

Layne hesitated, feeling as if she were being pulled apart. She wanted passionately to help Sahar. But she was afraid, more than she'd ever been in her life.

"Please, don't abandon me. You are my only hope," Sahar said.

"Saeed said you can come here."

"I will come there. That's better. A friend will drive me. His car won't be recognized."

Explaining the situation as best she could to the housekeeper, Layne stood watching from the glass doors of the foyer. Hardly twenty minutes passed before she saw the gates swing open and a gray sedan make its way past the huge fountain.

It stopped in front of the house, and Sahar leapt from the backseat. She pulled out two leather bags and a large suitcase. Her driver sped away, and she climbed the stairs, speaking a few words to one of Saeed's servants, who had hurried down to retrieve her luggage.

Layne held out her hand. "I'm glad you made it."

Sahar gave her a one-armed hug. "You are saving my life."

They went to the terrace and Sahar collapsed into a chair.

"Tell me what's going on," Layne said, sitting across from her. She poured a glass of water from the insulated pitcher on the table and handed it to her. "Do you want some wine, or brandy?"

"No. This is what I need." She drank and then rested her forearms on the table, desperation evident in her whole body.

"I am fleeing, Layne. One step ahead of the security police. I am about to be arrested."

"Today? Why? How do you know?"

"It's all a terrible mistake. Everything has gone wrong. I told you before that my people are struggling for reform against great odds. Some of them have been imprisoned. That will happen to me if I can't escape in time."

"What have you done?"

"I? Nothing. My only sin was in speaking out for truth. Six months ago, an international magazine in France interviewed me. I spoke against the injustice of our male guardianship laws. I begged that other countries bring pressure on our government to change."

"You must have known there would be consequences when the article was published. Why didn't you leave earlier?"

"That is the terrible mistake. They told me the article would appear two weeks from now. I meant it to be an explanation, a statement supporting our demonstration."

She pressed her palms to her temples and then raised her face to the sky in an agony of emotion. "This morning, my friend in Paris called to tell me the article was published there today. It will be here tomorrow. Word of it will be here today! I have no time.

"Our plan is in place. It will not be stopped. But if I am captured, security police will force me to expose these people who are working to change our country. Many lives besides mine are at risk."

"Your group is planning a demonstration? Why would that put lives in danger?"

Sahar held her gaze, as if she were compelling her attention.

"It is much more than you imagine. I can't tell you details, Layne. I beg for understanding. For the compassion others have been unwilling to give us."

Layne knew the "others" included Katherine Darius. And this was the only chance she'd ever have to make amends for that.

"I do believe in your cause, Sahar. I've never hidden my feelings about it. Hassan thinks I'm already one of your supporters. That's why he's after me."

"Perhaps," Sahar said, "but my uncle is directing Hassan's vigilance. He brought you here hoping you could find your mother's killer."

Layne didn't dare to believe the words. Or their promise that, after all this time, she was hearing the truth. "Are you sure?"

Sahar looked away. "Perhaps not. Some of the family say he arranged the killing of Katherine Darius because she was going to leave him."

The words were stunning. Among all possibilities, this seemed most plausible. Despite what Al-Amir told her, she never believed her mother had abandoned her family to embrace a wild passion with him.

His love for her seemed genuine, and her mother may have been carried away by infatuation. But Katherine Darius never really *belonged* to anyone.

"This speculation isn't helping, Sahar. If you know the truth, please tell me."

Still not meeting her eyes, Sahar said, "I don't know why you are here. I can say only that you are important to him."

"Not as important as you are. He won't let you be arrested," Layne said.

Sahar straightened, a fierce look in her eyes. "The decision is as good as made. He can do nothing to save me. Political activists at this moment are in prison for weeks, even years with no trial. Their families pay money, try to use influence. Nothing happens. They die there."

"If he can't help you, what can I possibly do?"

"Take me to your American Consulate. Your friend David Markam will tell them to protect me."

"This morning he said they can't give anybody asylum outside the States. I can try to reach him and ask, but it didn't sound likely they'd take you in as a political refugee either. What are you going to do if they won't?"

They sat in silence. The splashing of the fountain began to get on Layne's nerves, as if it were mocking them.

"The only thing I can think of is to call Saeed," she said. He offered to fly me out of the country. He can help you get away, too."

"Yes, that's what we must do! Saeed will help us. I didn't dare to tell you he is my friend. He is the one who built my company's water farm in the Eastern Province. I am seldom able to say so to anyone in this country. He has belief in our cause."

Layne hoped she was doing the right thing as she dialed the number Saeed had left for her. He answered immediately.

He listened and said, "I was afraid this might happen. Matter of fact, I've already started back to my house. Twenty minutes I'll be there."

Saeed looked hot and angry when he strode across the terrace and went to the drinks table. He swallowed a glass of water. "The worst has come," he said, his expression softening as he glanced at Sahar.

She blinked and looked down at her lap. "What have you heard?"

"I telephoned the security police on my way here." He sat down heavily on a chair.

"My friend Hameed confirmed it. He read some of the charges to me. *Suspicious contact with foreign parties. Activities damaging the security and stability of the country.* That means treason, Sahar."

"Do you think *I'm* the foreign party?" Layne said. "They're going to arrest us both?"

"There is a concern," he said gravely. "It's very likely you'll be detained. Or at least they will give you a bad time over it."

Sahar looked at them with frightened eyes, the muscles of her face working.

Getting up to pour himself a glass of tea, Saeed sighed and touched her shoulder before he sat down again.

"I have ordered my plane to be made ready. There's an airstrip I use, near my farms in the Eastern Province. We will land there. A car will be waiting to drive you to the coast."

"A boat?" Sahar said.

"Yes."

Layne listened, fear mingling with amazement. "You just made these arrangements?"

"We have known for a long while of trouble coming," Saeed said.

Sahar nodded.

"This is truly an emergency," he said. "Now that Sahar has told you of the plans for the demonstration, you must go with her, Layne. Hassan's vigilance makes it clear you've been linked with her. Neither I nor David will be able to protect you from the consequences."

Layne stood up. "I can't leave Thomas! If I escape, people will think he's part of this, this whatever is going on. They'll arrest him, too."

"He will not be harmed," Saeed said. "The Al-Amirs will protect him. They know his movements. Yours, they do not."

"I have to call David. To ask him what I should do," Layne said.

She went to the telephone in the foyer and dialed the number on David's card. The operator at the consulate told her he was not available.

Unable to keep the anxiety out of her voice Layne said, "He told me I could reach him there if I had an emergency. This is an emergency!"

The man repeated courteously but firmly that Mr. Markam was not available.

Layne hung up the phone and stared out at the green vines on the terrace. She needed time to think, to decide, but Saeed and Sahar were already standing in the foyer waiting for her.

She hurried upstairs, threw her clothes into the bag

Puja had packed for her, and came down to follow them to the Mercedes waiting at the foot of the steps.

The drive to the airport was surprisingly quick and uneventful. With tinted windows, they had a margin of anonymity. Even so, Layne felt fear every time a black sedan came near.

They went along what looked like a service road that led to a cement block building across the runway from the main airport terminal. Saeed parked beside the building and reached for Sahar's suitcases. Layne grabbed her own bag, and they hurried behind him toward a small plane.

He helped them aboard and got behind the wheel. While he went through the takeoff procedure, Layne stared out the window, forcing down the emotions that were welling inside her.

Just as the plane began a teetering run, she saw a black sedan coming across the runway. With a heart-stopping lunge, the plane leapt into the air. Below, the black sedan turned and headed back to the terminal.

Her head throbbing, Layne looked across the narrow aisle. Sahar sat staring ahead, her hands clinched on the armrests, and Layne knew she was terrified. This escape couldn't have been an impulsive decision. She must have known all along that a day like this could come if her plans failed. But that wouldn't make it any less devastating.

When the plane leveled off and settled into a smoother course, Layne said, "What's going to happen to your company? Will the women who work for you be arrested?"

Sahar shook her head. "I put the company in another woman's hands weeks ago. Our work will survive. Perhaps, one day—"

Hearing the despair in her voice, Layne knew she would go on hoping to gain freedom for women's lives. But she would not be here to see it come. Her heart ached for the loss of those dreams.

The plane lunged and began to ride airwaves. She searched around the seat, hoping Saeed had provided bags.

"Do you see any bags? For airsickness?" she said.

Sahar reached into the leather case at her feet and pulled out two large paper cups. She opened an insulated bottle, poured juice into one of them, and handed them both to her. "Use the extra one if you need it. In the other, this is mango nectar. It will calm your stomach."

"The plan is there!" Saeed suddenly shouted into the microphone of his headset. "I won't deviate." He listened and then began speaking in rapid Arabic.

An air pocket made the plane swoop, and Layne clapped her hand over the cup to keep the juice from spilling. In the moment of calm that followed, she had just enough time for a large gulp before the plane bucked again.

Saeed was talking now in short, angry spurts.

She leaned back and took deep breaths. The sick feeling eased a little and she closed her eyes, but when she opened them, everything in front of her began to dissolve in a gray haze.

"I feel so dizzy," she heard herself say from a faraway place.

"It will not be much longer," Sahar said, her words pulsing as if she were talking in a windstorm.

Chapter 23

David's boss was waiting for him when he got back to his office. Gerald Fitzwilliam's twenty-five years of Foreign Service, most of it in the Middle East and South Asia, had given him the comfortable look of a man who knew he belonged where he was.

He moved from behind David's desk to an armchair and sipped the iced tea he was drinking through a pair of straws. "We missed you at the country team meeting this morning."

"Yes, I apologize," David said. "Had to stop by my apartment to change clothes. I got a call from Khalil Hassan at the Ministry. Don't know if you've met him. He's state security, position's a bit nebulous, special high-level operations."

"Yes, I've met Mr. Hassan. Not a man I'd want to run afoul of. You went to see him about the messages Bin Yousef picked up at the satellite stations?"

David sat down at his desk. "That was one issue. Hassan thinks the activists are ready to make their move."

Gerald looked more surprised than he expected.

"We don't have intel to indicate that level of concern. Who are these people? Who's backing them? Do you have anything reliable?"

"Not much. From what I've heard, it's an eclectic mix. Intellectuals, businesspeople, mostly living abroad but with kinship ties to the kingdom. Size of the membership unknown, and it isn't clear who's directing things. I believe they're committed to moderating the country's human rights laws."

"Ain't gonna happen," Gerald said, his expression cynical. "It's 1400 on the Hijri calendar, not 1980. Hell, you wrote part of that last Human Rights Report. You know how far this government is from our policy objectives.

"If it's reform these activists are after, they couldn't have picked a worse time. With the hostage crisis in Iran still unresolved and the likelihood that we'll soon have an administration that's less sanguine about human rights than the current one, there won't be conspicuous political support for their agenda."

"They've got some valid grievances," David said.

"Yes, they do. And we'll keep on making our 'We are displeased with your treatment of such-and-such' statements. But we're not crusaders, David. Holding the line on what's been accomplished may be all we can do for a while. Not that I don't share your sympathy."

He closed his eyes and quoted his favorite diplomat:

There is nothing more difficult to take in hand, more perilous to conduct, or more uncertain in its success, than to take the lead in the introduction of a new order of things.

He sucked up the last of his iced tea noisily. "Machiavelli's right. Those who benefit from the current system aren't willing to budge. The ones who want change can't take the risks of forcing it."

David got up and stood by the window.

Aware that he hadn't reported his past week's activities as fully as he should have, he said, "There's another issue I'm concerned about. I mentioned the ethnologists Thomas Darius and his sister, Layne. Layne's befriended one of the activists, and that's brought her onto the radar of the security police."

One of Gerald's gifts was his appearance of untroubled affability. "Really? In what way has she 'befriended' them?"

David said nothing. What could he say? She's a woman on a hopeless quest, with a sense of justice so strong she might join a group of rebels? And incidentally, I've fallen in love with her.

Gerald's instinct was finely honed. "You're personally involved with these people, David? Not in over your head, are you? If the potential is there to compromise yourself or the mission, you'd better cut the ties," he said quietly. "Before it's too late."

David stared out at the concrete building across the street, outlined against the pale sky. "It's long past too late."

"Well, you know what you have to do. If you're involved with this woman, and she's mixed up with a bunch of activists, it's your problem too. It's a fast ride down a dead end road. Expulsion, persona non grata at best. Maybe worse if the local authorities get hold of you. That's assuming you don't get killed in the process."

"I didn't say she's mixed up with them."

"Didn't you? Remember what happened to the insurgents after that takeover at Mecca last year." He jerked his hand across his throat. "Beheaded. Those who weren't shot."

David turned and they stared at each other. Gerald rattled the ice in his glass. "Is Saeed Bin Yousef part of this group?"

"He's sympathetic to what they want to do, but I haven't seen any evidence of political activities. He's too busy with his own projects."

"Uh-huh. Let's hope so. It would be exceedingly unwise to underestimate this government's response to any threat, especially with that business in Mecca still so fresh. These folks don't play nice, my friend."

After a pause, he said, "Does Darius know how unsettled things are in this country right now? Do you think he'd change his plans if he did?"

"He believes he's got protection. I told you who arranged permission for his study."

"The Quiet Lion himself. Not something I'd have said was possible. Do you know why?"

David shook his head. "I tried to find out. But it didn't go well. I'm not likely to be invited to his house any time soon."

Gerald leaned back in his chair and regarded him with the worried look he had when he was mentoring.

"With Al-Amir's sponsorship, these Darius people ought to be all right once they're out in a Bedouin village. If some kind of rebellion erupts while they're en route, they could become targets."

His voice hardened. "If you've got any influence with them, tell them to get themselves out there. I don't want to supervise the retrieval of a couple of American corpses from the desert. Or negotiate the fallout from a frigging international incident!"

The image made David sick. "I've done everything I can to keep her from getting in any deeper. Layne lives by her own rules."

Gerald gazed at him thoughtfully. "A new experience for you. Tell me more about this Layne Darius. How much of a complication is she?"

David sat down and waited until he put his thoughts in order. "The presence of Dr. Layne Darius is a complication on just about every front. Aside from my personal feelings for her, the activist she's met is one of old Al-Amir's nieces. Her name's Sahar, and she's well known to the security police."

He paused, wishing he didn't have to tell him the most important reason Layne was in the country.

"And there's one other matter. Layne is the daughter of Katherine Darius, the journalist who disappeared at Al-Diriyah a few years ago."

"Don't tell me she's here to dig that up again?" Gerald said.

"Yes. She came as part of her brother's research team, but she's determined to know how her mother died. And somebody evidently doesn't want her to do that.

"Twice, she's been attacked. Apparently to warn her against delving into the past. Either time could have been fatal. Hassan has somebody following her, but even that hasn't stopped her."

Gerald's eyes narrowed. "She'd do well to heed those warnings. It's not likely she'll get what she wants anyway. This desert doesn't give up its victims like the sea does."

"I don't know what else to do," David said.

His phone rang. He answered and listened to terse sentences from Hassan.

"Thank you. Will you let me know as soon as you have an update?"

"Hassan," he said when he put the phone down. "Saeed's plane took off about two hours ago with Layne and Sahar Al-Amir onboard."

"Going where?"

"They've tracked a landing at Ha'il and a second one at a private airstrip on the east coast, south of Dhahran. No contact since then."

"Ha'il? Why the devil would he go up there? Could he be showing off one of his projects? You said he's got farms," Gerald said.

"Not in Ha'il. I don't know why he'd go there. But south of Dhahran, he's close to Bahrain. He must be trying to get them out of the country."

Slumped in his chair, he couldn't even think until shock slowly formed into a visceral fear for Layne. He rolled away from the desk.

"Something's wrong, Gerald. Really wrong. I'm going to see Hassan."

Chapter 24

Layne thought she heard a voice, words muffled and distant. She strained to listen. Gradually, there was only the noise, the steady gray noise inside her head.

Amorphous shapes swam in green light when she opened her eyes and became green against black when she closed them to let the nausea pass.

Tingling numbness. And cold, icy cold. She struggled to raise her head and fell back into blackness.

Minutes or hours later she was conscious again. Cold, so cold. She would never again be warm.

The noise was still there. This time pain as well. Stabbing at her temples, burning in her arms. She bent her knees to turn over.

Terror shot through her. Her hands and feet were tied. Black electrical cord cinched her wrists, cutting into her skin, binding her ankles, and tethering her to a drainpipe under a metal sink.

She was lying on a linoleum floor in a small room. Far above was a ceiling of acoustical tile. Two small windows set only an inch from the ceiling let in daylight. But what day?

She moaned, as much from the need to hear her voice as from the pain, and folded her body into a fetal position. Where was she? Where was Sahar? And Saeed? And where was David?

Memory came suddenly, the rush of airsickness on the plane, Saeed's angry voice talking in Arabic to the control tower. Something important he was saying. Did they force him to land?

She smelled the sweet, acidic scent of mango on her shirt and saw again the certainty in Sahar's face as she said, "Our plan is in place. It will not be stopped."

Our plan? Sahar made this happen? No, her uncle must be in charge. David said that, didn't he? Nobody but Al-Amir had the power to manipulate people as he chose. Or the arrogance to believe he could force a government to change because he willed it.

Looking at the cords binding her ankles, she understood why Al-Amir brought her to this country.

I'm alive to be the scapegoat. The blame will be on me. And Saeed. He must be a prisoner, too. If he fought them, he may be dead. Poor Saeed. His kindness, his dreams for the future.

Hot tears came and she lay in the wetness.

After a while, she wiped her face on her sleeve. Wincing at the pain in her neck muscles, she struggled to her knees, grasped the edge of the sink, and pulled herself up.

The room was not more than eight by ten feet. Some kind of workroom. On the Formica countertop, a roll of duct tape, a stack of computer paper, two empty plastic water bottles. In the corner farthest from the door, behind a partition, was a toilet, its disinfectant smell permeating the room. Her bag lay propped against the partition.

The jangle of a telephone sounded through the wall. She steadied herself against the sink and listened. It stopped in the middle of the third ring. Someone must have answered it. People were here. The people who had bound her and put her into this room.

"Hello!" she yelled, her voice a croak. Clearing her throat she yelled, "Who are you?" and waited. Only the labored noise she knew must be an air conditioner. Every now and then the motor sighed as if it were tired and about to stop.

No matter who put her into this room, she had to get out of it. She eased herself to the floor and rolled closer to the door. Tensing her muscles, she kicked the wood. The impact jarred her head and sent zigzags of pain through her temples.

Rocking to get momentum, she mashed her fingers under her spine, rolled over onto her stomach and lay seething, her cheek against the cold linoleum floor. Once again, she drew up her legs to kick, but she heard a faint sound. Footsteps! Adrenaline shot through her. She wriggled backward so the door wouldn't hit her if it opened.

A man, incredibly tall from her vantage point, eased into the room. He had on a thob, streaked with the same reddish dirt that caked his feet, their sides as cracked as his worn sandals. His goutra covered all of his head except the brown eyes that peered down at her.

"Who are you?" she demanded in Arabic.

Ignoring her, he turned, obviously eager to leave. "Wait!" she shouted. "I need—" She jerked her head toward the toilet.

He looked as if he wanted to refuse. Then he knelt again, smelling of cigarettes and sour sweat as he bent over her. The hands that grasped her arms were calloused but he worked quickly. Before she could do more than rub her bloody, swollen wrists he bound them again in front of her.

"This cord is hurting me," she said. "Do you have to do this? Who are you?"

He stared down at her, and the awful awareness came to her that he could do anything to her. She tensed, expecting a kick or a blow. He squatted beside her, untied the cord around her ankles, and unwound enough of the length tethering her to the drainpipe so that she could hobble to the toilet. He stood up and looked at her warily before he slipped out the door, locking it behind him.

"Damn," she said aloud. She glanced at her watch, grateful for a reference point. Three o'clock. Eight hours since she and Sahar left Saeed's house. If it was the same day.

She was still in the desert. Whatever brought the plane down must have happened soon after they took off.

With a struggle, she managed to stand. Leaning against the sink, she splashed lukewarm water on her face and let it run over her arms. The cord had made three deep cuts that were still bleeding.

She was propped against the sink when the door opened again, and the man came in. He seemed surprised to see her standing, but he put a small round tray on the counter and left without a word.

Smelling chicken broth, she lifted the piece of unleavened bread covering the bowl and stared at it. What if it was drugged?

How could she be any worse off if it were? She dipped the spoon into the broth. Inches from her lips, it turned in her fingers and hot soup dribbled down her shirtfront. She took the bowl with both hands and drank.

A telephone rang again. Chewing glumly on the bread, she listened to the silence. The man who brought the food was watchful but not overly anxious. She might be here for days.

The thought of it made her furious. Clamping the last bit of bread between her teeth, she jerked the cord around her wrists back-and-forth. It cut deeper into the wounds and made the bleeding worse.

Clinging to the countertop, she opened a drawer. Some sharp-edged thing must be in a room like this. Boxes of screws, a roll of toilet paper, half a dozen other totally useless things. In desperation she felt under the sink. Its metal edge was sharp and might actually cut with determined sawing.

Despite the cold in the room she was soon sweating. With one harder-than-usual jerk she lost her balance and the metal gouged a jagged line across the back of her arm. Her hand trembling, she watched the blood trickle through her fingers and drip into the sink. She held her arm under the water and looked at the cord. The plastic insulation was cut but the wires underneath had hardly been scratched. It would take hours. Cursing she renewed her sawing.

Her back ached from bending, and sweat and blood had mixed into a sticky mess by the time she decided it was hopeless. She turned on the water to wash and the cord slid down her arm a little. On impulse she hooked the cord around the faucets and pulled back with all her strength.

It was a slow process, and painful, but lubricated by blood, the cord began to move. She let go of the sink and jerked. Her hands slid free and she slammed against the wall behind her.

Another few minutes of struggle and the cords were off her ankles. She washed her arms, ripped one of her tunics into strips and wrapped the cuts. Tearing off pieces of duct tape, she secured the bandages.

She looked through her bag to see if there was anything else she could use. Nothing was missing. Even her purse with passport and wallet were there.

Whoever brought her here had just dumped her, without caring whether she could be identified.

She sat down on the floor to think. The only place she'd been in this country that had modern, prefab buildings and a huge air-conditioning system was the satellite earth station. Only one conclusion was possible. The coded messages Saeed intercepted were real. A rebellion had happened or was about to, and Al-Amir was in charge.

Why did they bring her here? Saeed would surely know about it. Unless some of the technicians had been recruited by Al-Amir. If that was true, and Saeed was alive, he might be in this building. But he would be making noise if he were conscious. She'd heard the man's footsteps when he came; a voice from another room would be even louder.

A telephone rang again. For a moment, she thought of trying to find that phone and call David. But the men here would know immediately if she used the telephone.

And how would David even find her? The desert was huge and she could be anywhere on it. The satellite stations were in several locations around the country. All of them out in the desert. Where scorpions roamed the sand at night.

She spent a fruitless few minutes discovering that the windows did not open and were too narrow to get through. Growing more desperate, she knelt beside the wall. It was made of rectangular pieces of fiberboard screwed into a metal framework. Her fingers slid over a screw head three times before she understood the possibility it offered.

If the panels could be attached to the frame, they could be unattached. She rummaged through the drawers. Finding a small screwdriver, she set to work on one of the panels. The first corner took forever but after that, it went faster. When a section of the panel was loose, she peered behind it and saw the back of an outer panel.

In frustration, she sat down on the floor and rubbed her aching wrists. The churning of the air conditioner made one of its frequent shuttering pauses, and the door next to her vibrated slightly. The door!

Removing bolts from hinges was the work of only a few minutes. She eased the door open. Her first glance at the room beyond confirmed where she was. Huge banks of telephone circuits, the clock on the wall, and the order wire receiver David used to call Saeed.

She drew back into her prison room. Was this the site she and Thomas went to with David? A sharp clarity came in the wake of shock. If David knew she was here, there was no one to help her. Thomas was all she had. Getting back to him was her only hope. After that, she would face whatever truth she had to about David.

Picking up her bag, she stripped off her filthy clothes, took out a skirt and tunic, and dressed quickly. Last of all, she put on the abaya and veil.

Reluctantly, she shed her sturdy shoes and buckled on the silver party sandals Puja had packed for her. Harder to walk in, but more likely what a local woman would wear. If she made it to the highway, she might be lucky enough to get a ride into a town. And not be killed in the process.

Filling the two plastic water bottles on the counter, she shoved them into the bag and stepped into the hallway.

Near the door to the outside was a large wall map, a duplicate of the one she had seen before. One location was circled. Not the one David took her to. This was in another part of the country, far away from Riyadh. Even that wouldn't matter if she could just get to a town, anywhere, to get help.

Cautiously, she opened the door and saw that she was at the back of the area, not more than five yards from the chain link fence. The satellite dishes were to the left. The office and sleeping quarters must be on the other side of this building.

She shivered, stepping into the hundred-degree heat from the frigid room. At first, she could barely breathe under the stifling veil. Squinting against the glare of sunlight reflecting off the fence, she crept along the side of the building and looked quickly around the corner.

Two Toyota trucks stood inside the fence and a smaller one was parked outside the open gate as if somebody had come for a short visit. Her first impulse was to run to the truck outside, hoping the owner had left the keys in the ignition, leap in, and race to the road.

The idea faded as soon as it came. Making it across the thirty or so yards between this building and the gate without being seen might be possible, but the men in the building would be after her as soon as the engine started. Even if she could escape from here, a few miles down the road there was bound to be a police checkpoint, and that would end it all.

She stared at the scruffy white truck, mesmerized by its promise of escape. What if she could reach it? And hide in the back? The decision to do it generated a reckless numbness.

Bending low and praying, she scuttled the few yards to the nearest truck. Crouching in its shadow, she waited. No one came from the building. Before she could think about the consequences, she bent again and ran to the truck outside the gate.

Flinging herself into the back, she landed on a pile of burlap bags and lay there, panting. Her courage was gone and trembling fear took over. The driver would see her the minute he came to the truck! If only she could shrink or hide. She picked up a corner of one of the bags. They were filthy, a noxious odor infusing the course material—goats or something worse, but she curled in a corner and spread them over herself.

The wait was almost too short. Within minutes after she'd settled, she heard men's voices talking in Arabic. One of the voices came closer, and she tensed to jump out and run if he saw her. The man shouted something, and there was another exchange of words.

The truck rocked when the driver got in, and the engine roared to life. Hardly believing he didn't even glance at her, she wedged her feet against the sides to keep from being thrown out of her nest as he backed down the length of the access road, made a wide turn, and lurched onto the highway.

Chapter 25

The truck had gone only a short way when she felt it slowing down. The military checkpoint! Preparing to be dragged out and arrested, she rehearsed phrases to explain why she was there. The driver paused only seconds, and she heard an exchange of insults and laughs. They knew the man. He was not stopping.

Afterward, he picked up speed, and gradually, the rhythmic jiggling relaxed her enough to push aside the bag covering her face. Breathing air, even scented with rotten dung, was a relief, and it dried the layer of sweat that bathed her face and stung the rims of her eyes. The sun was going down and the sky becoming pale, almost white.

She was near dozing by the time the truck made an abrupt turn off the highway and bounced into a pothole, slamming her head against the metal side. She braced herself again as they lurched over the dusty track. The truck slowed down, and panic gripped her. What if he knew she was in the back and intended to dump her out here, or rape and kill her?

The truck stopped, and a frenzy of dog barking

erupted. The cab door opened and slammed. Layne buried her head under the bags and willed herself to be completely still. The barking came closer and she felt the impact of jumping bodies and the scrape of claws inches from her head. The driver cursed the dogs and she heard what sounded like a strap on flesh, producing whimpers and yelps. Voices from a distance shouted at him, and he yelled back, his voice receding.

Layne raised the bag covering her face and breathed, grateful that the stench of the bags was stronger than the smell of her sweaty body. Shifting, she looked at her watch. Six o'clock. The drive from the earth station had taken nearly an hour.

For two more hours, she listened to sounds from the man's household, a recorded call to twilight prayer, and the settling down of evening. Finally, she had the courage for a quick look over the side of the truck.

Two makeshift huts of corrugated metal with pieces of fabric hanging over the doorways were about thirty yards away. A bedraggled goat was tethered between the huts and dogs crouched near the doorways. Rolling to the other side of the truck so the cab hid her head from the huts, she raised up and looked around. About a quarter mile away were twenty or so mud-brick houses, scattered over the gentle slope of a hill. A village. People who could help her.

But first she had to get past those dogs. If the driver spotted her, he might guess what she'd done. She had to be as far from the truck as possible before the dogs came after her. No one could see what a woman in an abaya looked like. She was just someone from the village who happened to be walking by. If the veil ever did offer protection, it had better do it now.

Climbing out, she scuttled several feet before the rangy desert dogs bounded toward her, snarling and barking. She shrank from them and shouted in what she hoped was plausible Arabic. Certainly the fear in her voice was real enough. Two men appeared in the doorway of the hut and stared suspiciously, but they called off the dogs. Women in the other hut lifted the door flaps to peer out. Stooping to disguise her height, Layne hobbled up the slope toward the houses.

Stands of palm trees, limp after the day's heat, suggested the village must have grown around a well or an underground spring. The houses, with doors carved of rough wood and small square windows, looked more permanent than the huts where the driver lived. He and the others around him might be transients who didn't mix with the village people very much. If luck stayed with her, he wouldn't hear about the arrival of a foreign woman until she managed to get away.

A few hardworking trucks like the one she came in stood at the edge of the village. There was no pavement but a dirt area had been flattened in the center of the cluster of houses. This was the market with a few stalls and a wooden shop. In the late twilight, the air still warm and the hour too early for a meal, several people were moving among the stalls.

Near the entrance of the shop, a kind of general store, a scribe sat on the ground behind his portable wooden desk, an inkpot, pens, and papers. He was busy composing a document, and a few men squatted around him, contributing suggestions. They glanced at Layne without interest when she sat on the rickety bench on the other side of the shop door. She drank warm water from one of her bottles and thought about her plan.

Thomas told her phone lines were just being set up in most of the kingdom, so this village probably didn't have telephones yet. Who she would call wasn't clear either. And after she called, she'd still be *here*. The first thing to do was get away from this village and the man who brought her.

She had no idea how far she was from Riyadh. For now, she had enough money to pay someone to drive her somewhere. It was just a matter of finding out who to ask.

This store seemed a likely starting place. Stooping under the low doorway, she went inside. The dimness smelled of resin and dust. She heard low voices but could see nothing through her veil.

Slowly, she began to make out a confused jumble of merchandise. Plastic housewares hung from nails, buckets stacked on the floor. Children's clothing, gaudy jewelry, and tools were arranged in a dusty display case. Behind the warped plank that served as a counter, a man of about fifty, in a thob and wearing a white *kufi* cap on his head, followed her movements with sharp eyes.

"As-Salaam-Alaikum. Forgive me for disturbing you," Layne said in faltering Arabic. "I am an American in this country for study. I came into some trouble. I was taken prisoner, and I escaped."

She lifted a corner of the cloth bandage to let him see the cuts, dried blood, and rings of dark bruises on her arms.

"I will pay a fair price to someone who will drive me to a city."

The shopkeeper listened impassively and then studied her as if he could see through the veil into her soul. He swung his head to the side and made a clicking sound with his tongue. "No one from the village goes today, madam."

"I can pay. Would some man not wish to earn?"

He pursed his lips. "Insha'allh," he said vaguely. "Perhaps."

Frustrated, she sat down on a wooden box and saw that several men and boys, even two women, were listening at the doorway. The shopkeeper told them of her predicament, embellishing the kidnapping part with his own details.

There was a general clicking of tongues and shaking of heads. Two other men joined the group and the story was relayed to them. One of the new men pushed forward. "The cousin of Ali visits today. He returns to the city tonight."

A chorus of *"Al-hamdu lillah*, Praise to God" filled the room.

"Where is Mr. Ali's cousin?" Layne asked, not as sure as they were.

Someone must have sent for him because within five minutes the crowd at the door parted and a tall, gaunt man in a brown thob pushed into the room. He surveyed her briefly and waited.

Again, the shopkeeper repeated her story. Ali pulled at his whiskers. His cousin Salim was visiting and would return to Riyadh tonight. He would ask if the foreign lady might ride with the women. Layne followed him back to one of the mud-brick houses.

Salim, a good bit younger than his cousin, acknowledged her with a dip of his head, and the two men squatted outside while Layne went into the house. It was a dirt-floored room with two storage niches and outside steps leading to the flat roof. She greeted Ali's wife and mother, Salim's wife, her teenage sister, and two small children.

The younger women were preparing dinner, and the smell of roasting meat filled the room. They brought her a bucket of warm water, and Layne bathed as best she could. Ali's mother made room for her to sit next to the mound of bedded coals where the meat was cooking.

Drawing a tin box from under a wooden shelf, she

began to clean the wounds with an astringent that burned fiercely. She expressed no sympathy. This thing had happened, and Layne had survived.

Dipping a gnarled finger into a small round tin, the woman spread dark brown oil into the cuts on her arms. Layne thought it must be the black cumin oil Sahar told her about, the Bedouins' all-purpose healing balm.

Feeling more comfortable and unafraid than she ever had in this country, Layne asked questions while the woman tied pieces of clean cloth over the wounds.

In this household, the family ate together around the fire mound, the men on one side and the women and children on the other. The grandmother urged her to eat the roasted goat and rice that filled the flat pan set on the mound. Layne needed no persuasion. She wrenched off a piece of meat with her thumb and two fingers of her right hand and ate what tasted like the finest food she'd ever had.

When the meal was over, the men went outside, to a village coffee house, she assumed, and the younger women prepared the children for bed. Ali's mother looked at Layne shrewdly.

"How do you come here?" she said. The story of the "trouble" had been relayed by the men. Now she wanted to hear the details.

Layne repeated her story. "I do not know how I came to be a prisoner," she said finally. "I fear my friends are dead."

The woman studied her and said nothing.

They sat in silence for a while, and Layne began to be nervous. The family showed no sign of preparing to leave. So long as she stayed in the village, the man who drove her here might find her.

Still more hours passed before she was sitting with her knees under her chin in the back of the small pickup with Salim's wife, her sister, and the sleeping children. The truck bed was padded with pillows and much cleaner than her earlier ride. When she felt the bump onto the highway, she relaxed.

They sat in companionable silence, the wind whipping their veils around their faces. Layne thought of pictures of her mother dressed in camouflage fatigues, reporting the news from a frontline position in the war in Southeast Asia.

What would Katherine Darius say if she could see her daughter shrouded in black and looking like part of a workingman's harem? She smiled to herself. "Write it all down," she'd heard her say so often. "It will make a great story!" It would, if she lived to tell it.

At the edge of the city, Salim stopped the truck and got out. "Where would you go?"

Layne realized the only place she knew was Al-Amir's house. And she didn't dare to go there.

She wanted to find David. The fears she had earlier still nagged at the fringe of her mind, but she willed herself to believe he would help her.

"To the American Consulate," she said and tried to explain what it was.

After a while, Salim was losing patience.

Resigned, she gave him Al-Amir's address. At least she'd find Thomas, and he would speak for her if he could.

Chapter 26

Her fear of what she might find at Al-Amir's house began to grow when they reached the wall along the side of the estate. The rusty gate, the way she went in her first night, felt safer than the front door. She tapped on the glass and asked Salim to stop.

Opening her bag, she handed Salim's wife all the money she had. She protested, but Layne said, "For the children," and climbed quickly out of the truck bed.

"Salim, *Baraka allahou feek*. Allah will surely bless you and your family for your kindness."

"Insha'allh," he said.

Pulling off the veil covering her face, she watched him drive down the street, taking with him her brief sense of safety.

Leaves crunched under her sandals as she walked along uneven ground, searching until she found the metal door. Running her fingers along the frame, she couldn't find the button Mustafa used. She pushed the door and gasped as it moved slightly, scraping across stone.

She eased the door open and slipped inside. The garden lights were out. Walking carefully along the uneven bricks, she could see only the dark mass of the house.

Suddenly her shin struck what felt like a bag of sand. Bending, she heard a voice muttering in Arabic.

Realizing this was a person huddled on the path, and a voice she recognized, she said, "Puja?"

Layne bent down and tried to pull her up, but the woman pushed her away, and went on rocking back-and-forth, muttering a kind of chant.

She squatted next to her. "Puja, what's wrong? Are you hurt?"

The chanting stopped but the swaying went on.

"Tell me what's wrong. Did someone hurt you? Please tell me," Layne said, trying to soothe her.

Finally, Puja raised her head. "Terrible ones come here," she said in her slurred Arabic and began to shake as if she were sobbing.

Shocked, Layne stood up. Terrible ones? The police? No, it must be the rebels, the people who forced Saeed's plane down.

If they were here, who had they come for? They must have taken over the house. Where was Al-Amir? Where was Thomas?

With difficulty, she kept from running inside. Grasping the woman's bony arm, she urged her to stand.

"How do the servants get into the house? I want to go to the kitchen," Layne said.

Puja tried to pull away, but she held her. "Show me the kitchen door."

In the best of times this woman hated her. Now, paralyzed by fear, Puja might even betray her.

Uttering a sound somewhere between a growl and a sob, Puja jerked free and shuffled toward the house. There was nothing to do but follow her and hope.

Reaching the left wing, she paused beside a narrow door, half-hidden by vines. "Servant door," she whispered.

Layne started to open it, but Puja clutched her skirt. "No go. He kill you. Kill master."

"Who is *he*? Who comes to kill the master?"

Puja looked up, her terror visible even in the near-darkness.

Layne waited, nerving herself for whatever she might find in the house. As she pushed the door open, she heard behind her softly, "*Allah maeak*. Allah is with you."

Fervently hoping that was true, she slipped inside, shed the abaya and scarf, and made her way through dark hallways to a steep flight of stairs.

Standing at the bottom, she tried to imagine where it might go. It had to lead to the second floor where her bedroom was. Climbing, she could think of no logical reason for going to that room, except that it was familiar. And nobody would know she was there.

At the top, she opened the door onto a dark hallway. Only a few feet ahead was the central staircase. Lights were on down below and a voice was speaking.

Saeed was speaking.

Layne felt weak with relief. He was alive. But why was he here? Was he a prisoner? Crossing the hallway, she dropped to a crouch and peered between the balusters.

Just inside the library, she could see Saeed sitting in the leather chair nearest the door. Soft lamplight shadowed his profile. He was still dressed in the clothes he had worn on the plane, but in his right hand, resting on the arm of the chair, he held a large revolver.

Although he spoke calmly, his voice lacked the genial tone it usually had.

"We have only about one hour to wait," he said. "At midnight, all satellite communication, telephones, television, radio in this country will stop. From the royals to the lowest menial, the entire kingdom will be cut off from the rest of the world.

"We will restore the system when we believe those in power have understood the vulnerability of their fortress. We do not mean to destroy, only to wake them up, break through the adamantine resistance to change."

"A fantasy. You have taken your plans from stories of superheroes with capes!" It was Al-Amir. Layne couldn't see him, but he must be in his usual chair on the other side of the lamp table.

Saeed bristled. "You're quite wrong. Our plan is meticulously laid. To the last thought. You, with your well-known advocacy for change, will speak for us, explain the meaning of our demonstration."

"Absurd!" Al-Amir said. His voice sounded irritable, as if he were speaking to a disobedient child.

"Anticipating your refusal, we have secured an incentive. Sahar was certain of your regard for the impetuous Dr. Layne Darius. If you refused to support our demonstration, at least you would not dare to speak against us so long as we held her."

"Where is Layne?" a voice out of sight behind the doorjamb said.

It was Thomas. Layne stretched out flat on the floor, straining to see.

"You have harmed Layne Darius?" Al-Amir said, his voice rising.

"Incentive, as I said. She was not harmed."

"What do you mean, 'she was'?" Thomas demanded.

"Dr. Darius, your sister is even more tenacious than I imagined. She escaped from her guards. Hours ago. She may have tried to make her way back to her zealous David Markam to warn him of our plans. Or, since reaching him was unlikely, she's alone in the desert. In that case, I will lend my assistance in finding her after our business is finished."

Pounding on the front door startled them all.

Saeed leapt from the chair. "Perhaps this is your ever-vigilant Hassan." He waved the gun in Thomas's direction. "Dr. Darius, you will open the door. Very carefully."

Watching her brother walk slowly across the entrance hall, Layne tensed to rush down the stairs.

In the library doorway Saeed raised the gun and aimed it at him.

Thomas opened the door and stepped back in alarm. David Markam strode into the light. A few feet behind him was Hassan, flanked by two men in uniforms. Assessing the situation with a glance, David motioned for Hassan to stay out of sight. Thomas stood at the open door, and David walked slowly toward Saeed.

"No farther, David," Saeed said.

David stopped and they faced each other across twenty feet of white marble.

"What are you doing, Saeed? Have you gone crazy?" he said.

Saeed lowered the revolver slightly. "David, faithful always. You've come in time to see the end. I wager you didn't expect such a dramatic finale as this. Stand by me! I will see you're given the credit your loyalty deserves. Together we will engender a new way of life for my people."

"You'll be executed for treason," David said.

Saeed shook his head, and David raised his hands in appeal.

"Don't throw away all the good you've done, Saeed. You can leave right now. I'll help you get out of the country."

"I may be forced to go, David. After our demonstration has its effect. Though perhaps I won't go. Soon, we will be deciding who comes and goes."

"If you fire that gun, you'll be a killer. No one can save you then."

"My own salvation is irrelevant, David. I learned that eight years ago when I put our lives into the hands of a woman who promised to help us," Saeed said.

"Our work, the future we fight for, that is the important thing. I tried desperately to tell Katherine Darius this. In the crucial moment, she closed her heart to us. 'A rebellion is news. The public has a right to know,' she said. She meant to reveal our names, our plans. She cared nothing for us, for what she was destroying.

"I tried to reason with her. I reached out, only to catch hold of her, to make her hear what I wanted to say. She whirled away and went over the wall of the tower. When I could do nothing, I buried her in the desert."

No one made a sound. Then, David took another step toward him. "Saeed, listen to me."

Saeed raised his arm again, the revolver aimed directly at his chest. "I can see you sympathize, David. You have always been an understanding friend. But you still mean to stop me—"

A sharp boom echoed in the high ceiling.

Layne screamed and plunged down the stairs.

Saeed's body slammed to the floor. He lay prone, his arms stretched out as if in supplication.

Hassan and his men rushed into the room with drawn guns. Thomas stood staring in horror, his hand gripping the doorknob.

David, as if in a trance, knelt down and laid his hand on Saeed's broad back, where a stain of blood was spreading across the khaki shirt.

Holstering his gun, Hassan went into the library. Thomas threw his arm around Layne, and the two of them, swaying, followed him.

In front of his chair, Al-Amir stood straight and fierce, the jewel-handled revolver still in his hand. He looked like a hunter who'd just shot a dangerous animal—shaken, but believing he acted in accord with necessity.

Layne turned back to David. His face dark with emotion, he stood up and gazed down at Saeed, his friend, and the man who had been seconds away from killing him. She wanted to go to him, to comfort him, but his jaw was clamped in unrelenting control, warning against any touch.

Hassan spoke to Al-Amir and then directed his men to take Saeed's body. They moved quickly, and as he was leaving, Hassan said curtly, "Dr. Darius, you and your sister will please remain in this house."

David came to the library doorway and said to Al-Amir, "Thank you, sir, for saving my life."

Still held upright by pride, Al-Amir said, "It was your arrival that saved us all. My act accomplished my own purpose." He dropped the ruby-handled revolver into its box on the side table.

Straightening, he looked at Layne, and she remembered the first time she'd seen him. His gaze would always be compelling.

"The fruits of the past cannot be denied," he said slowly. "Today, I saw the face of the man who killed Katherine. She has been avenged." He sat down, his legs seeming to buckle under him.

Thomas sat on the couch, looking stunned. Layne sat next to him and put her hand on his arm. "It's over," she said.

Eight years of aching to know, of useless hope. She would need time to learn how to go on with her life. For now, the relief she felt was so profound that she was ashamed of the strength of it.

She watched David sink wearily into one of the leather chairs, his face pinched with sorrow. This day of loss and betrayal had brought him more pain than she could imagine.

Al-Amir, his voice strong, said, "Bin Yousef is not the first man I have been willing to shoot.

"Had he tried to take Katherine from me, I might have killed Alexander Darius. And, for a few moments, Mr. Markam, I thought of killing you."

Challenge flickered in David's eyes. "The impulse was mutual, sir."

Al-Amir's mouth twitched. "Perhaps your motives were more admirable. You suspected me of being the man your friend was, the leader of this misguided group of idealists."

"I also didn't know what part you had in Katherine Darius's death," David said.

Looking at Layne's bandaged arms, he shook his head. "I even had the delusion that I could protect Layne."

"So there we were," Al-Amir said, "both of us learning what I should already have known when I wished to keep Katherine's daughter from you. She is truly her mother's child. A man may love her his whole life, but he will never possess her."

They both stared at her, and Layne was sure she saw in David's eyes a desire to prove the old lion wrong.

Chapter 27

There is no hurry, no bustle in the timeless existence of the desert. The rest of the world was far away. Hills and plains of red-gold sand, punctuated by scraggly abal bushes, stretched to the horizon as they had yesterday and would tomorrow.

It was twilight and evening prayers were over. In the flat center space of the Bedouin encampment, Mustafa and his male relatives sat talking around a mound of bedded coals, the smell of roasting goat pungent in the air. Behind them in the mud-brick huts, the women of the household were busy with the children and preparations for the meal.

After a day's drive across the desert with Mustafa, David was tired. He and Thomas sat a little apart from the other men. They could see Layne writing her day's notes under a date palm near the huts, her back resting against the trunk. The ever-present wind now and then ruffled a page of her notebook.

"Layne looks happy," David said. She also looked indescribably beautiful to him, and he ached to hold her.

"I know she was worried about not being accepted by the Bedouin women."

Thomas sighed. "There were some hard times in the beginning. Layne was an outcast.

"We use an Emic method of research, living as members of the family we're observing. But these women are indignant if any man or outsider so much as gathers dried sticks for the fire.

"They wouldn't let her do anything for a couple of weeks. She had to move carefully until they made a place for her. I'm proud of her. She's done as well as any researcher I've ever worked with."

A little girl of about five with a curly mop of dark brown hair ran out of the nearby hut. She pounced on Layne's lap. They held hands and sang a counting song until the child jumped up, tugging her into the hut.

"That's her little shadow," Thomas said. "She's teaching the child to read. Not without opposition from the family, of course. But she convinced them the girl should go to school when they're living in the settlement community. Layne can't resist challenging anything she thinks is unjust," he added.

"If she believes in a cause, not much gets in her way," David said.

They chuckled, and Thomas said, "I hope we'll see you back in Washington. I'd enjoy having somebody who knows the desert to talk to."

"If I have my way, you and I will have a kinship tie before long," David said, intensely aware of how much he wanted that.

Thomas smiled. "She won't make your life easy."

"I'll never be bored," David said ruefully.

He'd felt a sense of inevitability that baffled him the day he met her. Now, after four months away from her, there was no doubt left. He'd always love Layne Darius. What he didn't know was whether she was willing to share her life with him.

The sacrifices Foreign Service life demanded would make it hard, maybe impossible, for her to carry on her career. He knew what that meant to her. In the few hours they were alone before she and Thomas left Riyadh, they hadn't even talked about the future.

"Layne has thrived out here in the sands," Thomas said. "We work for what we need to eat and survive. There's quiet joy in this life.

'"She was badly shaken when she found out that Katherine had left our dad to live with Al-Amir. I knew she would be. That's why I didn't want her to know. She idolized her mother."

After a pause, he said, "You'll be good for her. She does love you."

"That's all I need," David said. But he knew Layne needed much more.

Getting up, Thomas said, "Why don't we go for a stroll?"

He called Layne, and the three of them walked

along a rough track that skirted the field of date palms behind the huts.

As soon as they were out of sight of the encampment, David said, "Turn your head, Thomas. I've got to do this." He pulled Layne into his arms.

Like that first day on the dune, a layer of his skin seemed to peel away when he let her go. He took her hand, warm and familiar, fitting his so well.

With his free hand, he pushed up her sleeve. "You've still got scars from those electrical cords. Damn, I hated them for hurting you."

She kissed his cheek, and linked her arm through his.

"Rotten experience all around," Thomas said.

They walked slowly, feeling the cool beginning of the desert night.

"I suppose you've been busy with the aftermath of Saeed's attemped rebellion," Thomas said. "How close did he come to bringing it off?"

"The shutdown of communications would actually have happened if Hassan hadn't put a massive response into action," David said. "Saeed had technicians at several of the stations ready to go when he gave the signal.

"It was a formidable web of conspirators. He even had a contact at our embassy in Jeddah who kept him informed. That's how he knew you two were coming before you arrived.

"Unfortunately for them, some of their people were too zealous to be competent. Al-Amir's head driver, for instance, was working for them. He's apparently the one who shot at you the first day, Layne, to scare you and stop you from doing any investigating."

"I thought he was watching me for Al-Amir. But he was working for Saeed? Did he try to kill Mustafa?"

"Seems likely. Though I think he intended to disable him rather than kill him. He wanted to be your driver so he could keep an eye on you all the time."

"That's why Mustafa was such a loner," Layne said. "He must have sensed that the other drivers were up to something."

David nodded. "I asked him why he waited outside of Al-Amir's house to warn you that night. He said the head driver told him you'd be arrested if you went into the house."

"That's irony for sure," Layne said. "I was mad at Puja for putting the abaya into the bag she packed for me and leaving out my underwear. But the abaya is what saved me!"

"What did Saeed believe his demonstration would accomplish?" Thomas said.

"His ideals were noble. I'll always believe that," David said. "He wanted to change the country's archaic laws, and he was convinced that a dramatic demonstration of the government's technological vulnerability would force a new way of thinking."

David still felt the bitterness of Saeed's betrayal. Even more, his own gullibility in trusting him.

They'd talked about these issues. Why did he never suspect that Saeed was actually laying plans? Or how desperate he would become.

"Do you suppose Saeed's death will be the end of it?" Thomas said. "How much support did he have?"

"Don't think we'll ever know that. A number of activists and assorted dissidents are working to moderate the government's policies. And substantial financial resources come from people who don't dare show their support openly. They will keep trying. No doubt of that."

"Their dreams are worth fighting for," Layne said. "I wish I had Sahar's courage. Do you know what happened to her?"

"After he left you at Ha'il, Saeed flew her to an airstrip near his farms in the Eastern Province. He evidently had a car ready to drive her to the coast and a yacht waiting there. She's gone into hiding somewhere. Probably have to live anonymously the rest of her life to avoid retribution."

"It's a terrible price to pay," Layne said sadly.

"She wasn't the only one who paid a price," David said. "The attacks on you came from Saeed's own guilt about what happened to your mother and his fear that you'd discover what he did.

"He really was a decent man," he said. "In many ways, one of the finest I've ever known. But his dreams were too ambitious and his people made mistakes."

"Mistakes on all sides," Thomas said. "The garage owner was a thief. The sabotage of our water supply and the setup at the Bedouin camp were probably engineered so Saeed could come to our rescue and establish contact with us. But why did he kidnap Layne? Why didn't he just take her out of the country?"

"Another desperate decision. When you were in the hospital, Al-Amir called Saeed to be sure Layne was safe. Saeed must have realized then how much Al-Amir cared about her.

"I think taking her hostage was a spur-of-the-moment effort to persuade the old lion to back their demonstration. Or, if that failed, to keep him from exposing them."

Shaking his head, Thomas said, "It's unfortunate that those in power in this government won't learn from all of this."

"They learned something," David said. "Security is tighter than it's ever been."

"Speaking of governments," he said to Layne, "I've got a message for you." He pulled out the long white envelope he'd been carrying in his shirt pocket and handed it to her.

"I was charged with delivering this to you as an official notice," he said, trying not to grin.

Layne took it apprehensively. "This isn't an order to be on the next plane out of the country, is it?"

David watched her face as she glanced through the letter. She laughed and then read it aloud.

Dear Doctor L. Darius:

This will inform you that his Majesty's government has elected not to bring charges against you for your flagrant disregard of the laws of this kingdom.

It is trusted that you will have learned more prudent behavior from your experiences. However, no future access will be permitted to you after your departure.

"It's signed by Hassan."

"The learning 'prudent behavior' part is certainly optimistic," Thomas said.

Layne smiled, but she must have given him a look he recognized. He said, "Enough strolling. I need to stretch my legs." He walked on ahead.

David drew Layne into his arms. She met his kiss with the same abandon that set him afire the first time he held her. They clung to each other, and he ached with awareness that every day would be this frustrating until they could be together.

"Waiting four months is going to be damned hard," he said, letting her go so he could bring himself under control.

"Four months? You can't drive out here again?"

"This was the only chance I had to see you before I leave. I won't be in country much longer."

He saw her tense. "Where are you going?"

"I've been reassigned to Washington. I didn't cover myself with glory in this posting."

"That's not fair, David. You had nothing to do with Saeed's demonstration."

"No, it's fair. I learned some lessons here, too. About people, and trust. If it hadn't been for my boss's intervention, I might not have a career anymore. Fortunately for me," he added, "Al-Amir decided to take my side, too. The old lion's still got teeth."

He wanted to tell her how much he loved her, wanted to be with her forever. But they heard voices of the men from the encampment on their way out to meet them.

Layne looked up at him, her eyes dark with longing. "I can't bear to lose you."

He held her close one last time. "When you get back to Washington, I'll be waiting for you," he said.

"Then I'll come to you, David. I'll be there."

ABOUT THE AUTHOR

Ann Saxton Reh, an educator and award-winning writer, has lived in many places, including Bermuda, England, Libya, India, Saudi Arabia, and Greece. Currently, she lives in Northern California, where she writes mystery novels and short stories inspired by her adventures.